Magda's lithe auburn beauty paid the
way for her survival as a girl.
Her reckless passion for life destroyed
the husband who made her a lady.
But it was a woman's courage that led
her to an atonement of self-sacrifice to
save the life of their daughter . . .

THE DAYS OF WINTER

The new novel by the author of
A WORLD FULL OF STRANGERS
and FAIRYTALES
Cynthia Freeman

Also by Cynthia Freeman

A WORLD FULL OF STRANGERS
FAIRYTALES
PORTRAITS
COME POUR THE WINE
NO TIME FOR TEARS

and published by Corgi Books

Cynthia Freeman

The Days of Winter

CORGI BOOKS

THE DAYS OF WINTER

A CORGI BOOK   0 552 11084 1

First publication in Great Britain

PRINTING HISTORY
Corgi edition published 1979
Corgi edition reissued 1981
Corgi edition reprinted 1981
Corgi edition reprinted 1982 (twice)
Corgi edition reprinted 1984

This book is set in 9 point Caledonia type.

Corgi Books are published by Transworld Publishers Ltd.,
Century House, 61–63 Uxbridge Road, Ealing, London, W5 5SA

Printed and bound in Great Britain by
Cox & Wyman Ltd., Reading, Berks.

For my mother and father with love. Without them, there would never have been Chapter One.

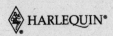
HARLEQUIN®

INTRIGUE®

As the summer comes to a close, things really begin to heat up as Harlequin Intrigue presents...

Big Sky Bounty Hunters: No man's a match for these Montana tough guys...but a woman's another story.

Don't miss this brand-new series from some of your favorite authors!

GOING TO EXTREMES
BY AMANDA STEVENS
August 2005

BULLSEYE
BY JESSICA ANDERSEN
September 2005

WARRIOR SPIRIT
BY CASSIE MILES
October 2005

FORBIDDEN CAPTOR
BY JULIE MILLER
November 2005

RILEY'S RETRIBUTION
BY RUTH GLICK,
writing as Rebecca York
December 2005

Available at your favorite retail outlet.

www.eHarlequin.com   HIBSBH

Susan Peterson

HARD
evidence

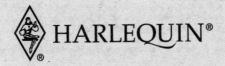

HARLEQUIN®

TORONTO • NEW YORK • LONDON
AMSTERDAM • PARIS • SYDNEY • HAMBURG
STOCKHOLM • ATHENS • TOKYO • MILAN • MADRID
PRAGUE • WARSAW • BUDAPEST • AUCKLAND

For my brother, Sam, who has lived through adversity and pain and come through it with his honor and integrity intact. May you find the peace, love and understanding you seek in this rough journey through life.

A special thanks to Christine Wenger for all her help with the "ins and outs" of Syracuse, New York. Any mistakes are purely the fault of the author's.

ISBN 0-373-22860-0

HARD EVIDENCE

www.eHarlequin.com

Printed in U.S.A.

ABOUT THE AUTHOR

A devoted Star Trek fan, Susan Peterson wrote her first science fiction novel at the age of thirteen. But as a hopeless romantic, Susan had to figure out a way to combine falling in love with a lifetime pursuit of total logic. After pursuing careers in intensive-care nursing and school psychology, Susan finally found the time to pursue a career in writing. An ardent fan of psychological thrillers and suspense, Susan combined her love of romance and suspense into several manuscripts targeted to the Harlequin Intrigue line. Getting the go-ahead to write for this line was a dream come true for her.

Susan lives in a small town in northern New York with her son, Kevin, her nutball dog, Ozzie, Phoenix the cat and Lex the six-toed menace (a new kitten). Susan loves to hear from readers. E-mail her at SusanPetersonHI@aol.com or visit her Web site at www.susanpeterson.net.

Books by Susan Peterson

HARLEQUIN INTRIGUE
751—CONCEALED WEAPON
776—EMERGENCY CONTACT
798—MIDNIGHT ISLAND SANCTUARY
860—HARD EVIDENCE

CAST OF CHARACTERS

Jack O'Brien—An ex-cop turned paramedic, Jack harbors serious guilt about his testimony against his foster father on charges of bribery.

Killian "Chili Pepper" Cray—Shocked when her former flame Jack O'Brien testified against their beloved foster father, Killian left Syracuse and vowed never to return.

Charlie Orzinski—Beloved foster dad to troubled teens for much of his life, he is now in a deep coma following a suspicious hit-and-run accident.

Handler Ortega—Local crime boss who'll do whatever it takes to get back vital information stolen from him regarding his criminal dealings.

Jeannette Renault—Former lover of Handler Ortega, and now married to a wealthy cardiac surgeon. Does this seemingly innocent suburbanite know more than she's willing to tell?

Craig Gibson—Charlie's lawyer, a man found murdered in Charlie's apartment.

Caroline Pratt—Gibson's law partner and known to represent Handler Ortega in a variety of shady legal matters.

Sweetie Pie—Charlie's nasty, mangy Maine Coon cat. Now Killian's responsibility.

Chapter One

If there was one thing I never expected to have to do in this lifetime, it was to stand over Charlie Orzinski and worry about whether he was going to live or die. Mainly because I've always believed Charlie was indestructible, the ultimate Man of Steel.

But the fact that he was in the I.C.U. of Crouse Hospital in Syracuse, N.Y., unconscious and hooked up to every machine known to modern man, showed me just how wrong I was. The trauma docs had given him less than a sixty-percent chance of survival.

Personally, I was betting Charlie had an ace or two up his sleeve, but something about the gray pallor of his craggy face told me death was a real possibility. And that was a possibility I wasn't prepared for. One I'd never be prepared for.

I reached down and slid my hand into his. His stillness frightened me more than the machines clustered around the bed. They seemed to diminish him, making his massive body, with its bull neck and linebacker shoulders, look small and insignificant beneath the stark white of the hospital sheets.

According to the nurses, he hadn't moved in three days.

Not for the day it took the hospital staff and police to identify him and not the following two days it took them to contact the only people alive who truly loved him, a ragtag
pack of former foster kids Charlie and his wife Claire had
raised over the years.

I was the last of the kids to get word, mainly because
they had to send someone into the backwoods of the Adirondack Mountains to reach me. As a deputy sheriff from
Essex County, N.Y., I'd been out traipsing through the
wilds of the Adirondacks, trying to locate some NYC
hump who had escaped from Ray Brook Minimum Security Prison.

Most of us had figured the idiot had counted on heading back to the city and his woman, but somewhere along
the line, he'd taken a wrong turn. A dangerous wrong turn.
He'd ended up stumbling deeper and deeper into the
remotest mountainous areas of the Upper Adirondacks.

Winter had hit the north country early and I had figured
we'd find the poor SOB frozen to some tree, solid as a
Good Humor Popsicle. He probably wouldn't be worrying about how much time he had to serve back at the Ray
Brook Country Club.

Shortly after the park ranger found me and informed me
of my foster dad's condition, I stumbled out of the woods,
jumped into my tiny electric-blue Neon and headed for
Syracuse, fighting a healthy dose of fear and guilt deep in
the pit of my belly.

Guilt because I'd told Charlie I'd never return to the city,
that I had written it out of my heart the day he'd been sentenced to eight years at Ray Brook Federal Prison in Ray
Brook, New York, for selling information and taking
bribes.

To my way of thinking, the city and the Syracuse Police Department had ruined his life, broken his heart and killed his beloved Claire. But Charlie, the only dad I'd ever really known, had always told me, *Never say never because that word will come back to bite you on the ass.* As usual, Charlie was right.

I laced my fingers through his and pressed my palm to his. I could feel the coolness of his skin beneath my own. I desperately wanted him to open his eyes, smile up at me and ask, "Where the hell ya been, Chili?"

But Charlie didn't move, and the heart monitor and other assorted machinery littering the Intensive Care cubicle continued to beep and click with maddening, mind-numbing regularity.

I moved closer to the bed and leaned down to whisper in his ear. "Come on, Pop, don't play possum. Wake up."

The respirator chugged on and the heart monitor beat out a steady pattern of life, but his eyelids didn't flicker.

"Could you tell me if there's been any change in Mr. Orzinski's condition?" a voice asked out at the nurse's desk.

I stiffened. It was a familiar voice. So familiar that it shot a charge of something sharp and unpleasant up the center of my spine, spreading out along the length of my shoulders and heating the back of my neck with black pepper anger.

I knew that voice almost better than Charlie's. But the difference was, this was one voice I had no desire to hear. Not now, not ever!

Still hanging on to Charlie's hand, I turned and peeked around the curtain. Jack O'Brien stood in front of the nurse's station, his upper body leaning casually on the counter top as he schmoozed the ward clerk sitting behind the desk.

One elbow was propped under his chin, and his powerful shoulders were hunched beneath a battered leather jacket, a jacket I'd bought him the first Christmas we'd dated.

I knew without seeing his face that his dark blue eyes, shaded by the longest, thickest eyelashes a man had the audacity to own, would be sending interesting chills down the pretty clerk's arms.

Sure enough, a flush of pink infused her cheeks and she smiled up at him with more wattage than was usually seen in a depressing place like the I.C.U. The Jack O'Brien I remembered liked using his charm to make women flutter. Obviously, he hadn't changed much in the nine years since I'd last seen him. And for more than one reason, that fact irritated the hell out of me.

To say that I harbored a deep-seated desire to return to the city and find Jack fat, or at least with a substantial beer gut, was an understatement. Unfortunately, he had developed neither.

His black hair, thick and longish with a familiar poetic curl to the ends, hugged the back of his neck and caressed the collar of his battered leather jacket, eliciting unwanted memories of my fingers shifting through those vibrant strands. Impatient, I pushed the thought aside.

Jack had always sported a dark, brooding look when it met his needs. It was his trademark. But even he knew his real charm was his charisma. It drew women and men to him like bees to honey—women to his dark beauty and men to his easy nature and laid-back attitude.

When he had been younger and gotten into mischief,

which, according to Claire, had been way too often, she'd tell him that he had the looks and temperament of one of God's dark angels—the ones who had fallen from grace. But no matter what he did, Jackie knew how to charm his way out of any kind of trouble. Even trouble with Claire.

She had been a pretty religious woman, but according to Charlie, Jack would just laugh and buzz Claire's cheek with those magnificent lips of his, pick her up and swing her around, and before he'd set her down, she would be all flustered and red. She'd swat at him and forgive him within seconds. Like everyone else in his life, she'd been unable to stay mad at him.

No one could stay mad at Jack. No one except me, that is.

As far as I could tell, the only clue that he was closing in on thirty-five were a few gray hairs mixed in with the dark strands along the sides of his head. The fact that they only made him look sexier set my teeth on edge. If there was one thing O'Brien didn't need, it was something that made him look sexier.

He leaned forward, his muscular legs, long and lean, spread slightly apart, showcasing a tight ass in worn jeans. Angry, I pulled my gaze up above his waist. No way did I want him turning around and finding my eyes glued to his ass. The Jack I knew would take too much delight in that particular scenario.

We had a history together, Jack and me. A very intimate history. But the last thing I wanted was for him to think I regretted walking out on him nine years ago when he testified against Charlie. It was his testimony that had put the final nail in Charlie's career coffin, information that guaranteed that he was stripped of his badge, gun and thirty years of retirement benefits with the police department.

The clerk behind the desk said something and nodded her head in my direction. I could see Jack shift his powerful body, and I ducked behind the curtain, breathing deep in an attempt to keep from passing out. Please let him have the decency to leave when he realizes I'm in the room.

I held my breath and waited.

A few moments passed and then, "Hello, Chili."

The voice was deep and gravel-rough around the edges. It was a sound so familiar that my traitorous nerve endings flared with a deep buried swoon of delight. I squashed the feeling with a viciousness that would have surprised even Attila the Hun.

"The name's Killian. Use it."

Chili Pepper had been my street name. We won't get into why; it's too embarrassing. But the nickname had stuck even after I went to live with Charlie and Claire.

Charlie had used the nickname affectionately, a clever, nurturing man's attempt to make the scrappy, defiant teen who had invaded his household with swagger, a vulgar mouth and piping hot anger, relax and realize her identity wasn't about to suddenly disappear simply because she'd ended up in the foster-care system. No one but Charlie had the right to call me by that name…. Okay, maybe Jack *used* to have that right, but not anymore.

My fingers tightened on Charlie's hand. *Wake up, Pop. Please wake up and rescue me before I make a fool of myself.* But Charlie slept on, oblivious to the fact that I needed him more than ever.

I lifted my head and met Jack's steady gaze. Air cramped in the back of my throat, squeezing it shut, hurting bad. I had to remind myself to breathe. His eyes were so dark, so deep and soulful blue that they seemed to sear right through me.

"It's good to see you," he said.

Yeah, right, I thought. Lie number one. Keep 'em coming Jackie boy. It'll just make it easier for me to keep my hate on.

"Can't say I feel the same way," I said.

He ignored the dig. "I'm glad they found you. I was worried when I heard you were out tramping around in the woods chasing down some poor sucker who took a wrong turn."

Lie number two. Jack O'Brien never *worried* about anyone or anything other than himself. I'd learned that fact nine years ago. "You're not welcome here, O'Brien. Do us both a favor and shove off."

I'd hoped to see a flicker of hurt in those beautiful eyes, but none appeared. He stared back at me with that familiar steady gaze, the one that used to make my knees melt and my body hum with a need so hungry and all consuming that I used to think I'd die if he didn't satisfy it.

"I simply came by to check up on Charlie."

"So, you checked. Time to leave."

He raised a single dark eyebrow, but didn't move. I gripped the metal bed rail and hung on for dear life. *He'll leave soon. Just hang on, Killian.*

"You look good. Mountain air seems to agree with you," he said as if we exchanged such pleasantries every day. "Things going okay for you?"

"Just fine. Thanks ever so much for asking."

He waited, the stillness of his body putting me even more on edge. I didn't bother asking him how he'd been. There wasn't any need. No one asked about the condition of perfection.

"How'd this happen?" I finally asked.

"I don't really know all the specifics. But they're calling it a hit-and-run."

"What's the matter, you aren't in the loop anymore down at the station?"

His eyes stared into mine, and a flicker of something close to pain or regret flashed through them. But it was hard for me to tell because the emotion disappeared so quickly.

"I'm not on the force anymore, Killian," he said. "I quit a few weeks after Pop was sentenced."

I swallowed hard. Now that was a surprise. Jack loved the force almost as much as Pop, maybe more. I wanted to ask what he was doing with himself, but that meant admitting I might actually be interested.

"I joined the fire department. I'm working as a paramedic."

"Interesting choice. Must be all that compassion and gentle caring you've got stored up, huh?"

Jack ignored my sarcastic dig. "I might not be part of the force anymore, but I know the guys will all be working hard to find out what happened. None of them will let it drop until they find the SOB."

"Yeah, right. Just like all you *guys* worked your tails off to clear his name nine years ago." I smacked my forehead with the palm of my hand. "Oh, wait, I'm getting that confused, aren't I? It's *you* who trashed Pop's name and got him sent to prison in the first place, wasn't it?"

"I gather from your tone that you're still having a hard time getting over that, huh?"

I met his gaze dead-on. "I'd strongly advise against holding your breath if you're waiting for any words of forgiveness from me, O'Brien. It ain't gonna happen." I glanced down at Charlie, my heart torn that he was the one getting the shaft again. "If you want to know the truth, I dream every night of you getting what you deserve."

"And what exactly is it that you think I deserve?"

"Believe me, you don't want to know. Now get out of here."

I fiercely willed him to go away, but he wasn't on my wavelength anymore. Once, not too long ago, people used to accuse us of being inside of each other's heads, finishing each other's sentences and laughing at jokes only the two of us heard. But Jack broke that thread when he'd incriminated Charlie to save his own skin.

"I talked with Elliot over at the Two-Four. You remember Elliot Standish, right?"

I nodded abruptly, concentrating on the rise and fall of Charlie's chest as the respirator blew air into his lungs, breathing for him, keeping him alive.

"Elliot says that they have two eyewitnesses. They're working from a sketch of the guy and a partial plate number." He shifted a little to the right, as if trying to catch my eye, but I avoided eye contact. I had to avoid eye contact. Jack's eyes had the power to reduce me to a puddle of emotion. I wasn't taking any chances, not now. Not when I was already an emotional wreck. I needed my wits about me. I needed to figure out what had happened to Pop and who had hurt him.

"Give them a few more days and they'll have something," he said.

I smoothed a wrinkle in the sheet over Charlie's chest, the starched fabric stiff and crisp beneath my fingers.

"Killian—?"

I glanced up. The angular planes of Jack's face had arranged themselves into an expression of concern, but I wasn't fooled.

Lie number three. Jack O'Brien was an expert at *appearing* concerned. It was another thing I had learned at Charlie's trial.

"What?" I asked.

His eyes narrowed a little as he studied my face. The dark midnight blue of his eyes in the dim light of the room seemed to slice through the space between us, lasering into me and cutting a clean precise incision directly through the center of my heart.

"Are you sure you're okay?"

"I'm fine."

He moved around the end of the bed, getting closer. It felt as though his powerful body was sucking up all the air around us, and I steeled myself against its influence. Closeness was not good. I needed to escape, get outside his circle of influence. But he didn't move, and I was frozen.

"Where are you staying while you're here?" he asked.

My fingers tightened on the rail of the bed, and bitterness rose in the back of my throat. "Pop's apartment, if you can even call it that. It's a certifiable hellhole."

I shot him a look that let him know exactly who I thought was responsible for the fact that our dad was sleeping in a one-bedroom rooming house with a rat problem that would keep the entire pest control industry in Syracuse busy for the next five years.

Charlie had lost the family home at some point during his trial. A house that had been in his family for several generations. The money had gone to pay for his defense.

"I thought about getting a hotel room, but Sweetie Pie needs someone to take care of him."

Sweetie Pie was the family pet, a fifteen-year-old Maine coon cat, half-blind, totally deaf and ornerier than a polecat trapped in a burlap bag while in fierce heat.

"You should have called. You could have stayed at my place."

I stiffened. Was he really that clueless? Did he actually believe that I'd take the freight elevator up to his loft apartment ever again? Or was he simply demonstrating his total insensitivity to what had happened to us in the past?

Sweet, painful memories of those late-night elevator rides flooded my senses, making me slightly woozy. Nights when we'd barely make it onto the elevator, let alone into his apartment before we were tearing at each other's clothes.

The elevator would chug upward, its gears and chains grinding and churning, as he'd press me up against the metal gate with his hardened body. His lips would travel over the pounding pulse in my neck and his clever hands would tear at my shirt buttons. My own hands frantically pulled and tugged at the waistband of his worn jeans.

We'd get to the top, push open the gate and stumble out, hobbling and hopping across the bare plank floor of his apartment, hanging on to each other and hampered by our clothing dragging down around our ankles.

Finally, we'd collapse onto the king-size mattress lying on the floor in the center of the loft. Jack didn't have a lot of furniture in those days. Besides, a bed seemed to serve any and all purpose in his life at the time. Knowing him, it probably still did.

Even with that bitter thought, my mind drifted back to

those crazy, hot, passionate nights. I'd lie on my back and suck in great gulps of air from the open skylight above, while his clever hands did wild and wonderful things to my body. And we'd lie there for hours, his powerful limbs entwined with mine, his lips whispering secret words in my ear as I screamed for a release I wanted so badly I could taste it even now.

My hands shook as I roughly pushed the thoughts aside, fighting to keep the emotions from ripping at my insides and showing on my face.

I met his gaze, and my anger heated to white when I saw the touch of sympathy sitting in the depths of those exquisite eyes. If there was one thing I didn't want, it was to have Jack feeling sorry for me. I wanted him on his knees hurting worse than me.

"Sorry, that wasn't very diplomatic of me, was it?" he said.

"Gee, you think?"

"Come on, Killian, cut me some slack. I said I was sorry. Can we call a truce?"

"Not in this lifetime." I tore my eyes away from his.

For a moment, I questioned if I was being unreasonable. But then rage pulled at me again. He didn't have any rights, in my book.

He had destroyed Pop with his testimony, telling the jury and the rest of the world that Charlie had sold important police information to the local crime boss, taking huge kickbacks in return.

He'd come to Claire's funeral when she died of cancer a week into Charlie's trial, but he stayed in the back, aware that he was no longer welcome inside the magic circle of young adults who clustered around Charlie in a show of support and infinite sorrow.

At one point, Charlie had reached out to him, but Jack was quick enough to catch the warning glares from the rest of us. He disappeared a short time later, never making it to the graveside service.

"None of the others have mentioned you lately. Have you talked to them?" I was referring to our five foster siblings.

"The reason he hasn't mentioned us is that we never see him," a new voice piped in.

I turned to see Shawna, one of our former foster sisters, watching us from the doorway. She stood with both hands planted firmly on her narrow hips, a fierce expression of protectiveness stiffening the dark mahogany planes of her proud face. The thick gold ring punched through the center of her lower lip glittered in the muted lights of the room as she glared in Jack's direction.

"Jack knows he isn't welcome around here."

"Good to see you too, Shawna." Jack's expression showed no reaction to her bristly greeting. "As disagreeable as ever, I see."

"You ain't even seen disagreeable, big brother." She turned away from him and concentrated on me. "Brian told me you'd arrived. I came down right after work. Couldn't get away earlier. Another supervisor retired, and I've been picking up the slack. Damn hiring freeze."

She scowled and then moved over to stand next to me. "How's he doing?"

"No change," I said, leaning down to hug her. She clung to me for a few seconds, her head nestled against my shoulder as if trying to soak in some of my strength. I'd always envied Shawna her petiteness. Without meaning to, she had always managed to make me feel like an Amazon.

"The docs been in today?" she asked finally, stepping back.

"Earlier. They didn't have anything to say. The usual grunts and nods. Which seem to be the typical way of imparting information around this place."

Shawna nodded and rearranged the sheet lying across Charlie's chest. Her nails, long and meticulously painted, showed bloodred against the white linen. "Drake and I are taking the night shift. He told me to tell you to go home and get some sleep. You and Courtney have day duty."

I sighed. Did they really think I was going to leave Charlie's bedside? "I'm fine right here." I nodded toward the cushioned high-backed chair in one corner of the room. "I'll catch some Z's right over there if I get too tired."

Shawna shook her head. "They only allow two of us in the room at a time."

"Then I'll sleep out in the waiting room."

"You're not going to do Charlie any good if you're dead on your feet," Jack said quietly from the end of the bed.

I bristled. "No one asked for your input."

It was Shawna's turn to sigh. "Look, as much as I hate to admit it, Jack's right. You need to keep strong."

Jack moved toward the door. "When Pop wakes up, will you at least give me a call?"

"Sure," Shawna said.

I let her do the talking. If I had my way, he'd be the last person I called to tell the good news, but in this case I bowed to Shawna's diplomatic skills.

He zipped his jacket, pulling up the collar in preparation for heading outside. His gaze shifted to me. I stiffened.

"Take care of yourself, Killian." His tone had a certain softness to it, as if he were trying to connect with me. To reach out and touch the part of me that had once loved him.

"You, too," I said curtly.

He walked out and Shawna shot me a quick look. "Still haven't gotten over him, have you?"

I stiffened. "What makes you say that?"

"The fact that your hostility has an undeniably passionate edge to it."

She looked me up and down and shook her head knowingly. "No doubt about it, sistah, you're still holding a torch for that one."

"Boy, are you living in a dream world."

I glanced away so she couldn't read any more of the raw emotions flickering across my face. Shawna was only three years older than me, but she had a tendency to take on the role of the all-knowing older sister, a trait that never ceased to annoy me. Basically, I hated her uncanny ability to read me.

"Well, he's gone and that's all that matters for now." She picked up a small package on the bedside table and slipped out a premoistened swab. She leaned over the rail to moisten Charlie's chapped lips around the adhesive tape securing the breathing tube in his mouth.

"Jack's been pretty decent about staying out of our way these past few years. I can't really fault him for wanting to stop by and see Pop now." She glanced up, her dark eyes wistful. "Pop never hated anyone in his entire life. He didn't even fault Jack for testifying against him in court. He forgave him—told all of us to forgive him, too."

"Guess I'm not as kindhearted as Pop," I said. "But then, he's always been soft when it came to dealing with

Jack. In fact, he was too kindhearted toward all of us. None of us deserved him. Or Claire."

Shawna reached up and touched my shoulder. "Save it, sweetie. He's gonna pull through this. He's too strong to give up." She swallowed her own obvious pain. "Craig Gibson, Pop's lawyer, stopped by yesterday. Charlie has a health proxy and a will. He appointed you as the executor of his estate and gave you power of attorney."

I couldn't hide my surprise. "Me? Why me?"

Shawna shrugged. "I don't know. I just know that the suit who stopped by here said for you to get in touch with him as soon as you arrived."

She glanced over at the clock hanging over the head of Charlie's bed. "Too late now, but he wants to see you in his office tomorrow morning at 9:00 a.m. sharp. Something to do with Charlie's will." She patted my arm. "Now get some rest. You need to be fresh for Pop in the morning."

I nodded, shrugged into my oversize down jacket, zipped it up and headed for the door.

"Oh, wait," Shawna said.

I turned back.

Her face had that worried, indecisive look she got when she wasn't sure she wanted to share her information. Big sister syndrome—what degree of truth do you tell the little ones?

"Just say it," I said.

"Some weird stuff has been going on."

"Weird how?"

"People showing up in Pop's room who no one knows. And it's always when one of us isn't right here in the room."

I walked back over to the bed. "You're talking about people who aren't hospital staff, right?"

Shawna nodded. "One time, I came back in after going down the hall for ice and the hose from his respirator was off—just laying on his chest. He couldn't breathe. His lips were blue."

Fear tightened in my belly. "What did the nurses say?"

"They said the hose pops off like that sometimes. But an alarm is supposed to go off. For some reason, it didn't happen that time." She paused for a moment and then continued, "When I asked if anyone had been in the room, they said some guy stopped in for a quick visit. No one knew his name and by the description, it didn't sound like anyone Pop knows."

From her expression I could tell there was more. "Tell me the rest."

"Well, when I came in last night, Craig was on the phone in the hall and when I walked in the room, some guy was leaning over the bed fiddling with Pop's IV tube. Soon as I walked in he dropped it and said something about it looking fine and hightailed it out of here. None of the nurses knew who he was."

"Have you told the police all of this?"

Shawna nodded. "They told me I was overreacting. They won't put a guard on him no matter what any of us say."

I pulled my cell phone out of my pocket and punched in a number. "Then we'll get our own. Dickie Petrova from the old neighborhood opened his own security business. We'll use him."

"That's going to cost us a mint, Killian."

I shrugged. "I'll pay for it."

Dreams of upgrading my cabin in the woods on my tiny piece of heaven right outside Keene Valley flew out the window like a puff of wood smoke escaping from a cast-iron stove, but I didn't care. Pop's safety was more important, and he would have done it for me, for any of the kids. That and more.

Until I found out what was going on, Pop was getting twenty-four-hour protection. And his lawyer was going to have a lot of questions to answer tomorrow when I arrived at his office. Something was going on and it didn't add up to a simple hit-and-run case.

Chapter Two

The front doors of the hospital slid open and a frigid wind whipped up Crouse Street, stirring up scraps of trash lining the sidewalk and spraying my face with small, gritty grains of dirt-encrusted snow. I reached up and brushed a hunk of hair out of my eyes.

A sense of disorientation hit me for a moment as I stood on the front walkway. I'd grown up in Syracuse, on the west side. A part of the city not many people visited. When I'd been sent to live with Charlie and Claire, I'd discovered a whole new Syracuse, one I hadn't really known had existed—the world of suburbia.

Suburbia had been a place with elegant Tudor-style homes, tiny, manicured front lawns and neat wooden porches with wide, comfortable porch swings. Fussy potted plants and starched white lace curtains sat in the front windows, and antique boards painted with cute little sayings about angels and sunflowers hung on the front double doors. Claire had worked hard to keep up with the neighbors. No one had outdone Claire when it came to decorating.

I breathed in the familiar grime and reminded myself that living in a city needed some getting used to. It wasn't suburbia and it sure wasn't the Adirondacks.

Even though it was early evening, the temperature had already dropped down into the low teens. A frigid night in Syracuse. Now there was a big surprise.

I found myself wishing I was back on Giant Mountain, sitting under a canopy of stars, next to a roaring campfire and listening to the cold north wind rustling the pines.

It took a minute to get my bearings, but finally I turned right and headed across the street toward the parking garage. Snow crunched under my hiking boots.

My head was a little woozy, no doubt from the stuffiness of Charlie's hospital room and then the sudden exit into carbon-monoxide-polluted air. Breathing crisp mountain air for the past few years had its advantages.

Of course, the fact that I was still recovering from sharing the same breathing space as Jack O'Brien might have something to do with my current respiratory difficulties. I'd gotten out of his breathing space just in time.

Unfortunately, I had spoken too soon. The deep rumble of an idling Harley sounded from the left and a second later, the front tire of the powerful machine nudged my left toe.

Steeling myself, I glanced over. Sure enough, Jack sat in the saddle, his legs spread wide to balance himself, his helmet sitting between his legs. The expectant expression on his face told me he'd been waiting for me.

"Most sane people know when to put their cycle away for the winter, O'Brien," I said, stepping around the front of the bike, determined to get to the garage and my car.

He laughed agreeably. "Gets harder and harder for me to do every year."

"Yeah, arrested development can do that to a guy." I shot the comment over one shoulder as I tried to push past him.

"Killian, wait." He caught my elbow and whipped me around easily.

I shrugged his hand off. "We said what we needed to say to each other inside."

"I just wanted to try and get you to reconsider your plans to stay at Pop's place."

"Where I stay isn't any of your concern."

I started to turn away again, but he reached out again, stopping me.

I folded my arms, hopeful that it would provide protection against the flush of awareness that shot through me when those long fingers clamped on my forearm.

Damn, I hated my body and its immediate reaction to his touch. It was like a memory of him, of his hands on my body, had been scorched into every cell and nerve ending of my being.

"I'm willing to sacrifice my couch in your honor. You know the west side isn't a place for you to be hanging out."

I almost laughed at that. Yeah, right, I had only cut my razor-sharp baby teeth on the goings-on over on the west side. Jack knew that only too well.

I'd lived on West Belden Avenue most of my life. Until Social Services stepped in, anyway, yanking me out of my heroin-addicted, straight-vodka-swigging mother's custody and plunking me down on the porch steps of Charlie and Claire's rambling, historic house. For me, it had been like landing on Mars.

Thirteen years old, ornery and disagreeable, smelling like pot plant, dog slobber and dirty laundry. But Claire hadn't blinked an eye. She'd simply opened her door wide and welcomed me into that huge, rambling house of theirs.

"I'm perfectly capable of taking care of myself. Speaking of which, did you know that Shawna and the others suspect that someone has been coming into Pop's room uninvited, possibly fooling around with his life support equipment?"

"One of the nurses mentioned that they made a complaint."

Yeah, when you were flirting with her, no doubt. I gritted my teeth. "Well, I believe Shawna and respect her concern. I've hired on Dickie Petrova for added security."

Jack rolled his eyes. "Ah, jeez, Killian, Dickie Petrova? You know he can't find his way out of a paper bag. Would you please let me take care of things?"

I moved past Jack. "You had your chance and you blew it. I'm taking care of things now."

I crossed the street to the parking garage and Jack didn't follow. I didn't even bother to glance over my shoulder as I stepped onto the elevator.

Jack seemed to get the message that I didn't want his help, and he made no attempt to follow. For that I was thankful. Thankful, that is, until I stepped off the elevator onto the third floor of the parking garage.

Damn! The lights were out on this end of the garage. A sprinkling of glass shards among a few rocks laying beneath three of the closest light poles told me that some punk, bored with having to wait around for his family, had taken a couple of pot shots at the overhead lights.

I looked around. The inside of the garage was murky and the hair on the back of my neck stood on end. My training kicked in, making me instantly cautious.

I walked down two rows and found my grime-encrusted car tucked in between a silver Lexus and a black Cadillac

Escalade SUV. My sturdy little electric-blue Neon looked pretty lonely among all that luxury.

I pulled my key out but before I had it in the lock, I felt, rather than heard, someone come up behind me. I stiffened.

"Don't scream and don't turn around," a voice whispered in my ear.

I tightened my hand on the key. At this point, it was my only weapon. I shrugged and allowed my purse to slide off my shoulder. I shoved the purse back toward the disembodied voice. "Here," I said. "I don't have a lot of cash, but whatever's there is yours. And you're welcome to the credit cards, too."

I didn't mention that the cards were almost maxed out. Let the jerk find that out for himself.

A hand grabbed the purse but immediately heaved it onto the pavement. Concern shot through me. When a robber didn't want your purse, that was not a good sign. If he wasn't looking for cash, then there was only one other thing he'd want from a single woman in a dark parking garage. I wasn't about to give that particular item up without a fight.

As inconspicuously as possible, I shifted my weight onto my toes. But the guy seemed to anticipate the move and he hit me hard between my shoulder blades, sending me stumbling forward against the hood of the car.

I used my hands to keep myself from hitting face-first. He pressed against me with his bulky body, pushing my head down until my cheek rested against the cool metal.

"Don't even think about running," he said.

"I wasn't," I lied.

My heart pounded against my rib cage and fear thickened in the back of my throat. The guy wasn't going to make this easy. He was a pro, someone who had done this before. He knew what to look for.

"What do you want?" I asked, desperately trying to keep myself from panicking.

"We want what belongs to us." His hand held me tight against the car. I couldn't move.

"Tell me what it is and if I have it, I'll give it to you. I'm not looking for trouble."

"We want the key and the package."

I shoved my key chain in his direction. "Here, take them. Take the car. Just leave me alone."

He took my keys but I heard them hit the pavement alongside my purse. "These aren't the key or the package we're looking for."

"Well, they're the only ones I've got," I said.

He snorted in exasperation and grabbed my collar, hauling me to my feet. Reaching around me, he yanked open the door of the Escalade. "Get in and push over behind the wheel."

I locked my knees, digging my heels into the pavement. *Don't ever let an abductor take you to a new location.* I'd heard that particular warning more than a few times from Charlie, Jack and every other police officer I'd ever worked or trained under.

"Just tell me what you want, and I'll give it to you," I stalled.

He didn't answer, but instead crowded in behind me, using his thickly muscled body to nudge me into the car. "I said to get in and get behind the wheel." He shoved me between my shoulder blades, sending me stumbling against the open car door.

I stepped up and bumped my head on the door frame.

A stinging pain shot across the top of my scalp. I swallowed against the tears that sprang to the corners of my eyes and slid across the seat.

I reached for the opposite door handle, but before I could grab it and jump out, a hand reached across the front seat and clamped down on my shoulder, anchoring me firmly to the seat.

I jumped, and my fear hit a new high. My abductor had an accomplice. My chances of escape had just taken a rather significant nosedive.

"Don't even think about jumping out," a voice said, the sound low and grating, like granite stones rattling in a metal cage.

How had I missed that there was someone else in the car? I was getting careless. Too many years living in the mountains and not enough time keeping my city radar switched on high.

I grabbed the wheel and peered into the rearview mirror. The shadowy figure in the backseat wore his cap low on his forehead, shading his features. His shoulders were wide and bulked up beneath the expensive leather coat. He used two fingers to flick the back of my skull, sending another flash of pain shooting through my head.

"Keep your eyes front and center," he ordered.

"What do you want?" I tried to keep the fear out of my voice. "My boyfriend is going to be here any minute."

Mr. Biceps laughed, and it wasn't anything light or airy. More like the low rumble of a diesel truck. "You ditched O'Brien down below. Ain't no one coming to your rescue, little sister."

He knew Jack. Apparently Jack was still hanging with an interesting crowd.

The shooter slammed the passenger side door closed and shifted around to face me. He had a fleshy nose with a boatload of nasty-looking moles and other assorted blemishes spread out across his cheekbones and neck. The guy was in serious need of a dermatologist.

He wagged the gun in the direction of the ignition. "Start it up. We'll go somewhere a little less public to conduct our business."

He glanced over his shoulder at his buddy. "The Bay Street exit, right, boss?"

The figure in the mirror nodded and then settled back, apparently content in his belief that Mole Face had things under control. I let him think that as I leaned forward and started the engine.

"Back it out nice and slow," Mole Face instructed, settling his own shoulder back against the passenger side door, a small smile puckering his full lips.

"Where are we going?" I put the car in reverse and backed out. The bottom of my foot itched to floor it, but something told me I needed to bide my time, pick my opportunity carefully.

My passengers had the attitude of thugs who'd done this drill before. Something told me that there wouldn't be any second chances. It was now or never.

Up ahead, I could see the ramp leading to the top of the parking garage. Patrons of the garage had to go up to the roof to start back down again. I eased the SUV into Drive.

"Take the back exit," Mole Face ordered, resting the butt of the revolver on his right knee. He was feeling pretty confident, sure that I was frightened enough to do what he asked.

I shifted my left leg closer to the door and carefully slid

my left hand off the wheel, resting it on my thigh. I nodded my head agreeably. "Whatever it is that you two want, I'll give it to you as long as you don't hurt me." I put a little extra plaintive pleading into my voice, hoping they'd concentrate on that rather than the fact that my left hand was now resting on the door handle.

"Just shut up and drive," the backseat thug said.

I headed for the ramp, bracing my left foot against the frame of the car as I stamped my right foot down on the accelerator. The car engine roared, and the vehicle jumped as if goosed.

Both men fell back against the seats, and the gun flew out of Mole Face's hand, hitting the dashboard. With a grunt, he scrambled to reach it. But the revolver slid to the floor, skittering across the floor and settling beneath my feet.

"Slow down!" Mole Face shouted.

"It's stuck," I said, pretending to pry at the bottom of the gas pedal with my foot but instead stomping on it harder.

Mole Face bumped up against me as he blindly groped along the floorboards for his gun. I ignored him and jammed the accelerator flat to the floor. The engine screamed and we hit the top of the ramp going sixty-five.

Come on! Come on! I chanted inwardly, my fingers gripping the steering wheel with a white-knuckled grasp. I willed the car to go faster.

The engine roared, building up more speed. Seventy. Eighty.

We raced across the top level of the parking garage, directly toward the opposite end and a line of cars.

I aimed for the tiny red sports car and when the SUV hit the back end, it reared up and over the little car's trunk. In seconds, we were airborne.

I yanked open the driver's side door, tucked my chin and threw myself out sideways. Blackness closed in around me as I twirled and spun in midair.

There was a whirlwind of flashing lights and then pain as I struck the pavement with my left shoulder. Lucky for me, my oversize down jacket provided me with some extra protection.

I rolled and then hit something hard but with a little give to it. Pain shot through my entire body and then darkness settled over me.

GROGGY, I blinked and opened my eyes. I was laying up against the rim of a tire. It had broken my fall, probably keeping me from getting seriously hurt.

Cautiously I sat up and looked around. The Escalade had gone over the side. There was nothing left except the smashed sports car with the M.D. plates. Some doc was going to be royally ticked when he came out after a hard night's work to find his little plaything a total wreck. Guess more than just his malpractice insurance would go up this year.

I pulled myself to my feet, grimacing a bit when I moved my left shoulder. I'd taken my full weight on it when I fell. It was going to be more than a little sore.

Limping slightly, I walked over to the low wall at the end of the garage and looked over. The Cadillac lay on its side, steam rising up from the engine. After experiencing the speed that monster vehicle had mustered in such a short time, I figured I needed to consider buying one when I won the lottery someday. Nice wheels.

No one moved inside the SUV. If Mole Face and Biceps were still alive, they didn't appear to be in any condition to climb out. Unfortunate for them, but lucky for me. Charlie would be proud. I had managed not to get myself moved to a new location.

A motorcycle's engine echoed inside the parking garage, tearing upwards toward the top floor. I glanced around, suddenly desperate to disappear. I didn't want to have to answer any questions, and I didn't have any doubts as to who was riding the bike.

Sure enough, a few seconds later, Jack skidded to a stop. He yanked off his helmet, jumped off the bike and headed toward me, throwing the helmet over his shoulder. It hit the side of his bike and rolled a few feet away.

He ignored it, his face angry. "What the hell is going on?"

I shrugged. "Someone must have jumped the wall in a misguided attempt to avoid paying their parking fee." I nodded toward the end wall. "He sailed right off the side."

Jack walked over to view the mess below. He shot a suspicious glance in my direction. "Something tells me you're involved. Wanna come clean?"

"The two gentlemen in the car thought they had my permission to take me for a ride. I disagreed." I shrugged. "So, we parted company on unfriendly terms."

"What did they want?"

"I'm not really sure. But they were under the impression that I had something they wanted. A key and a package of some sort."

A few minutes later, the sound of a siren told us the police had arrived. They were crawling all over the SUV below in a matter of minutes.

"You're going to have to make a statement."

I shrugged again, ignoring the nagging pain in my shoulder. "Not my fault they took the short ride off the side of the parking garage. They shouldn't have told me to drive while holding a gun on me."

Jack shook his head. He wasn't convinced I'd told him everything, but he wasn't in the mood to argue about it right at the moment. "You'll make your statement and then you'll come with me. No way are you staying alone at Charlie's."

I bristled at his commanding, no-nonsense tone. Who the hell was he kidding? His place was *not* the safest place for me. Not when my traitorous body hummed like a well-oiled machine with every glance from those dark blue eyes of his. Nope, more like his apartment was the most dangerous place on the planet for me.

Before I could open my mouth to argue, he grabbed the extra helmet off the back of his bike and jammed it none too gently on my head. "Don't be stubborn. Those men weren't playing around. You need a safe place to stay. I'll take you over to Pop's place, we'll pick up Sweetie Pie and then you can sleep at my place tonight. Tomorrow you can make whatever other arrangements you want."

His fingers, warm and infinitely more sexy than my own, worked the straps of the helmet, brushing the soft skin at the underside of my chin.

I clenched my back teeth, my toes curling in the bottom of my boots. God, give me strength to ignore the tingle shooting up the center of my spine.

As hard as it was to admit it, I knew was right. I was tired. We could call a truce for tonight. We were both adults. No reason we couldn't both handle staying in the same apartment for one night. We were strong. Responsible.

Ha! Who was I kidding. It wasn't Jack I was worried

about. I was the one who'd been living in Upstate New York, where every man seemed to live for his rifle, his snowmobile and Genesee Beer. A good woman was usually the last item on his list of life necessities. Right now, even O'Brien was looking too good to pass up, and that thought scared the hell out of me.

A SHORT TIME LATER, my statement having been given to the police, Jack and I were headed down Pine Street on the west side. Overflowing garbage cans lined the streets. One could only hope that the city sanitation department was headed in this direction tomorrow morning, or else the entire west side looked as though it might get buried under a mountain of Glad trash bags and empty pizza boxes.

Charlie's apartment was in one of the old row houses that lined State Street, one of many elegant old homes that had slowly deteriorated into dilapidated ruins, propped up with plywood and cheap siding.

As financial times had gotten leaner, a lot of the original owners had divided their houses up into multiple dwellings, cramming as many people in as was humanly possible.

Charlie occupied a small one-bedroom apartment on the third floor of one such house. The owners were two elderly Polish ladies, sisters who had probably lived in the neighborhood since its creation. From the age of them, I figured they had both been born in the house.

Jack parked his bike at the curb, turned the front tire in and took off his helmet. He rested the helmet in front of him, balancing himself on two legs, his expression a bit horrified as he surveyed the garbage littered front yard.

I figured from his expression that this was his first visit to Pop's new residence. A touch of resentment rumbled in

the pit of my stomach, and that little voice in my head reminded me bitterly that it was all his fault Pop lived in such
a dump.

I shut the voice off. He and I weren't going to make it
through the night if I had him roasting on a spit before
midnight.

I hopped off and jammed my own helmet on the back
of the bike. He followed suit and climbed the rickety steps
onto the front porch. He glanced over one broad shoulder.
"Are you coming? I don't have a key, so we need yours to
get in."

I followed him into the front hall, the smell of frying
sausages, sauerkraut and onions hit me hard and made my
stomach rumble. Memories of dinner at the Orzinskis'
house swam into my consciousness—Claire standing over
the stove, sautéing onions while Charlie read her sections
of the evening paper.

I pushed the thought aside. Obviously the PowerBar
earlier hadn't been enough. Suddenly, I was starving.

A door to the right swung open and a short, squat
woman with pure white hair and a bulldog face peered out.
"Who are you?" she demanded.

Jack smiled that charming, one-sided dimpled grin of
his. "Evenin', ma'am. We're here to pick up Charlie's cat."

The woman opened the door wider; her expression was
suddenly a map of concern. "How is Charlie? Edith and I
have been beside ourselves with worry about him. We
were going to take a bus down to the hospital to see him,
but money has been a little tight this month."

"Who's out there, Patty?" another voice called from inside the apartment.

"It's some friends of Charlie's here to pick up that insufferable beast of a cat of his. He's still in the hospital. Gonna be there for a while longer, it seems." She glanced at us for confirmation and Jack nodded.

There was the sound of something thumping on the floorboards of the hall and a tall, skinny woman with gray hair and a sour expression appeared. She leaned heavily on a thick cane. "You sure they're legit? Awful lot of people claiming to be Charlie's friends been popping out of the woodwork lately, asking to get into his apartment."

Jack reached into his back pocket and pulled out his wallet, flipping it open to show his badge. "I'm with the Syracuse Fire Department. Charlie's a real good friend of mine." He nodded in my direction. "This is Killia—"

"Oh, we've met Killian," the shorter sister said, smiling sweetly in my direction. "Sorry, dear, I didn't recognize you in the dark hallway."

She glanced up at the dim bulb. "We keep meaning to get stronger lighting out here, what with all the riffraff hanging around the neighborhood and stumbling into entryways without an invite. But somehow we always forget to tell Charlie to do that for us."

She sighed. "Charlie's been very good to us. He was always willing to do a few chores. Help us out when we needed something done."

"Sounds like he won't be helping us again any time soon," Edith grumbled. She turned and thumped back down the hall of her apartment, mumbling under her breath.

The shorter sister smiled apologetically. "You'll have to excuse Edith. She really does care about what happens to Charlie. She just isn't the type to show her true feelings."

I nodded but had a strong feeling that if Edith had the

opportunity to get anywhere near Charlie's bedside, she'd whack the soles of his feet with her cane and tell him to get his lazy ass out of bed. No doubt Charlie would be grateful she hadn't scrounged up the extra money to take the bus down to the hospital.

Patty shot a quick glance over one shoulder and then shuffled her swollen, slippered feet out into the hall. She pulled the door shut after her. "Sorry for all the questions, but my sister is right. Lots of people been claiming to know Charlie lately. I never knew the man to have so many friends."

"What did these *friends* say they wanted?" I asked.

Patty shrugged. "A few asked if he was home. A few of the recent ones wanted me to let them into the apartment." She reached up and scratched her powder-white ear. "Personally, I can't figure it out. Charlie doesn't have two nickels to rub together. He doesn't have much and I can't say I can believe they stopped by to feed that ugly, disagreeable cat of his."

"Did you recognize any of them as visiting here before?" I asked.

Patty's bulldog forehead wrinkled even more. "Can't remember anyone specific. One fellow had a bad case of pimples—in serious need of a good scrubbing. And his breath wasn't any prettier than his face. Charlie might be poor, but he isn't the type of man to let his personal hygiene go."

The hair on the back of my neck ruffled. "Did you let him into the apartment?"

Indignation crossed Patty's face. "Of course not! What kind of rooming house do you think we run around here?" She fluttered her stubby eyelashes in Jack's direction. "Of course, if the request comes from one of Syracuse's fire-men, heroes that they all are, then that's an entirely different story."

I snorted at the description of Jack as a hero, and he shot me a look of exaggerated woundedness. I merely raised an eyebrow and frowned. He might be welcomed eye candy for a little old Polish lady on the west side, but he wasn't fooling me. He sighed and turned back to Patty.

"Mind if Killian and I take a look around?"

"You go right ahead, sir. Just lock up when you're all done." Patty smiled and disappeared back into her apartment.

Jack and I took the worn stairs to the third floor. I could hear muted voices behind the walls of the other apartments we passed and the smell of dinner cooking.

My stomach rumbled loud enough for Jack to shoot me a quick glance. "Hungry?"

"A little."

"We'll grab some King David takeout on the way home."

My heart squeezed with pain. Our favorite meal—Middle Eastern—hummus-and-fried-veggie patties on pita bread. We used to set up a picnic in the middle of the bed and chow down like two wild beasts and then roll over and make ourselves hungry all over again.

"I'm more of a hamburger and French fries type of gal, nowadays," I said stiffly.

Jack shrugged. "McDonald's it is, then."

We reached the third floor and stopped.

Charlie's apartment door yawned open on its hinges. Apparently whomever the Stanziki sisters had last refused entrance hadn't accepted no for an answer. They'd simply kicked the flimsy door open and walked right in.

Jack and I stepped around the hanging door into utter chaos. If I'd judged Charlie's place to be a hellhole earlier in the day, it now looked as though even Satan had deserted the place, but not before he'd had a major temper tantrum.

Every piece of furniture was smashed, slivers of wood and metal littering the threadbare carpet. The tiny twelve-inch black-and-white TV—where Charlie had gotten a real black-and-white TV was beyond me—was now screenless, shards of the glass spread across the carpet. The lamps lay broken on the two cheap end tables among ripped magazines and scraps of newspaper.

Through the archway into the tiny bedroom off the living room, I could see clothes, mostly worn jeans and stained T-shirts, hanging out of the thin plasterboard dresser.

The mattress, stained and sagging in the middle, was ripped up the center, the rusted springs and thin padding bubbling up between the tear like the guts of an eviscerated pancake. I swallowed hard.

Jack lifted his hand, pushed me back against the wall and started to shoulder his way past me. I shoved back, reaching inside my coat and drawing my gun.

"If you don't mind, I'll go first," I said, brushing past him.

"Stay here," I mouthed silently.

He frowned, none too pleased. When I stepped inside, he pulled up close on my heels. I was annoyed that he didn't listen, but I didn't take the time to argue. I didn't want to warn anyone if they were still in the apartment.

I poked my head into the small kitchen to the right of the living room. Actually, it wasn't a kitchen, but a pathetic notch in the wall that served as a cooking nook.

The few dishes that had been sitting in the sink earlier lay smashed on the counter, every cabinet open and the contents dumped. All the drawers were open, their contents dumped onto the narrow strip of cracked linoleum.

The door on the tiny apartment refrigerator stood open; food and beverages, mostly opened bottles of beer and a pitcher of orange juice, dripped down off the racks. The putrid smell of spoiling food, probably tuna fish meant for Sweetie Pie, filled the tiny area.

"Damn!"

I jumped. The expletive had come from the bedroom. Jack had taken off on his own. I turned and ran in Jack's direction, a burn of anger at his stupidity eating at the lining of my stomach. He didn't have a weapon and he could have put himself in a great deal of trouble.

As I rounded the corner to Charlie's bedroom, I realized fairly quickly that someone other than Jack was the one in deep trouble. The kind of trouble you don't ever get out of.

Chapter Three

In the center of the cramped bedroom, near the closet, sat a wooden, straight-backed chair. But it was what was tied to the chair that almost made me lose the PowerBar I'd scarfed down earlier that afternoon.

The guy didn't fit the overall decor of Pop's apartment. He was too uptown for that. His expensive three-piece suit looked as though it might cost in the range of a two years' salary for me. Unfortunately, he'd bled out all over the front of the suit.

The multiple stab wounds to his neck and chest looked as if someone had taken their sweet time inflicting them. A puddle of congealed blood pooled at his feet.

I almost gagged, but I held on. I told myself I'd seen worse, and I had. Maybe not murders, but car wrecks in the steep Adirondack Mountains could produce some pretty horrific scenes.

Jack swore and I could see him shoot me a quick assessing glance. He was probably worried that I was going to take a header directly into the middle of the crime scene.

I clenched my teeth and swallowed hard. I nodded my head to let him know that I was okay. No way would I give him the satisfaction of falling apart. I was the cop on the scene, *not* him.

"Do you know him?" he asked.

I shook my head, going for the casual look. "You?"

"Nope."

I stepped forward and pulled a rubber glove out of my back pocket. Pop always taught me that a cop was always prepared, on duty or off.

I donned the glove with a quick snap of rubber and then carefully lifted the man's jacket to extract the victim's wallet and flipped it open.

"His name is Craig Gibson." I couldn't keep a touch of surprise from filtering through my voice.

Jack gave me a sharp glance. "So you *do* know him?"

I nodded. "Kind of. Shawna said that Pop's lawyer wanted to meet with me tomorrow. She said his name was Craig Gibson."

"Guess your meeting won't be going off as planned."

I closed the wallet and slid it back into Gibson's pocket.

Reaching into his pocket, Jack pulled out a cell phone and quickly punched in a number. "Yeah, my name is Jack O'Brien. I'm at 354 Pine St., third-floor apartment. Number 3A. Notify homicide they've just caught a new case. And tell 'em to bring the coroner."

He rattled off a few other details as I backed out of the room. I retreated to the kitchen and leaned over the battered metal sink. Turning on the tap, I splashed cold water on my face.

I'd seen enough gruesome car accidents to typically handle the blood and gore without any real show of emotion, but for some reason seeing that guy tied up and tortured that way affected me more than I'd figured on.

When I came up for air, I found Jack standing next to me, regarding me with that familiar, quietly assessing look of his.

"You okay?" he asked.

A sharp retort hovered on the tip of my tongue to cover up how off-kilter I really felt, but I kept quiet because I knew he'd be able to see right through me. So I simply nodded.

"The locals aren't really going to let you get involved in this case," he said. "You wanna wait downstairs with the sisters until they want a statement?"

I thought about the current condition of my stomach and the combined smells of Ben-Gay, sausage and sauerkraut leaking out from beneath the Stanziki sisters' apartment door. "I'm fine. Just got a little shaky there for a minute due to an empty stomach."

He shrugged those broad shoulders. "Fine by me. Just don't touch anything. Homicide gets a bit touchy when people fiddle around with their crime scene."

"I'm not an idiot, Jack. We do have crime scenes up there in the wilds of northern New York."

Before he could respond, I turned on my heel and marched out into the drafty hallway. I figured I'd spend some time poking around out there, see if Pop's guests had left anything interesting.

The window at the end of the hall was open partway and a cold breeze touched the side of my face, sending a chill through me. The Stanziki sisters wouldn't be too pleased to see that. Precious heat was slipping out beneath the window sash like water over a dam. But it might have been how the perp got into the apartment if there was a fire escape attached to the side of the old house.

I walked over to the window and bent down to take a look. An indignant screech greeted me. Careful not to touch the sill and mess up any fingerprints, I leaned out the window.

A huge beast sat hunched on the railing of the ancient fire escape. Yellow eyes glared accusingly into my own.

"Awww, Sweetie Pie," I cooed. "We forgot all about you in the ruckus, didn't we? What are you doing out there in the cold?"

He blinked and then let out another indignant yowl. Obviously, he was royally perturbed. But then, anyone who knew Sweetie Pie knew that was a permanent condition.

I leaned out farther and gathered his mangy, hairy body into my arms and pulled him inside. He latched on to my slick, nylon jacket with his claws, their sharpness shredding the nylon and letting loose a few feathers.

His oversize head, with its mangled, gnawed ears, bumped the bottom of my chin, and he nestled closer, shoving his head up against the hollow of my throat. His fur felt cold in my hands, his body heavy. I couldn't help but wonder how long he'd been sitting out there waiting for someone to come home and rescue him.

I moved back to my position outside the front door of the apartment, stroking Sweetie Pie's bulky body as a way of reassuring him that everything was okay. He was pretty tense, his fur standing on end, but after a few minutes I could feel him begin to relax.

I leaned up against the wall again, sliding down to sit on my heels. Some of Syracuse's finest had arrived and they swaggered into the apartment, a thick wave of testosterone following them in. A few nodded in my direction, but most were focused on what was going on inside Pop's place.

As I sat cooling my heels in the hall, I itched to get in there and get involved. But I knew police etiquette. I needed an invitation, and none of the guys in there seemed to recognize me. Not that I could expect them to; I'd been gone a long time.

As my tension rose, my hands tightened around Sweetie Pie's plump body, and he gave me a quick nip on the tip of my thumb as a warning. I concentrated on taking slow calming breaths and slipped a hand beneath his collar to keep him from jumping down and taking off in a huff.

The soft leather of the collar caught my attention and I glanced down. An unexpected lump of hot emotion filled the back of my throat. It was a hand-tooled collar, with clever cat prints lovingly carved into the leather and painted black.

I knew without question that it had been one of Charlie's creations, a favorite hobby of his—leatherwork. From a metal ring, a tiny pie charm hung off the collar and the name Sweetie Pie and Charlie's address were engraved on the back.

I fingered the pie charm as if I could reach into Pop's head and figure out what had happened in his apartment, but it was a useless gesture. Instead, I watched the drama inside the apartment unfold.

For years, I had dreamed—no, prayed—that the brothers on the force would ostracize Jack after his testimony against Pop. I had wanted them to shun his traitorous butt for what he'd done to Pop. And from the cool, studied nonchalant way they greeted him, it was pretty obvious my wish had come true.

Strangely enough, witnessing what I'd prayed for didn't bring me any great pleasure. I actually found myself feeling sorry for the guy.

Growing up in a cop household had taught me well how important a cop's fellow officers were, and when Pop had been convicted, I'd watched in dismay as his buddies ostracized him—cut him out of the brotherhood. Now Jack was getting a taste of how it felt, and something told me that he'd been feeling it for quite a while.

The detective in charge snapped a few questions at Jack and then turned in my direction. His smile was warm. Elliot Standish. I hadn't seen him come in.

He walked over, his hand out in greeting. "Hello, Killian. It's good to see you. I'm sorry you had to return on such a sad note." He nodded his head in the direction of Pop's bedroom. "Not to mention coming to your dad's house and finding that mess."

"Not a great homecoming, I agree," I said, standing up and shaking his hand. Over his shoulder, I could see a touch of resentment flicker across Jack's face. He hadn't missed the fact that he'd been pushed aside.

Standish took my arm and lead me back into the apartment. "Give me a rundown of what you observed when you entered the apartment. Don't leave anything out."

He and I took a slow, methodical walk through the apartment for the next fifteen minutes, while Jack was left to cool his heels in the hall.

"Any feeling for why Gibson would be here in Charlie's apartment?"

I shook my head. "I was going to meet the guy for the first time tomorrow. Apparently, he's handling Pop's affairs—his health proxy and his will."

Standish's right eyebrow, more weathered and gray than I remembered, took a leap upward. "Charlie had the money to hire Craig Gibson?"

"Apparently. You saying the guy charges more than Pop could afford?"

"Let me put it this way—he's out of my league, your league and Charlie's league all put together. He and his partner take on only the highest profile cases here in Syracuse and the surrounding areas. Usually, dealers with money to burn."

I whistled softly through my teeth. "So the question is where would Pop, a guy who is essentially down to his last nickel, get the money to pay for a guy like Gibson? And what would Gibson be doing making a house call?"

"Bingo." Standish glanced over at the gnome looking guy hunched over the body. "Got any thoughts on how he died, doc?"

"My professional opinion is that he bled to death," the coroner said dryly.

"No kidding, doc," Standish said. "Can you get any more specific?"

The coroner pointed to a series of bruises on the dead lawyer's jawline and upper chest. "They worked him over pretty good. And then they started in on him with the knife. Whoever was wielding the knife knew what he was doing. He made sure the guy didn't exsanguinate too quickly." The coroner straightened up, grunting slightly and placing a hand against his lower back.

"I'm getting too old for this," he said. "Whoever did this wanted information. And he went about getting it in a slow and methodical manner. You want anything more specific than that, you're going to have to wait until I'm done with the autopsy."

He nodded his head and two of his staff wheeled a gurney with an open body bag on top into the room.

Standish jerked his head toward the living room. "Let's get out of their way."

We moved back out into the living room where a crew of CSI workers swarmed over the area, busy dusting everything for prints.

"You ready to go?"

I glanced up to see Jack standing next to me. He and Standish glanced at each other, but neither spoke. I had learned from Jack earlier at the hospital that he was actually on speaking terms with Standish, but their current coolness toward each other told me that their friendship was probably on the sly. No doubt Standish didn't want any of his fellow officers knowing he associated with someone who had actually broken the blue wall.

"Yeah, I'm ready." I turned to Standish. "You'll call me as soon as you hear anything?"

Standish nodded and wandered off to talk to a few other officers congregated in the kitchen area.

Jack swung a small cat crate in my direction. "You're going to have to put the beast in here. We'll never get him across town otherwise."

Sweetie Pie's ears immediately went back and he hissed. I wasn't sure if it was Jack's presence or the appearance of the cat crate. Whichever it was, Sweetie Pie wasn't happy. Jack was smart enough to know that he best not try to hustle Sweetie Pie into the crate. He left that job to me.

As we trooped back down the stairs, I asked, "Why would Pop hire a lawyer known for working for the dregs—drug dealers?"

Jack shrugged. "Guess we'll have to ask him when he wakes up."

A few minutes later, we were on his bike, the cat crate sitting snug between us as we headed across town. Sweetie Pie yowled his discontent the entire way.

THE ELEVATOR to Jack's apartment was different from the one I remembered from nine years ago. Apparently, the loft had become a bit more upscale over the years. Gone was the freight elevator ambience, replaced with a sleek, metallic-looking interior filled with mirrors and recessed lighting.

"Impressive," I said, shifting the cat crate to my other hand and glancing around.

Jack pressed the button for the fourth floor and then leaned one shoulder against the wall as the elevator started upward. "The place went co-op about five years ago. It was either move out or buy in. So, I bought in." He grinned. "Kind of strange to be a home owner."

"Don't tell me you're getting domesticated."

He laughed. "Hardly. The place is made up mostly of singles. But we've made a lot of improvements to the building over the past couple of years. You haven't seen the place in a while so it'll look pretty different."

Haven't seen the place in a while? Who was he kidding. I hadn't stepped foot in his apartment since the day I got word that he'd reported to work and ratted out Charlie.

That single thought sent a flash of guilt rumbling through me. What the hell was I doing here? Hadn't I sworn this would never happen?

It was hard accepting the fact that I was even standing in the elevator next to him. The rest of the family would probably tar and feather me and ride me out of town on a rail if they knew where I was at this very moment.

The elevator slid to a smooth stop and the door opened.

Jack's apartment was directly across the hall. He unlocked the heavy door, leaned in and flicked on a switch.

Soft light flooded the interior. He stepped aside and motioned for me to go first.

My heart kicked up a few beats as I brushed past him. I was careful to keep my arms close to my sides. I didn't think I could handle any contact between us after our forced intimacy on the back of his bike.

The feeling had been uncomfortable and incredibly awkward, like having to be the maid of honor to your usher of an ex-boyfriend during your best friend's wedding. You can't back out and you can't let everyone know how stupid you feel.

I forced a bit of a swagger into my step. It was all an act, but what else was I supposed to do—except wonder what the hell I was doing casually walking into O'Brien's apartment. Apparently, I'd lost connection with my last fully functioning brain cell.

Of course, Jack seemed oblivious. He moved about the cavernous room, turning on lights and talking as he went. "Make yourself at home. I'll let you take the bed."

He nodded toward one end of the room that had a large Japanese-style screen set up to partition off the bedroom area. "I've been sleeping on the couch lately, anyway."

A glimmer of self-amusement touched one corner of those exquisite lips and my heart tumbled just a little. I pushed the feeling deeper and concentrated on what he was saying.

"I'm on call. I could get beeped at any time. It's just easier this way." He ran a restless hand through his thick black hair. "I haven't been sleeping too well lately and will just end up keeping you awake. I've got a touch of insomnia." He gazed at me, his eyes telling me he knew I'd understand.

I nodded noncommitedly, not wanting to let on that I

knew exactly what he meant. But there was no denying that I knew. Hard, fast memories flooded my brain with the force of a dam breaking. Memories of sleeping next to Jack, my butt pressed tight against his hard belly, his strong arm wrapped securely around my chest, resting directly below my breasts.

He'd always been a light sleeper, a person who prowled the apartment at all hours of the night. When we'd slept together, I used to hear him get up and leave the bed, and sometimes I'd go in search of him, finding him slouched in a chair or standing in front of one of the huge windows overlooking the dark street below. The soft light filtering in from the street lamps would caress the hard, muscular lines of his body, and the beauty of him would always take my breath away, leaving me with a painful ache of need deep inside me.

Just the thought of those times made the ache creep into my belly, catching me off guard. I blinked, trying to regain my equilibrium, but the memories continued to wash over me.

Jack would always chalk his restlessness up to work, thoughts about a case pressing in on him. I used to lean up against him and gently massage his shoulders, molding my body to his and soaking in his warmth and strength.

It never seemed to do much in the way of getting him to relax, but it always seemed to have a nice effect on our love life. At times, his insomnia had meant marathon sessions of wild and wickedly delicious tumbles in the twisted sheets.

Startled, I shook myself. Memories like that were going to have to be off-limits if I planned on staying even one night under the same roof as Jack. They were too dangerous. I needed to stay focused on the here and now—no more trips down memory lane.

"I'm not taking the bed, Jack." I moved over to the couch and swung my duffel bag and Sweetie Pie's crate up onto the cushion. "I'll be fine on the couch."

"Same old Killian, huh? Incapable of ever doing what someone asks of her?"

I stiffened. Bullheadedness had always been my badge of honor. But it was the one thing that kept me whole and sane in a crazy world that changed at a moment's notice. Leftover stuff from my early life.

"Apparently not," I said, leaning down to open my backpack and rummage through the contents. I wasn't sure what I was looking for, I just knew I couldn't look at him right then.

"There's no privacy out here in the living room. At least the bedroom is partitioned off."

He paused for a moment and then added quietly, "I'm asking for my benefit, Killian, not yours. It would just be better if you had some privacy."

The soft tones, rich and husky, filtered across the space between us and lifted the hair on the nape of my neck as if I'd been touched on the tenderest part of my skin by the calloused tips of his long fingers.

I lifted my head and met his gaze across the length of the room. Those dark blue eyes burned with an intensity capable of opening a hole right through the middle of my chest and stabbing the center of my heart.

I struggled to breathe as he waited.

Finally, I shrugged and swallowed hard against the sudden dryness in the back of my throat. "Fine. You win. I'll take the bed."

He smiled that slow, easy smile of his and the intensity of his gaze softened a bit, as if he knew even before I spoke that he'd won. I tightened my fists and pulled my duffel bag closed with a fierce tug.

Damn it, he'd done it to me again, manipulated the hell out of me and he hadn't even broken a sweat.

I, on the other hand, had a fat bead of sweat rolling merrily down the valley between my breasts, making its way toward my belly button.

I ignored it. No way was I touching any part of my anatomy with Jack O'Brien's smoldering eyes sparking like heat lightning across the length of the loft.

I knew without him saying anything that he was more than a little aware of my current predicament. Damn his psychic hide. I had thought the little thread of connection between us had died a long time ago. Apparently I was wrong.

I reached down and opened Sweetie Pie's crate. He slinked out gingerly. I'm sure he wasn't used to the degree of cleanliness that permeated Jack's apartment. Charlie appeared to be a bit less of a fastidious housekeeper in his older years.

"He's going to need a litter box."

"I'll take care of it," he said.

I yanked my bag off the couch and slung it over my shoulder, wincing slightly.

"Shoulder still hurting?"

"I'm fine."

"Doesn't appear that you're fine. You took a pretty bad fall. Better let me take a look at it. If you need to have it X-rayed, we're going to have to head back over to the hospital."

"What, you're a doctor now?"

"No, but in case you've forgotten, I'm a paramedic."

"I'm fine. A hot shower will take care of it. You don't mind if I use your shower, right?"

"Help yourself. Towels are in the cabinet behind the door. Shampoo and soap are on the shelf in the stall. I'll check the shoulder after you shower."

The slight smugness touching one corner of those perfect lips made me clench my back teeth. He turned away, his attention on the expensive-looking stereo equipment lining one side of the wall.

As I entered the bathroom and slammed the door shut with a quick kick of one foot, the smooth, soothing tones of Norah Jones slipped from the speakers and filled the loft.

I groaned aloud and leaned my head against the door of the bathroom, closing my eyes in frustration. Oh, God, was he doing this on purpose? Was he looking to ignite me into a single roaring flame of sexual desire?

I bent over the tub and turned on the cold tap. Forget the hot shower. I was going to need to freeze out the scorching heat coursing through my bloodstream if I intended to go back into the same room as Jack O'Brien and converse like a rational, coherent human being.

Chapter Four

When I opened the bathroom door twenty or so minutes later, clouds of steam drifted out into the open space of the loft and hung there.

My skin, flushed and heated from the hot shower, was wrapped in a thick bathrobe I'd found draped on a hook on the back of the door. The cold shower idea hadn't lasted longer than two seconds. I was a wimp, plain and simple.

The bathrobe was Jack's, and I knew putting it on was a major mistake. Why? Because the slightly tangy scent of his aftershave wafted up to fill my senses.

But I hadn't had much of a choice. I had the habit of sleeping in panties and men's summer undershirts. Not exactly what I'd call body-concealing clothing, and I hadn't thought to bring a robe. I'd packed in haste, and I definitely hadn't planned on having a sleepover at my ex-lover's apartment.

The loft appeared empty, the soft, mellow tones of Norah sliding out of the speakers like warm, sticky honey. Maybe he'd gone out for a run. From past experience, I knew he often ran at night. If that was the case, I'd have time to climb into bed, fall asleep and not worry about the fact that his long, lean, deliciously muscular body lay only inches away from me on the living room couch.

"Feel better?"

I whirled around to see him stand up from his crouch next to the cast-iron stove in one corner of the loft. He'd laid a fire and lit it. Flames shot through the balled-up newspaper and licked the edges of the perfectly stacked kindling. The smell of dry wood burning filled the room, and I had an overwhelming urge to run for my life.

Things had the feel of spinning out of control. Norah Jones on the stereo, a romantic fire, a hunk of a man and me in a bathrobe, feeling every nerve ending screaming for release. This was a lethal combination, one to be avoided at all costs. I was in serious trouble.

"I'm feeling fine," I lied. I turned and headed straight for the partition. Sanctuary lay behind the screen.

"I had some Chinese delivered while you were putting a major dent in my hot water supply."

I noticed the familiar cluster of white cartons sitting on the coffee table in front of the couch. The smell of sesame chicken, teriyaki pork and fried rice, combined with the sweet smell of burning wood, told me escape was no longer possible.

My stomach rumbled, reminding me that I hadn't had anything since the PowerBar in the hospital.

"Maybe I'll have a little," I said, edging over to sit on one corner of the couch—the corner furthest from Jack.

He brushed off his hands and came to stand a few feet from me. I knew his eyes were on me, taking in the fact that my wet hair, curly and in disarray, covered the collar of his robe, the brilliant red in sharp contrast to the white.

He didn't speak, and I didn't dare look up. If I looked

up, I knew I'd be pulled into something I couldn't handle, something I wasn't equipped to deal with now or any time in the near future.

I was beginning to think Shawna was right—Jack O'Brien wasn't as far out of my system as I had tried to convince myself. Obviously, I was going to require the services of a good exorcist.

He waited as if expecting me to say something, but when I didn't, he sighed and sat down on the floor across from me, the coffee table sitting securely between us.

He folded those long muscular legs beneath him, and I pulled my gaze off of them, concentrating on his hands. His hands, something I'd always loved, were big, with veins thick and strong crisscrossing the back. He effortlessly opened the cartons and dished out generous helpings of everything for the two of us. I knew not to look up. Knew not to make eye contact.

"Here."

He handed a plate to me and when I reached for it, I winced in pain, the shoulder reawakening in spite of the hot soak in the shower.

"Shoulder still bothering you, huh?"

"It's fine. Just a little twinge. Nothing a good night's sleep won't cure."

"We should have stopped at the hospital and had the E.R. doc take a look at it. We were right there."

"We had other things to do," I said, lifting a healthy chunk of sesame chicken to my mouth and stuffing it in. I chewed, figuring if I ignored him, he'd leave me alone and let me eat in peace. But as usual, I was wrong.

He climbed to his feet and moved over to stand next to

me. Next thing I knew, those long fingers were pulling aside the thick cotton of the robe.

"Hey!" I protested.

"Relax, Chili, I'm not planning on ravaging you right here on the couch. I just want to take a look at your shoulder—see if it's bruised and in need of attention tonight."

I flung down my fork. However I realized he wasn't going to back down until I humored him, so I shrugged the robe half off my left shoulder, clutching the front to keep everything else from falling out and embarrassing me even more.

Jack settled onto the arm of the couch. I could feel the warmth of his skin through the cloth of his jeans a few inches from me. He leaned in, and his fingers gently probed my shoulder. "Does it hurt here?"

I nodded, wanting to add that it hurt somewhere else, lower down, somewhere sweet and deliciously wicked, but I managed to keep that thought to myself. I bit my bottom lip.

His hands moved up over the top of my shoulder, the calloused tips of his fingers probing and kneading my heated flesh.

I could only hope he thought my flushed skin was due to my hot shower and not the burning need that sang in my ears and sent my blood roiling.

Please God, I thought, *make him stop now. Please don't let me fall into a million shattered pieces of wanton need right here in front of him. Please don't let me embarrass myself any more than I already have.*

I wanted to shut down. To turn off my emotions. But most of all, I wanted to block the craving flood of need that threatened to swamp my entire body. I knew it wouldn't take too much more and I'd be over the edge, a whimpering, begging fool.

"Okay, slip your arm out of the sleeve and let me see if you can move it." His voice was so matter-of-fact, as if he'd asked me to pass the vegetable fried rice.

I wanted to protest, to refuse, but instead I dutifully did as he asked. The cool air of the room touched my forearm and puckered the little hairs on my arm.

At least, I told myself, it was the cool air and not the sensuous glide of Jack's hands on my sensitive skin. Skin that seemed to recognize the touch of his hand like a memory etched into every one of my nerve endings. A memory never forgotten, never erased.

He gently bent my arm and moved it upward. I cringed a bit, but the pain wasn't so bad that it eliminated any of the other interesting feelings I was experiencing elsewhere in my body.

"You've got a small bruise right here." He lightly touched the upper line of my shoulder blade, and then ran his finger along the edge to the side of my neck. Goose bumps pebbled my skin, and I struggled to suppress a shiver.

"It doesn't hurt," I lied.

"It's not a serious bruise, and you're moving it okay. You'll live."

His casual tone and the fact that he obviously wasn't feeling any of the sensations I was feeling angered me more than I cared to admit.

"I told you I was fine." I pulled my arm away and stared up at him defiantly, not wanting him to know how much his words—his touch—affected me.

He smiled that quiet, all-knowing smile of his, the one

that told me he knew *exactly* what I was feeling, and lifted up the sleeve of my robe expectantly.

As I shifted on the couch, ready to shove my arm back in, the oversize strap of my thin undershirt slid down my upper arm, and I knew without even looking down that the top of my left breast was now fully exposed.

My gaze didn't leave his, and I didn't dare look down. My cheeks flushed with heat. But then I had my revenge. I saw it in his sea-blue eyes. A flash of something needy. Something red-hot. Gotcha, I thought.

Oh, he fought against it. Gave it the old college try. One corner of his mouth tightened and he took in a deep breath, as if to fortify himself against something.

But in the end, he couldn't resist, couldn't keep his own gaze from drifting downward to caress my exposed skin with a gaze so heated, so sensuous that it sent a quiver of something dark and forbidden coursing through my belly and lower still. Damn, how was he able to do this to me with a single glance?

"I've missed you," he said, his voice barely above a whisper.

"I've missed you, too," I admitted softly.

As soon as the words were out of my mouth, I wanted to snatch them back, grab them out of midair and stuff them back in my mouth.

How could I betray Pop this way? How could I admit to still having feelings like this for the man who had betrayed everything I believed in? The man who had hurt the single person in my life who had always been true, honest and straightforward. The only man who had believed in me and supported me when I was least able to believe in myself or in my own worth.

But Jack seemed oblivious to the pitched battle going on inside of me. The outer rim of blue, the darkest midnight blue of his eyes, deepened, and he slid down off the arm of the couch to sit next to me.

I took a stuttering breath that seemed to catch and flutter in the back of my throat.

Now was the time for me to run, to get as far away from him as was humanly possible. But I was frozen, trapped by the intense look of hunger and fire on his lean face.

He bent his head and softly touched his lips to mine. It was a simple touch that sent licks of something hot and delicious racing through me. Without thinking, I opened to him, and his tongue slipped inside to lightly caress the tip of my tongue. And then, when I thought I might be able to pull away, to escape, he slid his tongue slowly down the length of my own, and I knew I was lost.

Oh, Lord, it was like coming home. I melted inside, like a soft spring thaw that seemed to liquefy my entire body, my entire soul.

He gently pushed me backward, and I lay back on the cushions, my spine suddenly liquefied mercury. It was if all my strength, all my power, had disappeared into nothingness.

He followed me down, pressing the full length of his body upon mine. I could feel every sharp, hard angle of his muscular frame molding itself to my softness, and it was like being covered with a down comforter, thick and heated to a core temperature that was almost more than a body could bear.

Time stretched between us and a strange lethargy came over me. His mouth seemed to be everywhere at once. On my lips, against the hollow of my throat, between my breasts and on them, gently sucking on my nipples and sending currents of something mind-blowing coursing through me. A touch so intimate, so familiar that my body responded with no thought, no reason.

The doubts of a moment ago vanished like a whisper of forgotten smoke. I reveled in his touch, basked in the feel of his big hands slipping between the front opening of the robe and traveling over my body like two coals of heated stone.

I arched my back and felt the hardness of him pressing urgently against my belly. Something wild and abandoned escaped from the back of my throat, and I wrapped my legs around him, pulling him closer, wanting him inside me.

And then, something chimed, startling us both. Jack swore softly against my lips and then drew back. He lifted his lips off mine, millimeter by millimeter, as if reluctant to stop. But stop he did.

Groggy, slightly confused, I shook my head, feeling as though I were coming out of a drug-induced stupor.

He reached a hand back and grabbed his beeper off his belt, checking the number. Leaning over, he picked up the portable phone and punched in a number.

I dipped my head, secretly running the tip of my tongue over my bottom lip, savoring the last lingering taste of him. I knew without question that I wouldn't be tasting him again anytime soon. We'd stepped over the line, and we both knew it. Such a slip wouldn't happen again.

"O'Brien," he snapped curtly into the phone.

He listened for a minute, the lazy, sensuous look in his dark eyes changing to something hard and urgent. "How long ago?" He nodded and then said, "I'm on my way."

He hung up the phone and stood, the warmth of his big

frame immediately withdrawing, leaving me feeling strangely vacant and alone.

"I have to go out for a while. One of the regulars called in sick and they're short a paramedic. Big accident out on the interstate."

I nodded and pulled my robe closed with trembling fingers. "Don't worry about me. I'm headed for bed."

He considered this for a minute and then shook his head, a fan of dark hair drifting down onto his forehead and tumbling into those beautiful China Sea eyes. "Really bad timing, huh?"

"Actually, I'd say it was perfect timing. You and I were about to make a very bad mistake. One we won't be making again."

He stared at me for another moment, as if testing to see if I'd back down, but then he shook his head. "You're right, of course."

He strolled over to the closet and lifted out his jacket. "Lock the door and stay put," he ordered as he let himself out. "I'll call if I'm going to be late."

"Don't bother. You'll just wake me up." I wanted to laugh. Yeah, right, he'd wake me up. If I could get to sleep now, it would be a miracle.

He shut the door, not bothering to comment.

I stood alone for a minute, my head still reeling. And then, I did something stupid. I walked over to the window to watch him leave. I knew that it was childish, but I needed to get one last look at him before he disappeared from my sight.

Something told me that if Jack had his way, he'd make sure he didn't return until late tomorrow morning, hoping I'd be out of his apartment by then.

He'd been as surprised and shaken by the kiss we'd just shared as I'd been, and we both knew only too well that we'd overstepped a line drawn in the sand nine years ago. A line that had stood between us for way too long for us to ignore it now.

I knew without a doubt that I needed to go to the lawyer's office alone tomorrow. Even though Gibson was dead, I needed to get a look at Pop's will. I knew someone at the man's office would be able to help me out. If I had the money for a hotel, I'd probably have gotten dressed and left right then. Doing that would save both of us a lot of anguish and recriminations in the morning.

I leaned against the windowsill, peering down at the darkened street. It had sleeted a little earlier and the pavement was slick. Puddles of half-frozen water pooled in the uneven cracks of the sidewalk, and I knew without even stepping outside that ice was forming around the edges. By morning, the puddles would be frozen solid, tiny skating rinks to trip up unsuspecting pedestrians.

Jack appeared, and I watched him head for his bike, his long legs eating up the sidewalk with ease. The heel of one boot hit the center of one of the puddles, breaking the ice and sending a spray of icy water up the back of his jeans. He was oblivious.

He swung one leg over the seat and then glanced up at the window. A small smile quirked one corner of those perfect lips, the ones that had done such interesting and erotic things to my body less than five minutes ago.

It was obvious he enjoyed the fact that he'd caught me watching. I folded my arms across my chest, pretending I'd simply stepped over to the window to check on the weather, but I knew I wasn't fooling anyone. Myself included.

He shoved two fingers into the front pocket of his jeans and pulled out the key, sticking it in the ignition. With one hand he revved the engine and then lifted the other hand to wave to me.

Stubbornly, petulantly, I didn't wave back. His grin widened. That only got me more angry, and I think I scowled down at him. But he didn't seem bothered.

He swung the bike away from the curb and did a quick U-turn, roaring off down the street, headed somewhere. Determined to save the world. Anything to avoid being cooped up in his apartment with me.

As I watched his retreating back disappear around the corner at the end of the street, my attention was diverted by a car pulling up across the street. A black Town Car purred down the street and slid into the spot directly across from the loft. The headlights snapped off, but no one got out.

A strange feeling of being watched prickled the back of my neck. I stepped back away from the window, for the first time cursing Jack and his lack of curtains. Moving over to the side, I peeked out again.

Inside the car, there was a brief glow of something red. Whoever was inside was lighting up a cigarette. The end glowed for a moment and then the window on the driver's side slid down just a hair. Smoke drifted out into the cold night air.

Someone was watching the apartment. I knew it without question. I could even feel the crawl of the person's gaze from below searching the blank windows of Jack's apartment, settling finally on me.

I ran over to the door and checked the locks. I locked and relocked the dead bolt a few times just to be sure. My hands shook.

As I headed back toward the window and the car sitting outside, the phone rang.

I froze, my heart hammering a harsh, staccato beat against the flat of my breastbone.

My gaze darted to the window. Was the car still out there?

The phone rang again, shrill and demanding.

Should I answer it?

It could be Jack checking up on me. Or it could be the hospital trying to reach me about Pop.

I picked the receiver up on the third ring.

"Hello?" My voice sounded hesitant even to my own ears.

"Hello, Killian." I didn't recognize the voice. It was deep, with a slight South American accent. "Spending a bit of time alone this evening, are you?"

"Who is this?"

"A friend of your father's. A friend who wants what belongs to him."

"My father is in the hospital. You'll have to contact his lawyer."

The voice on the other end of the phone laughed, but it was a rough sound as if the person wasn't used to laughing a great deal. Almost rusty-sounding. "Oh, I don't think anyone will be contacting your dad's lawyer. Something tells me that maggot is burning in the same hell all good lawyers go to when they depart this world."

The room tilted slightly and I dropped down to the floor to keep from keeling over. My stomach twisted and I felt slightly nauseous. How did he know Gibson was dead? The news hadn't even hit the papers yet.

"What do you want?"

"I want whatever your daddy left for you to keep safe for him, Killian."

"I don't know what you're talking about. He hasn't left me anything."

Well, he'd left me his damn, crazy cat to take care of, but that was beside the point. As if on cue, Sweetie Pie sauntered over and rubbed up against my thigh. When I reached down to stroke his ear, he took a swipe at me. Somehow I didn't think the nut job on the phone was really interested in lobbying for the job of caring for Sweetie Pie. A cat lover he wasn't.

"Well, I suggest you figure out what it is I'm looking for because unlike the two idiots who botched things up this afternoon, I'm not so stupid. I get what I want. And I want it within twenty-four hours."

"And if I don't figure out what you want by then?"

"I come and get it the hard way, sweetheart. And you won't like the hard way one little bit. In fact, I'll have you screaming worse than that boyfriend of yours gets you going when you're doing the wild thing. You think about that real hard, sweet stuff."

The phone line clicked.

"Hello? Hello?"

Nothing, the line hummed.

I pressed my finger on the Disconnect button and then almost jumped out of my skin when the phone rang again.

"Listen, you crazy dirtbag, don't be calling here anymore and threatening me!" I yelled into the receiver. "I already told you I don't have what you're looking for!"

A stunned silence met my rant, and then Jack's low, soothing tones filtered across the line. "I just called to remind you to dead bolt the front door. Is something going on that I need to know about?"

I tightened my hand on the receiver. Damn. I was losing it. I mean really losing it, and I didn't want Jack to know how badly I'd been rattled by the call.

I took a deep breath, giving myself a minute to collect my thoughts. I didn't want him running home, thinking he needed to rescue me.

"I'm fine. The phone just startled me."

"What's going on, Chili?" The gentleness in his tone and the actual slip of him calling me *Chili* made me have to wait another beat before answering.

He waited as if realizing I needed the time to get my emotions under control. I appreciated that more than he knew. Being strong, being in control, was a major issue for me. I think Jack understood that better than anyone.

"Right after you left, someone pulled up outside the apartment. They parked right across the street. No one got out." I sucked in another deep breath. "I'm pretty sure someone is watching me from inside the car."

"It's probably just a couple of lovebirds getting a few extra gropes in before the girl has to go in and face an irate dad," Jack said. "No reason to panic."

Every muscle in my body tightened in defense, and my teeth clamped down with a vengeance. Oh yeah, so much for him understanding. He'd dismissed my concerns as if I were some kind of hysterical female worked up about a few unexpected bumps in the night. I didn't like having my concerns dismissed so casually. I was a trained observer.

"So then you've got a real good excuse for the threatening phone call I just got too, right?"

He was silent for a minute and then asked, "What phone call?"

"The one I got right before you decided to call and harass me about locking the front door."

"Who called you?"

I paced the hardwood floor. "How the heck should I know? He didn't identify himself—harassing phone callers usually don't, you know? He just threatened me."

My tone was edgy, not in the least forgiving that he was now treating my complaint with some concern. "He told me that if I didn't give him what he wanted he'd be coming for it himself. And interestingly enough, the guy knew that Gibson was dead."

"Tell me exactly what he said, word for word."

So I explained the call word for word, and Jack was silent for another minute. I figured he was deciding exactly how he was going to word his apology.

But I was wrong. He didn't apologize.

"I'm on my way home," he said. "Don't answer the phone. Don't open the door and stay away from the windows. I'm calling Standish and telling him to send a patrol car over to check out the vehicle parked across the street. Stay put!"

He clicked off.

The authoritative tone of his voice and the fact that he then hung up on me only served to tick me off even more. The nerve of him.

I threw the portable onto the coffee table. Damn domineering, bossy, chauvinistic so-and-so. He acted as if he were still a cop rather than a paramedic.

How had I managed to forget that particular flaw in Jack O'Brien's personality? Ever since I've know the man, he hadn't shown the ability to understand the concept of admitting when he was wrong. An actual apology to someone was next to criminal in his book.

I dropped down and crawled across the hardwood floor to the bank of windows lining the street side of the apartment. Grabbing hold of the windowsill, I cautiously poked my head up and peeked down to the street below.

The car was still there, the driver's side window still cracked open, smoke drifting out in a steady stream. Obviously, Jack was way off on his assessment of a little hanky-panky going on in the front seat of the car. No one would have any time to be groping body parts in that vehicle. Not when the person sitting in the driver's seat was chain-smoking up a storm.

As I watched, a car turned the corner, the headlights headed down the street. It was a police cruiser. Smoke belched out the tailpipe of the black sedan.

The driver had noticed the police car, too. He'd turned on the ignition, getting ready to bolt. But the cop wasn't having any of that. He pulled up next to the Town Car, blocking it in.

I rose up a little higher to get a better look.

The driver's side window of the police car slid down and the cop hooked an arm over the door. He waited until the Town Car's driver lowered his own window.

I squinted a bit, trying to get a look at the guy sitting behind the wheel, but he kept back in the shadows. There was no way to see into the back seat of the car; the windows were tinted and the light on the street was poor.

The cop and the driver seemed to talk for a few moments and then the cop reached out a hand, making a *gimme* motion with his fingers. Probably asking for license and registration.

I gnawed on my bottom lip, worried. It made me nervous that the policeman was being so casual, so easygoing. Pop, myself, even Jack, would never have parked face-to-face with some unknown perp in a car.

We would have approached the perp's car from the rear, kept back from the driver until we knew we had things under control or our backup had arrived.

Suddenly, the driver of the Town Car stuck a hand out. Unfortunately, he wasn't holding his license and registration. Even from here I could see the revolver in the guy's hand.

I jumped up and pounded on the window. I screamed a warning to the cop.

But it was too late. Two quick pops and the policeman slumped over the wheel of his cruiser. The perp's hand disappeared back inside his own car, and a second later he jumped out the passenger side door.

He was chunky with a fireplug build. Five foot five at the most. He stopped for a moment and glanced up at the window toward me. The street light hit him full on, and I memorized every feature of his tough face, storing it away. Young. Twenty-five. Maybe as old as twenty-eight. Dark complexion with buzz-cut hair and a square chin. His nose was long, hooked at the end. The eyes were hooded beneath thick brows.

He seemed to realize he'd made a mistake and ducked his head, sprinting off down the street and tossing the gun overhand into a Dumpster as he passed.

I ran for the portable and punched in 911.

Chapter Five

As soon as I made the call, I did something I knew was stupid. Something so risky I knew I was making a mistake, but I did it, anyway.

I grabbed my jacket out of the closet, shoved my bare feet into a pair of Jack's L.L. Bean boots and ran for the elevator.

As I jabbed my finger on the down button, my brain screamed at me to rethink what I was planning to do. But I didn't care. First and foremost, I'm a cop, and a cop's daughter.... Okay, a former cop's foster daughter. But a cop's daughter nonetheless. No self-respecting cop or cop's daughter would allow a fellow policeman to lie out there alone after being gunned down by some thug. I needed to get to him.

No way could I allow him to wait alone, his precious life's blood leaking out of him. I knew without question that I owed him something and that something was my presence, even if it was to simply hold his hand until his fellow officers arrived.

When I pushed open the front door and stepped out onto the sidewalk, my feet skidded on the sheet of ice coating the sidewalk. The cold night air had frozen everything, making walking as treacherous as a two-year-old on single-blade skates on a skating rink for the first time.

Clutching my coat around me, I felt the chill of the night breeze slip up beneath the cloth of Jack's robe. I wrapped the coat tighter around me and practically skated across the street to the still running police cruiser.

Even through the closed window on the passenger's side, I could hear the radio squawking like a crazed chicken. The dispatcher was firing out requests for backup while trying to raise the man slumped over the wheel.

I ran around the end of the cruiser, clutching frantically to the cold metal side in a desperate attempt to keep myself from falling. When I skidded to a stop next to the driver's side, I reached in and pressed my fingers to the man's neck.

Relief washed over me. Beneath the tips of my fingers, I could feel a steady pulse, but I drew my hand away covered with blood. My heart pounded in my ears. It wasn't a small injury. The guy was hurt bad.

I yanked open the door and pulled him out of the car. He was heavy, deadweight, falling sideways, his arms flopping uselessly as I lowered him onto the pavement.

I grunted under the heft of his weight, scrambling to keep from being pinned beneath him. I rolled him onto his back and his hat fell off, revealing short, cropped brown hair, and a sweet innocent spray of freckles across the bridge of his pug nose.

His mouth was a perfect circle, making him look as if someone had taken him totally by surprise. Which, from my post at the window, was pretty much accurate. The kid hadn't expected the thug to pull the gun. He hadn't even known what hit him. I called him a kid because he couldn't have been more than twenty-two. Twenty-three at the most. Straight out of the academy, most likely.

I checked his pulse again. Still steady. I leaned down

and pressed my ear to his chest. He was breathing. I sat back on my heels and checked him over. Blood was spreading down his left arm, soaking his armpit and entire sleeve. He'd been hit all right.

I unzipped his jacket and yanked his shirt open.

I sucked in a breath of relief and glanced heavenward. Thank you, God. The kid had been smart enough to wear his vest. Rookies sometimes got cocky, forgoing their vests for a cleaner, sleeker look, and sometimes the veteran officers left theirs off due to its weight and the bulky feel beneath their uniforms. But the smart ones never forgot.

The bullet had missed his chest and entered the fleshy portion of his upper shoulder, right next to the end of his vest. He was going to be fine. He was damn lucky.

Off in the distance, I could hear the sirens getting closer.

I grabbed the kid's hand in mine and leaned down to whisper in his ear, "Just hang on, kid, they're on their way. Your buddies are on the way."

I SAT ON A PATHETICALLY worn leather couch situated in the far corner of the Syracuse Police Department's squad room on the third floor. Someone, the heavyset sergeant with kind eyes, had given me a blanket to wrap myself up in. But for some reason, I couldn't stop shivering. Kneeling on the cold pavement must have lowered my body temp too low to ever warm up again.

I pulled my legs up close to my chest, clasping my arms around them tightly and tried to conserve some warmth. Deep inside, below my ribs, I was shaking so hard I thought everything in me might suddenly shatter into a thousand pieces. It felt as though I would never be warm again.

Through gritty, grainy eyes, I stared across the squad

room and spied Standish huddled with a few of his police buddies. They seemed to be arguing about something.

But at this point, I hardly cared. I'd been up over twenty-nine hours by now, and I was exhausted. If someone asked me my name, I wasn't sure I'd be able to give them a straight answer. My mind would probably go blank, which, in a sense, would be a sweet blessing.

I knew someone was going to want me to look at some mug shots or work out a sketch on the computer with a police artist, but I wasn't sure how much longer I could keep my eyes open. Or even think clearly enough to be of any help to anyone.

The blanket must have started to work because suddenly I was feeling a little warmer. The warmth started at my toes and then spread over my entire body. I leaned my head back against the butter-soft leather and closed my eyes. I just needed to rest them for a minute.

I drifted. It was pleasant, and everything around me softened. The voices of the men arguing on the other side of the room seemed to fade and blend into the background. I must have fallen asleep because the next thing I knew, someone was shaking my shoulder and calling my name.

My eyes snapped open and I straightened up. Jack.

I rubbed my eyes, trying to hide the relieved tears brought on by his unexpected presence. "Where'd you come from and how long was I out?"

"Elliot called me. Told me you might need a ride home." He looked about as weary as I felt. "He said you've been asleep for about an hour or so." He put a hand under my arm and started to guide me up.

"Don't they want me to look at some mug shots?" I protested, more than a little miffed at myself for the warmth that flooded through me at the welcome sight of his familiar face. Why was my heart betraying me when I needed to keep him at arm's length to protect my sanity?

My defences going back up, I reminded myself that I didn't like being taken care of, especially by someone I'd written off years ago.

"No need to worry about the mug shots. According to Elliot, he got a call from the hospital. Bobby Zander came around right before he went up for surgery. He was able to tell the captain that he recognized the guy who shot him. A small-time thug by the name of Iggie Dansk. He isn't connected to anyone. A freelancer, from what I hear. They already have a warrant out for his arrest."

Standish moved over to stand next to Jack. "We'll have the guy in custody by morning."

His voice was filled with a familiar confidence. A confidence I'm sure he'd used when he'd told my foster siblings that he'd find the idiots who ran over Pop and put him in a coma. But the tone didn't foster any big degree of confidence in me. Not when he wasn't making any progress in that department.

"Why do you think the guy was hanging outside Jack's apartment?" I asked, trying a new line of questioning.

"Either someone hired him to watch Jack, which I think is highly unlikely since he didn't appear interested in following him when he left on a call," Standish said. "Or he was hired to keep an eye on *you*."

"But why?" I frowned, more than a little confused. "I'm not getting any of this. I haven't visited Syracuse in over nine years. I have no connections here except for Pop and my foster siblings. And if Pop or the others want to see me, they make the trip up to the Adirondacks. I don't come here."

"So I've noticed," Jack said, his voice reaching out and caressing me with a soft accusation that was hard to miss.

I ignored the comment. What did he want me to say? He already knew only too well why I didn't visit—him, and the painful memories that went along with him. But I didn't bother to bring him up to speed. There wasn't any sense in going over ancient history in the middle of the Syracuse Police Department.

Standish seemed to recognize that another level of conversation had taken over, one he wasn't party to.

From the look on his face, I could tell he was relieved not to be a party to it. Like most cops, emotions made him antsy.

He shifted uneasily. "Look, I'm going out to see if I can't pick up that little weasel, Iggie, at one of his usual haunts. I'll catch you two later." He winked at me. "Take care, Killian. It's good to see you, even if it's been under such rotten circumstances."

He sauntered off, a cop walk I was only too familiar with. I wanted to call him back and use him as a buffer between Jack and myself. But he was gone before I could even open my mouth.

"Come on, you look like hell," Jack said, reaching down again to pull me up off the couch. "I'm taking you home. You need a good night's sleep."

"Thanks for the compliment." I brushed his hand away and stood up on my own. I kept the blanket wrapped over my shoulders, resisting the urge to reach up and try to run my fingers through what I knew was a rat's nest of a hairdo. "Did you find out anything new about Craig Gibson?"

"Such as?" he probed.

"Like, were you able to pump Standish for any reason

why Gibson was in Pop's apartment in the first place? Or why Pop hired him?"

The light in Jack's eyes seemed to darken for just the briefest of seconds, as if he were working hard to keep me from picking up on what he was thinking.

It was a familiar look. One I'd seen a million times before when we dated. Times when Jack worked to keep things from me when he wasn't sure I could handle whatever it was he was dealing with on the job.

It was a look I knew Claire had seen in Pop's eyes just as many times. Over the years, I'd learned that cops protected their loved ones—hid things they felt were too gritty. Too real. And even though Jack wasn't a cop anymore, he still had the look, the attitude. I did not appreciate that attitude at the moment. He seemed to forget I was the cop now, and he was the one sitting on the sidelines.

"Spit it out, O'Brien," I snapped.

He had the decency to look surprised, as if he didn't know what I meant. But in the end, he told me, "I don't know why Pop hired him, but I got it from a good source that Gibson was up to his proverbial eyeballs defending some pretty seedy characters. His partner is on retainer with Handler Ortega."

Something ugly and bitter rose up into the back of my mouth. "Ortega?"

Jack nodded. His gaze, openly concerned, searched mine. He knew only too well what that name meant to me, the memories it elicited. "Look, Chili, I'm sorry, but the D.A.'s office confirmed it. Gibson and his partner work for Ortega."

I dropped back down onto the couch, my knees no longer able to support me. It felt as if someone had drained all of the blood out of my body in one fell swoop. I was light-headed, slightly dizzy.

The color must have gone out of my face because Jack gently pushed my head down near my knees. "Take a couple of deep breaths."

I brushed his hand away and sat up. "I'm fine." Even though I wasn't. I didn't dare stand up or I knew I'd end up on my ass in front of the entire squad room of detectives. "Pop would never have anything to do with anyone who works for Ortega."

"Standish got it right from the D.A.'s office, Chili. He knows what he's talking about. Gibson's firm is on Ortega's payroll."

The last statement sent the blood rushing back through my system. Anger was a great motivator. A stunningly good impetus.

I stood up and brushed past Jack. "Get out of my way. I need some fresh air. You're just trying to justify your actions against Pop—your testimony that screwed him to the wall."

I tried getting ahead of Jack, but his long legs easily kept pace with me. As we walked out of the squad room, his hand came up and he pressed his palm against the small of my back, an unconscious, normally chivalrous move to guide me through the double doors.

I knew he didn't mean anything by it, but I felt myself stiffen inside, constructing and reinforcing the wall that I knew I was going to need to keep in place in order to keep him at a safe distance.

I could feel the heat of his hand radiate through the blanket, down through the cloth of my jacket and through the cloth of his robe, directly into the pores of my bare skin beneath. It was hot enough to scorch the skin of a tender peach, and that's exactly how I felt—as tender and vulnerable as a peach ripe for the picking. Damn him. Damn him for still being under my skin, stealing my breath and making my heart race.

I walked a little faster, breaking contact without saying a word. He didn't touch me again as we took the elevator to the first floor and walked out into the cold night, headed for the parking lot.

The silence between us was heavy, leaden with nine years of hurt. But perhaps even worse than that, the silence was soaked with memories of such distrust, such unmentioned anger and rage, that I was sure it was a wall I'd never be able to dismantle. Even if I wanted to, which, somehow, I was pretty sure I didn't.

Not when Jack O'Brien had helped to convict Charlie Orzinski of selling classified information to top drug dealer Handler Ortega and now wanted me to believe that Pop was using the same sleazebag lawyer as Ortega.

LESS THAN TWENTY minutes later, I leaned my head against the wall of the elevator leading to Jack's apartment, my eyes closed. My knees felt as though they might give out at any moment. I'd now been awake for over thirty hours straight.

"We need to call the hospital when we get upstairs," I said.

"I called when I arrived at the station. Drake said there's been no change."

Sweetie Pie padded over to greet us, hissing at Jack when he made the mistake of leaning down as if to pet him. He then wound his body around my legs, purring a greeting that let me know he wasn't happy about being left alone for so long.

I bent down and picked him up, smoothing down his thick, unmanageable fur as his purr increased to the decibel of a small hedge clipper running on high.

When Jack reached over to stroke his head, Sweetie Pie

let out an even more vicious hiss and took another quick swipe at him. It left a nasty gash on the back of his hand. "Damn! Why does that cat hate me so much?"

"He happens to be an excellent judge of character."

"Oh, so you're saying he's judged me to be a louse and won't have anything to do with me because I testified against Pop?"

There it was, the unspoken resentment that hung between us unspoken for so long. Known by us both, but never truly addressed with words.

"Well, now that you mention it, I'd say that's a pretty good reason for him to hate your guts."

"I did what I had to do, Chili." He sucked on the gash and then shook his hand in a useless attempt to take the sting out of the cat claw wound. "It wasn't like I went in there and ratted on him for any personal gain or everything. Internal Affairs dragged me in for an interview. What did you expect me to do?"

"I expected you to tell the truth and let them know that Charlie Orzinski would never sell out the department."

He sighed, the sound heavy and resigned. "I couldn't do that. It would have been a lie. Pop sold information to Ortega. There wasn't any way around that. They had him dead to rights. Even Pop knew that. Why do you think he gave himself up the next day?"

"He gave himself up because he couldn't believe the young man he loved like a son had sold him out. He didn't want to see you dragged in front of the ethics committee and accused of lying, of purposefully damaging the reputation of a fellow officer."

I stared across the room at him, trying with every ounce of my being to make him understand how he had betrayed the man who believed in him, who would have done anything for him.

"He loved you, Jack. He loved you more than any of us. He believed in you. Adored you more than he could have adored a biological son if he could have had one. But you let him down. Duped him when he needed you most. Kicked him when he was at his most vulnerable. Was I supposed to forget all that?"

Tears stung my eyes and the fact that they appeared so easily frustrated the hell out of me. I wanted desperately to be strong. To represent Pop's side of the story without losing it and wimping out. I wanted to rub Jack's face in his betrayal.

But instead the tears came, leaking from my eyes and trailing down my cheeks to the corners of my mouth. I could taste their saltiness on my lips, and the bitter taste of them hardened my heart against him even more than before. I could not, would not, let him in. He was the enemy.

As if sensing my despair, Jack reached out and gently wiped one of my cheeks with the back of his hand. The touch of his skin on mine seemed to melt the bitterness, and that only me made me feel more impotent, more of a betrayer to Pop.

I didn't want Jack's comfort. I didn't want his sympathy. I wanted him to speak out, to admit his ultimate betrayal of the man who loved us so much that he'd do anything to protect us.

Jack's hand slid down over my shoulder, pressing against the middle of my back as he pulled me close. The incredible strength of his body was more than I could fight. My hip bumped against his and I fit against him as if I'd been made to be there, soft, gentle curves to his sharp edges.

He bent his head, his lips touching the curve of my ear. "I didn't want to hurt him, Chili. I swear to you. I thought if Pop told the truth and gave the D.A. what they wanted— Handler Ortega on a silver platter—they'd cut him a deal. That they'd let him off with early retirement. It's what they told me they'd do if he came clean."

"How could he cut a deal with them when he didn't do what they said he did? Why would you ever believe that Pop would admit to something he didn't do?" I spoke the words against the cloth of his shirt, my lips moving against the hardness of his chest.

"He was guilty, sweetie. I know you don't want to believe this, but he sold the information to Ortega. There's no getting around that."

Sweetie Pie took that moment to take another swipe at Jack, his claws ripping a nice strip of flesh off the side of his neck.

Jack jumped back, his hand going to his neck. "For pity's sake, can't you control that crazy beast?"

Concern swept through me at the sight of blood trickling down the side of his neck and staining the collar of his shirt. I pulled Sweetie Pie close and trapped his vicious claws with a strategically placed forearm. As hurt as I was with Jack's betrayal of Pop, I'd never wish any harm on him.

"Sorry. I think he's just out of sorts. He misses Pop as much as I do." I headed for the bathroom. "I'll get some antiseptic and a Band-Aid."

Tending to Jack's wound was the least I could do, even though I knew it was going to be difficult touching the very face that a few moments ago had been pressed so tightly against mine, sending threads of need through my entire body. Lord, give me strength.

"I'm okay," he protested. "Just keep the attack cat under control."

I grabbed the necessary items out of the medicine cabinet, deposited Sweetie Pie on the side of the tub and closed the door, effectively cutting off his yowl of protest. Better to keep the two beasts out of each other's hair for the next few minutes.

Pouring a bit of antiseptic on a sterile gauze pad, I motioned for Jack to take a seat on the couch. He didn't argue.

I pushed aside his collar and gently swabbed the gash.

He jumped. "Hell and damnation! What are you using—lighter fluid?"

"Plain old peroxide. Stings a little, huh?"

"More than you can imagine." He glanced up at me and shot me a sly grin. "Might feel better if you kissed it."

I wasn't fast enough to squash an answering grin, but as appealing as the suggestion was, I knew it was a trap I couldn't afford to walk into. "Behave or I'll be forced to pour the whole bottle on you."

"Okay, okay, I'll behave." He tilted his head. "You know, you used to be a lot more fun. I think becoming a hard-ass cop has killed your sense of adventure."

I ignored the comment and covered the cut with a Band-Aid. "There, all better."

I marched back to the bathroom and replaced the peroxide bottle. Bending down, I scooped up Sweetie Pie and headed for the partition.

"Where are you going?"

"To bed. I'm beat and I have a long day ahead of me tomorrow. I'll keep Sweetie Pie with me."

"How predictable."

I turned around. "What do you mean?"

"Running off and using the cat as protection."

I laughed. "Well, you did say he was an attack cat. Think it'll work?"

"You tell me," he said softly.

His gaze met mine and my mouth went dry. I pried my tongue off the roof of my mouth and swallowed hard.

"Good night, Jack."

"Good night, Chili. Sleep well."

I ducked behind the partition and flopped down on the bed. Every nerve in my pitiful body was on fire, naming me for the chicken I knew I'd become.

Sleep well? Who was he kidding?

Sweetie Pie was my last hope. I could only pray that the ill-tempered beast would take up residence on my chest and keep me pinned to the bed for the entire night. I had no illusions about who was the weak one when it came to staying put.

Something told me that it was going to be a long, lonely night with only a mangy cat and my memories to keep me company.

I WOKE THE NEXT MORNING without the alarm, a longtime habit of mine. In fact, I'd never had to set an alarm clock in my entire life. It was as if I could go to sleep at night and preprogram my brain to the exact time I wanted to get up.

Part of that was growing up in a chaotic household where you never knew who or what would be coming at you at any point and time. So, I had learned to sleep light and wake up at the slightest noise. Even the years of living in the safety of the Orzinski household hadn't changed any of that.

The digital clock on the bed stand flashed 5:30 a.m. My

appointment at Gibson's office wasn't until 10:00 a.m., so I had the time to roll over and catch a few more hours of sleep, but I knew there wasn't much hope of that happening. I was a creature of habit and my inner time clock said it was time to get up.

I decided to tip toe out to Jack's kitchen, make a pot of coffee and plan my day. I pulled on his robe, tightening the belt around my waist, and made my way across the cool plank floor in bare feet.

As I passed the couch, I realized there was no need to tiptoe. The blankets were neatly folded at the end, with a pillow on top. There was also a note in Jack's scrawling handwriting.

I got a beep last night. One of the guys asked me to sub for him. I'll sleep at the station tonight. I figure that would make things a little easier on you. You can take care of Sweetie Pie and not worry about where you're going to stay. Use whatever you like. Standish is going to put a cop outside to keep an eye on things. I'll meet you at Gibson's office today at 10 a.m.
Jack
P.S. Make sure that damn cat doesn't claw up my new couch!

Okay, I admit it. A twinge of regret shot through me as I folded the note up and stuffed it into the pocket of my robe. Sure, I was still mad at him, but there was no denying the electricity that ripped through space between us whenever we were near each other.

But I shrugged. Jack was right. The new arrangement would work out a lot better. I needed all my attention on

Pop's health and on solving the mystery surrounding his attack. I couldn't be doing that if I was thinking about Jack and a relationship that went sour nine years ago. I made a mental note to call Gibson's office and change the appointment to 9:00 a.m. I wanted to get in and out before Jack even made an appearance.

Yanking open one of the industrial stainless steel cabinets in the kitchen, I located the coffee can and set it on the counter. Maxwell House coffee. I smiled. Exactly the kind of coffee Claire used to make Pop every morning. Not surprising that Jack drank the same thing. No fancy designer coffee for him—just plain, dark roast coffee made so strong it would peel back the hide of a rhino's back end.

I measured out the right amount of coffee, poured cold water into the back of the pot and turned it on. As the machine started to drip, I headed for the bathroom and a hot shower. I was halfway there when the phone rang. I couldn't resist grinning.

It had to be Jack checking up on me. He knew I was an early riser, and he probably thought I wouldn't be able to find my way around without some prompting from him. Funny how guys think women are clueless when it comes to finding their way around their apartments. They don't realize we have the place scoped out, mapped and committed to memory two minutes after entering.

I grabbed the portable up out of its cradle. "Yeah?"

"You realize of course that the message last night was meant for you?"

It was the same smooth, velvety dark voice from last night's threatening phone call.

My heart jumped a beat, but I managed to keep my voice cool. "I got your message loud and clear. But unfortunately, it doesn't mean a thing to me because I have no idea what it is you think I have of yours."

"Perhaps you'll figure it out today," the voice said smoothly.

"Perhaps. But then again, maybe the police will figure out who you are and come after you today." I paused to let that sink in and then added, "You do realize that they know who the little thug was that you hired to shoot that cop? Not too long before they connect him to you."

The reptilian sound of his laugher slithered over the wires. "Rest assured, that particular inconvenience has already been taken care of. And you'll be joining him if you don't return what belongs to me."

In spite of the twist of fear that slid up the column of my spine, I worked to keep my voice bland. Unaffected. "You're going to have to give me a better clue than that, buddy. I'm not following you too well."

"Oh, I plan on doing that, sweet stuff. In fact, I plan on sending you all kinds of messages. Messages that get you to realize that I mean business and want what belongs to me."

The phone clicked down and I allowed myself a quick, shaky breath. I thought about calling Jack and blabbing about what had just occurred, but then I remembered it didn't make any sense.

Standish was the one I needed to call. Jack wasn't a cop anymore. There wasn't anything he could do. A small voice in the back of my head told me that the reason I wanted to call Jack had more to do with needing to hear his soothing voice than it had to do with him doing anything about the phone call.

And since I'd already decided the two of us needed to

steer clear of each other, I dialed the number Standish had given me last night. Reality was definitely the pits sometimes.

GIBSON & PRATT'S OFFICE was located in the historic Landmark Building on South Salina Street in the middle of downtown Syracuse. The downstairs portion of the building housed the Landmark Theater, the last remaining fully functional theater in the city.

Big stage, plush seats and tons of gold leaf and gilt to satisfy the wealthy clients who had nothing better to do than spend their time raising money to keeping the elegant old lady in optimum repair.

I'd gone there once with Claire when I was younger, to see a Christmas showing of *The Nutcracker.* I'd sat there in awe through the entire performance, positive that I'd stepped into something out of the *Arabian Nights.*

For ten weeks after the show, I'd taken ballet lessons. Charlie had paid for the lessons and sat in the audience for a rather painful recital at the end of ten weeks. Over ice cream sodas at Friendly's, the two of us had laughingly decided that a gawky, five-foot-seven, thirteen-year-old tomboy wasn't prima ballerina material. I was happy to get back to the pick up game of baseball in the vacant field down the street with the boys. But I never forgot the theater.

From the looks of things, the offices above the theater rented for more money than I even wanted to guess at. Apparently, Gibson & Pratt were doing quite well for themselves.

"Pretty swanky office space," I muttered to myself as I climbed out of my vehicle and stood on the sidewalk looking up. Earlier, I'd taken a cab to the hospital, stopped in to see Pop and called Gibson's office and made arrangements to meet with his partner. I'd also picked up my Neon.

Stepping off the elevator, I entered the lobby. It was open space, with oversize windows and an airy, upscale feel to it. Thick, handwoven rugs covered hardwood floors buffed to a high gloss, and fresh flowers—orchids and glades—were all over the place, situated in an assortment of expensive-looking crystal vases.

The furniture was modern white, giving everything a clean, sterile look. Not too comfort-inducing, but I had no doubt that the decor made a distinct impression on the clientele—mainly, that they were going to pay through the nose every time Gibson & Pratt jotted down a billable hour or two in their files.

The receptionist gave me the once-over with a pair of slightly contemptuous, meticulously made-up sapphire-blue eyes.

I sighed inwardly. Obviously my appearance didn't fit with her idea of what kind of person should be occupying space in front of her desk.

Her smile, polished and professional, had a slightly condescending slant to it. A kind of obviously-you're-lost-but-I'll-direct-you-to-where-you-really-want-to-go, twist to one corner.

I brushed aside my irritation. Too bad I didn't have Jack along. With his charm and good looks, he'd have the receptionist groveling on the floor in two seconds flat, trying her best to accommodate us.

"May I help you?" she asked, her voice low and husky. I wondered why the hell my voice never sounded like that no matter how hard I tried to force it down an octave or two.

I swept a quick glance across to the etched silver name-plate on her desk and smiled politely. "You most certainly can, Heather."

She waited, a bored look on her face. Obviously, my charm wasn't going to have the same effect on her as Jack's would.

"I'm here to speak to Catherine Pratt," I said.

"Is Ms. Pratt expecting you, Miss—?"

"Ms. Killian Cray. I called earlier. I had an appointment with Mr. Gibson for 10:00 a.m. Ms. Pratt's secretary told me it would be fine if I came in at nine to meet with Ms. Pratt instead."

A shadow of distress flickered briefly on the woman's face, indicating that she'd already received the news of Gibson's appointment with the coroner. I had to give her credit; she recovered quickly.

"One moment, please." She keyed her phone pad with a set of bright red, wicked-looking claws and spoke into the receiver softly. A moment later, she rested the receiver back in its cradle and glanced up at me. "If you'll have a seat, Ms. Pratt will be with you shortly."

I wandered over to the tiny sitting area to the right of the receptionist's desk and plopped down on the expensive-looking white leather couch. The cushion whispered a soft sigh beneath me as I sank down. Definitely a little more high-class than the couch in the police department's squad room. Maybe I needed to seriously consider attending law school at night.

Across the room, a door opened and a tall, fashionably thin woman dressed in a killer pin-striped suit and three-inch spiked heels stepped out into the lobby. Her hair, a perfect honey blond, was cut blunt to her chin and pin-straight. She smiled across the room, her ice-blue eyes hard and flat without a trace of warmth.

The smile, however, was a different story—that was wide with a forced warmth to it. Definitely faked. Something told me this was a woman prepared for battle. A woman ready to make sure I didn't get an ounce of information out of her that she didn't intend to give in the first place. A line had been drawn and I stood squarely on the opposite side.

I knew without a doubt that she was Catherine Pratt. She'd come out of her den to escort me personally into her office. One look and I knew she was a shark of the finest and deadliest kind.

Sharp and professional, she looked like the type who could chop, fillet and swallow a guppy in a matter of seconds. I could only hope I wasn't one of those guppies she was sharking for. Something told me if Catherine got those shark teeth into me, I'd be ancient history before I'd even felt the first chomp.

She smiled, flashing those great white teeth and held out a hand. "Ms. Cray, I presume."

I wrapped my hand around her elegant, perfectly manicured one and shook it. "It's a pleasure to meet you, Ms. Pratt. Thank you for seeing me on such short notice."

She seemed to size me up and dismiss me all in a single glance. I tried telling myself it was because I'd only gotten about three hours of sleep and looked like hell. But the fact that I was dressed in my typical, non-uniform outfit—wrinkled cargo pants, a T-shirt and fleece under an oversize down jacket—might have had something to do with her reaction.

I was definitely not in Ms. Pratt's league when it came to fashion, and she had recognized that fact in less than two seconds flat. She glanced inquiringly over my left shoulder.

"I was under the impression that Mr. O'Brien would be accompanying you."

"I'm afraid he was otherwise engaged."

Her gaze jumped back to meet mine. There was no missing the flicker of interest that darted in and out of their depths, and I knew instantly that she was acquainted with Jack and there was, or had been, something between them. Funny how an ex-girlfriend could tell that about her former lover.

Not that I was surprised. Catherine Pratt was right up Jack's alley. Poised. Sophisticated and sexy as all get-out even in a lawyer's suit. I had little doubt the woman wore imported black lace French underwear under that pinstriped suit, and my fertile imagination told me that Jack had seen it on more than one occasion.

"Will he be joining us soon?"

I affected a look of dismay. "No, I'm sorry. He couldn't get out of a previous engagement."

"How unfortunate." Her expression told me she was more than a little disappointed, but she recovered quickly. "Well, then, let's get started. If you'll follow me, we'll talk in my office."

I followed her trim figure into an exquisitely appointed office with a bank of windows overlooking a narrow side street below.

As I settled into one of the leather chairs situated directly across from her massive, meticulously organized, cherry oak desk, Ms. Pratt said, "I'm not sure how much help I'm going to be. Craig and I are partners—"

She paused a moment to look properly distressed and

then continued, "—*were* partners. But as we both have very busy schedules, we never had much time to discuss or collaborate on cases. Especially ones that weren't complicated or detailed cases."

"So, Charlie Orzinski's case wasn't what you'd call a complicated case?" I asked.

"Not in the least." Catherine used one fingernail to flip open the file sitting in front of her. "As far as I can tell, Craig did a fairly straightforward will and power of attorney document for Mr. Orzinski. He also drew up a health proxy."

She glanced through the file quickly. "There's nothing unusual or unexpected here." She glanced up at me. "In fact, it would appear that your foster father was a man of very limited assets."

She lifted up a white envelope. "There's a letter here but the instructions read that it is to be mailed to you only upon Mr. Orzinski's death." She tucked that back in the file. "I'll be sure that's done when and if Mr. Orzinski doesn't respond to medical treatment."

She turned to another page and lifted a green card. "Apparently he also has a safe-deposit box at First Federal Trust. Craig doesn't have the items listed here, but the value has been estimated as sentimental." She glanced at me again. "Personal items, perhaps related to your foster father's marriage or job."

She handed me a manila envelope. "This has the location of the box and the key. The box was originally opened under the name of Jennifer O'Brien." Catherine glanced up at me. "Any relation to Jack O'Brien?"

"Not that I'm aware of."

"Well, apparently Mr. Orzinski obtained possession of

the box from Ms. O'Brien upon her written request to my partner."

Although I'd never admit it to Catherine, the name O'Brien was too much of a coincidence. Jack's biological mother, perhaps? A shadowy figure that Charlie and Claire never talked about and Jack refused to admit any interest in. He'd been adamant that he had no desire to go looking for his biological family. His attachment to the Orzinskis had been complete.

Catherine continued, oblivious to my mental musings. "When your foster father set up the will and health proxy with Gibson, he included a provision that should he become sick or die, you were permitted access to the safe-deposit box. Your name is included on the access card."

I nodded numbly and laid the envelope on my lap. Catherine continued to flip through the final few pages of the file. "From the health proxy your foster father had drawn up, it would appear that he's pretty adamant about not wanting any heroic efforts made to prolong his life should he be incapacitated in some way."

She glanced up at me again. "You mentioned that Mr. Orzinksi is currently in the hospital."

I nodded.

"Well, if he isn't able to make his own decisions, that puts the ball firmly and legally in your court, Ms. Cray. You are currently your foster father's decision maker on all aspects of his life—including any health-care decisions."

"As you said, pretty straightforward," I said softly, my insides crumbling under the weight of what I considered an impossible task.

How could I make decisions like that? At the moment, I felt barely capable of making decisions on what kind of toast to have for breakfast, and now I was left making life-and-death decisions for a man I cared about more than anyone could imagine.

Charlie must have been nuts when he picked me for this job. Why hadn't he chosen Jack? Or if he'd been out of sorts with Jack, why not Shawna? Or even Richard? I shuddered. Hard to believe I'd actually consider my oldest foster brother, Richard, more qualified to do the job than me, but there it was.

I blinked hard, holding back a sudden rush of unexpected and decidedly unwelcome tears. I dug my nails into the palms of my hands. No way was one single tear escaping from my eyes while I sat in front of this barracuda.

Catherine stared coolly across the desk at me as if waiting for the inevitable to happen, her expression expectant, as if this was something she was actually going to enjoy. But thankfully, I was able to disappoint her. The tears dried up. "The only other item in the file is the letter from Mr. Orzinski that I mentioned is to be mailed to you only upon his death." She glanced up at me. "Please notify me of any changes in his medical condition."

The words were cold, with no inflection of regret or compassion. Not that I'd expected any from this woman.

I tried another tack. "I don't mean to sound crude here," I said, glancing around the office. "But you look like you run a pretty high-class operation."

Catherine smiled indulgently. "If you're asking if my practice is successful and thriving, then the answer is yes. Craig and I have been doing quite well."

"So how was my foster father, a man who, as you so delicately put it, had limited assets, able to afford a lawyer of Craig Gibson's caliber?"

"Good question." Catherine pulled her computer keyboard over and rapidly typed something in. She stared at the screen for several minutes. "It would appear that Mr. Orzinski had a benefactor."

"A benefactor? You mean someone else was paying his bill?"

Catherine nodded, her perfectly cut hair swinging along the side of her chin and emphasizing the sharp cut of her jaw.

"Who?" I inquired.

Catherine's eyes shadowed for a moment as she considered my question. "I'm sorry, but I don't think I'm at liberty to divulge that information."

"You mean I have to go through the process of convincing the police to get a court order? This is a serious assault case we're working on here, one that appears to be connected to the shooting of a young police officer. You wouldn't want the local police and D.A.'s office to think you were putting unnecessary roadblocks in their way, would you?" I didn't have a legal leg to stand on, but I decided the bluff was worth a try.

Catherine's ice-blue eyes froze to a filmy whitish cast as she considered my challenge. Finally, she smiled, the slide of her lips stiff and decidedly unfriendly. "Feel free to speak to the D.A. for that warrant. I'll be happy to cooperate if he is able to get one."

My back teeth tightened down with disappointment. It had been worth a try, anyway. As I prepared to get up, Catherine's secretary appeared at the door.

"I'm sorry to interrupt, Ms. Pratt, that package you've been expecting has arrived."

Catherine immediately stood up, her expression distracted. "Excuse me for a moment. I'll be right back."

She followed her secretary into the outer office.

I sat quietly for a moment and then jumped out of my seat. I rounded the end of her desk and leaned over the keyboard of her computer. A few key strokes and I had the document she'd been viewing a moment ago up on the screen.

I stared at a list of billing hours and the charge for each. For such a simple case, Pop's account showed that he'd managed to charge up quite a legal fee. His final total was $15,000.

"Jeesh, remind me to forget about making out a will or a living health proxy," I grumbled to myself. "Either Pop had a more complicated will than Pratt indicated or Gibson was bleeding his benefactress dry."

I ran my finger across the screen to a name and address of the payer. Mrs. Jeannette Renault.

I quickly returned the screen to its previous document and sat back down. I didn't recognize the name. Glancing over at the shelves, I noticed a Syracuse phone book. I got up and pulled it down, thumbing through to the white pages. The only Jeannette Renault was listed with a Dr. Edgar Renault. I flipped to the yellow pages and looked up Edgar Renault, M.D. He had a prominent ad listing him as a cardiac/thoracic surgeon.

I straightened up. Time to make a house call and talk to the Renaults. I quickly rifled through the white pages until I found the Renaults' home address: 2389 West Lake Rd., Skaneateles.

I whistled through my teeth. I knew from experience that West Lake Road overlooked Skaneateles Lake. Houses out there started at about 1.5 million dollars and that was for a run-down shack with no land.

The residents of Skaneateles were the crème de la

crème. Everyone with half a brain knew that. The town was something out of a storybook. In fact, around Christmas, residents dressed up like characters out of a Charles Dickens novel and paraded around reenacting Christmases past for the tourists.

There was no doubt in my mind that Mrs. Jeannette Renault had the dough to pay for Charlie's legal bill. The only question was, why would she do that?

I tore out the sheet with the Renaults' home address, replaced the phone book on the shelf and headed for the door. As I breezed past Catherine Pratt and her secretary, sorting through the contents of a small box sitting on the secretary's desk, I smiled.

"I'll be heading out. No sense in taking up any more of your time. Thank you for meeting with me."

Catherine didn't bother to hide her relief. "Tell Jack O'Brien hello for me. And tell him not to be such a stranger."

"Yeah, I'll be sure to mention that first chance I get," I said with a touch of sarcasm. Right after I grilled him on exactly how well he knew Ms. Catherine Pratt. He might be my "ex," but there was no denying the tiny twist of jealousy sitting in the pit of my belly.

But at the moment, I was more interested in examining the contents of a certain safe-deposit box located in the First Federal Trust Bank. And then, I had a burning desire to take a buzz out to Skaneatales Lake for a nice little chat with Mrs. Jeannette Renault.

O'Brien would have to wait.

Chapter Six

I pulled up to the curb in front of the First Federal Trust Bank, a small branch located in a rectangular red brick building on the corner of Seymour and West Street.

A seedy-looking pool parlor stood directly across the street, along with an even more dilapidated apartment building with a sagging porch and paint so chipped and peeling that the underlying wood was more visible than the former gray paint that had once covered the place.

A tiny sporting goods shop butted up against the other side of the bank. From the number of Sale signs and All Merchandise Must Go posters plastered across the front windows of the shop, I figured it was about to go under. Too much competition from the big malls and not enough athletes in the neighborhood to support it.

A single glance around told me that the area wasn't a prosperous one. The multiple-dwelling houses situated along the street were fairly pathetic. They had a used-up appearance, sadly lacking in a fresh coat of paint or decent aluminum siding. There was a dreary film of dirt and grime covering almost everything, giving the place the appearance of something out of a Tim Burton film.

It wasn't hard to see that this was a working-class neighborhood, the kind where both adult members of the household struggled to hold down two or three jobs, raise a pack of kids and keep their heads above the avalanche of bills that filled their mailboxes each month.

As I opened the car door, I reached into my jacket and fingered the key sitting deep inside the pocket. Still there, along with the neatly folded document giving me Pop's power of attorney. It didn't matter if I had the key, if I didn't have the document; the bank representative wouldn't allow me access to anything.

I pushed open the bank door and entered the lobby, noting the two lines in front of the open teller windows and the two desks off to the left, both occupied by people chatting with the men sitting behind the fake, cheaply made wooden desks. Busy place.

A maroon-colored velveteen rope hanging from metal poles sectioned off the desks from the main lobby. I sat down in one of the chairs lined up behind the rope. I figured if I wanted to gain access to a safe-deposit box, I'd need to talk to one of the desk jockeys, not a teller.

Purely a guess on my part. Dealing with safe-deposit boxes was all new to me. I didn't own a single item I thought would ever require the security of a bank vault.

Of course, that immediately made me consider the fact that Pop wasn't exactly in a position to own anything important or valuable that needed locking away, especially considering that he lived in a rat-hole apartment and cooked in some greasy spoon for minimum wage.

"May I help you, miss?"

I glanced up to see the man directly across from me looking in my direction. The couple who had been seated in front of him had vacated the area, leaving Mr. Dimestore

Suit with his perfectly knotted tie unoccupied. The cheap plastic nameplate on his desk identified him as Harold Egan.

His smile was benign, patient but decidedly bored. No doubt he took one look at me and had already figured out I wasn't one of the bank's more prosperous customers. Although, considering the condition of the neighborhood, I couldn't imagine anyone walking in who would fit the description of prosperous.

I stood up and approached his desk. "Yes, please. A safe-deposit box here in the bank was originally opened under the name of a Jennifer O'Brien. Charles Orzinski now retains ownership of the box. I have power of attorney of Mr. Orzinski's belongings and I'd like to examine the contents of the box, please."

"I'll need proof of this action," Mr. Egan said.

"No problem." I reached into my pocket and pulled out the required paperwork. Harold glanced over the document quickly and then nodded, turning his body slightly to access the keyboard of his computer. He typed in something and then sat back. "Everything seems to be in order. I'll just need to see some personal identification."

I slapped down my driver's license and badge. The badge got the most attention. Harold straightened up a little and his tone took on a touch more respect. "Of course, Officer Cray. I'll escort you to the vault personally."

The bank vault sat at the back of the building down a short flight of stairs.

"Did you ever meet Ms. O'Brien or Mr. Orzinski?" I asked, curious as to how often the O'Brien woman or Pop had visited the bank.

"No, I'm sorry, I can't say I've ever had the pleasure."

Harold checked the sheet he had printed off. "According to the check-in sheet, the last time someone was in was—" one eyebrow rose slightly "—over twenty-two years ago. It was the same day Ms. O'Brien first rented the box. There's been no visits since then." He glanced over at me. "That's quite a time span."

I nodded but didn't elaborate. How could I? I had no idea what was going on or what could possibly be in the box.

Whatever sat in the box was dated material. It couldn't be what the voice on the other end of the phone was looking for. That material sounded a lot more urgent than something that had sat in a tiny bank vault for over twenty-two years.

A few minutes later, I was sitting in a small cubicle with two very large safe-deposit boxes sitting on the small built-in shelf desk in front of me. Apparently Pop had more things to secret away in a bank vault than I had figured on.

I slid the key into the box and turned it. For some reason, my stomach twisted. Acid pumped into my system as if a dike had broken somewhere deep inside me. I swallowed against the hot, burning sensation, feeling slightly nauseous. I felt as though I could down an entire roll of Tums and a gallon of Mylanta.

Whatever I found in the box, I wanted desperately for it to be something that would help me exonerate Pop. But a little voice in my head was preparing me for it to be otherwise. Why else would he hide it away like this?

I opened the lid and I stared into the box. The acid in my stomach flooded the back of my throat. The metal box was jammed with neatly stacked bills.

I closed my eyes for a minute and braced myself. No way was this a good sign. I reached in and touched the top stack of bills lining the length of the box. The bills were real, the feel smooth with an underlying oily feel. They weren't new or crisp bills. They were used. Soft. Untraceable. I riffled through the first few packs. Not one bill was less than a hundred dollars.

I slammed the lid shut and closed my eyes again, my fingers trembling on the edge of the box. Did I really want to look any further?

I could simply relock the box, shove it into the hands of the bank representative and leave. No one had to know about the existence of the cash. No one but me and Pop.

Even the lawyer had admitted that there was no paper trail saying what sat in the bank box and Uncle Sam wouldn't get to know until and if Pop died and the contents of the box went to the estate.

Was it Ortega's money? Was this what he wanted back? Hell, I'd gladly stuff it into a sack and deliver it to him personally if that was the case. But I also knew that Ortega had more money than God himself. Why would he be concerned about a few hundred thousand in cash? Even he couldn't be that greedy…could he?

I slowly opened the other box, hoping for something other than cash. Something told me I was going to find the same thing.

I was right. Cash filled the second box, too. I sat back with a sigh. There could be no other explanation than that Pop had been taking bribes as accused. Pain squeezed the center of my heart.

No, it wasn't possible. The money had been planted here, an attempt to make him seem guilty. But then why hadn't it come out at the trial. It would have been one more nail in Pop's jail-sentence coffin.

As I contemplated the stacks of bill, I notice the upper edge of a brown envelope alongside the money. Curious, I reached in and pulled it out. It wasn't thick. A simple brown envelope. The flap was not even sealed shut.

I lifted the flap and peeked inside. A handful of photos sat at the bottom. I tipped the envelope upside down and the pictures slid out, fanning out on the Formica surface of the built-in shelf.

They were black-and-white photos, probably old mementoes. Old photos of Charlie and Claire? The thought made me smile in the midst of my pain. Maybe there would be something decent about these two boxes after all.

Eagerly, I sorted through them, my confusion growing as I spread them out in some semblance of order. There wasn't one photo of Claire. There were quite a few of Charlie. A very young Charlie—about age twenty-two or twenty-three.

A few showed him sitting at a restaurant table or at a bar, his police cap pushed back on his head at a cocky angle, a self-conscious, almost sheepish smile on his mouth as he stared directly into the lens. He wasn't a big drinker, not that I ever remembered anyway, so seeing him at a bar was a bit surprising.

But the most surprising photos were of a woman. She was quite striking, a tall blonde with a kick-ass figure that would make even Catherine Pratt green with envy. They were old photos, the woman dressed in clothing reminiscent of the Seventies. I didn't recognize her, and in most of the photos her face was blurred, not very clear.

But it was the final few photos that helped me to put things together. She was holding an infant of about six months or so; the little guy was dressed in short pants and a T-shirt. His chubby hands were tangled in the woman's blond hair, and in one of the photos, he was staring over his shoulder at the camera, smiling, his cheeks dimpled and his blue eyes dancing with mischief.

Jack. The pictures were of Jack and his biological mother. What were they doing in the safe-deposit box? Why hadn't Charlie and Claire given them to Jack?

A SHORT TIME LATER, I was back out on the front sidewalk. I was surprised to see a familiar figure, one broad shoulder leaning casually against one of the light poles, arms folded and his expression distinctly displeased. I stopped dead.

Jack. How had he found me? He was in uniform, a pristine white turtleneck with a navy-blue medical insignia embroidered in the center. A navy-blue jacket with SFD over the left pocket and a pair of neatly pressed black pants completed his outfit. A stethoscope was looped casually around his neck.

Behind him, doubled-parked next to my Neon and effectively blocking me in, was a white-and-red rig with Syracuse Fire Dept. Ambulance lettered along the side.

The driver sat staring straight ahead, ignoring the interaction that was destined to erupt directly in front of him. No doubt Jack had coached his partner to keep his eyes front and center. In other words, to mind his own business.

"Why didn't you wait for me?" Jack demanded.

I shrugged. "You made it clear in your note that you'd be working these next few days. Gibson had scheduled the appointment with me. I figured I could handle it alone."

I brushed past him, headed for the driver's side of my car. Unfortunately, I couldn't resist giving him a slight dig as I passed. "Catherine Pratt was more than a little disappointed you didn't show. You might want to scoot over to her office and smooth those ruffled feathers of hers. I think she might suspect you're avoiding her."

"How do you think I found out about your little trip over here to the bank?"

I nodded. "Figures. So much for lawyer confidentiality. Guess she really does have a thing for you."

A definite frown of annoyance popped up between his dark blue eyes. "Contrary to what you're insinuating, Catherine Pratt and I have only met a couple of times in court. Nothing more, nothing less."

"A bit of close cross-examination between friends, huh?"

He shook his head, his annoyance taking on an appearance of weariness at this point. "Where is all this hostility coming from, Chili? You're hissing like a female cat in heat ready to take on the competition."

I stopped dead in my tracks. All right, now he'd done it. Pushed my button harder than he needed to. No way was I letting that comment go by without a response.

"Dream on, lover boy."

"Mind telling me where you're headed in such an all-fired hurry?"

"Actually, I do mind. It's none of your damn business." I used my remote to click the locks and climbed into the driver's seat, putting my hands on the wheel and staring straight ahead. I figured he'd get the message at some point and push off.

I was wrong.

The passenger side door opened and Jack climbed in next to me. The interior temperature of my little car seemed to increase by about twenty degrees and I hadn't even turned on the heater yet. I resisted the urge to unzip my coat.

"Get out," I said.

"Not a chance." He waved a hand in the direction of his partner and the ambulance moved off down the street. "Someone needs to look after you when you get unreasonable like this. And I'm guessing that person is going to be me. I'm coming with you."

Realizing it was futile to argue, I started the engine.

"So, where are we headed?" Jack asked.

"To Skaneateles."

"And who are we visiting out there in Skaneateles?"

"A woman by the name of Jeannette Renault."

"Any particular reason why?"

I flicked on my blinker and pulled smoothly out into traffic. "She's the one who's been paying Pop's lawyer's bills."

"Nice of her." He was quiet and then asked, "What was in the safe-deposit box?"

For a brief moment, I considered blurting out everything I'd found. But something stopped me. Jack had always been pretty closemouthed when it came to his biological family, and I quickly decided I needed to get a better handle on what the pictures meant before discussing it with him.

As for the cash, keeping it a secret was personal. I needed to digest the significance of all those neatly stacked bills before telling Jack or anyone else about them. The thought of Pop taking bribes was simply too hard to accept.

"Just some personal stuff—pictures, mainly."

I tightened my hands on the wheel waiting for him to press the issue. But he didn't and I breathed a silent sigh of relief.

I hopped onto Route 81 South and got off at the Lafayette exit, taking Route 20 West. Things were as barren out this way as I remember. Lots of hills, curves and winter-desolate dairy farms.

We were only a mile down Route 20 when it started to snow. The light fluffy stuff blew across the two-lane road, making visibility poor. I concentrated on driving and Jack brooded quietly in the corner. I figured he might be starting to regret his decision to take a ride with me. By now, he was way overdue and his partner would only be able to cover for him for so long.

Although it was only about fifteen miles to the village of Skaneateles, the ride seemed to take an eternity. Mainly because the ice on the road made the going slow and the tension between us didn't help to make the time pass any quicker.

But as we got closer to the village, the trip seemed worth it. Cute, incredibly neat colonial homes popped up along the side of the road. When we turned onto the main street, we were met with trendy shops and upscale restaurants.

Overlooking the lake was a park with a pristine white bandstand, its pointed, shingled roof harkening back to days of slow walks in the park and ladies in long dresses with parasols.

Snow covered the railings of the bandstand, but I could picture it in the summer with people sitting on the grass or blankets, listening to music as the sun set over the lake.

In spite of the cold weather, people wandered along the sidewalks, glancing in the windows and darting in and out of the shops. It was like entering a different world, slower, more peaceful.

I turned onto West Lake Road and drove past all the elegant houses populating this side of the lake. Each house the ones visible from the road were more incredible than the last.

The Renaults were about a half mile down the road. Apparently, Dr. Edgar Renault was doing quite well for himself. Slicing open the chests of wealthy patients appeared to be reaping the guy more than a few jingles.

The driveway to his house looked to be about a quarter of a mile long, winding through a grove of trees leading up to a huge Southern-style plantation house sitting overlooking Skaneateles Lake. A bit pretentious, if you asked me, but then I was used to living in an ill-heated log cabin.

I glanced over at Jack. "After visiting Pratt & Gibson's office, I thought I might consider going to night school to become a lawyer. After getting a look at this place, I think I might reconsider and go to med school."

Jack shook his head. "You're a cop, Chili. You like being a cop. You're no different than Pop or me." He paused for a minute and then added, "Although you could do whatever you set your mind to. Pop always said that you were the one with more than two brain cells sparking off each other."

I laughed, and a fond memory of Charlie and Claire popped into my head. The two of them used to line us kids up in the living room on report-card day and check each card individually. They praised accomplishments and got on our backs for blatant evidence of goofing off.

Jack was already out of the house by the time I got my turn to stand in the Orzinski living room on report-card day. He was working part-time, attending Onendoga Community College and applying to the Police Academy.

When I first arrived at the house, I'd been the princess of darkness, an outright troublemaker. Ditching school, mouthing off to teachers, smoking in the girls' room—and on more than a few occasions in the boys' room—breaking curfew and giving the assistant principal major attitude. Those were my big accomplishments. That, and a reputation for rolling the perfect doobie had been my claims to fame.

But Charlie and Claire never got flustered, angry, or embittered. They never gave up. They simply started setting limits, reeling me in like a largemouth bass with a terrible hunger for something they had—a gentle nurturing love for a terribly wounded teen. A teen who had never learned to trust anyone.

I'm still not exactly sure how or when they actually managed to break through and build a bridge over that wounded ability to trust. Earlier in my life, before I hit my teens, I'd been in and out of more foster homes than I could remember, places that had been only too glad to see me vacate the premises when the caseworkers came back to reunite me with my mom.

My file had been thick with remarks from social workers and court-appointed psychologists about my incorrigible behavior. I'm not sure, but I think the social workers had to use two file drawers just to keep my file in.

My frequent absences from my mom's custody were due to her numerous binges. Straight scotch when she was able to hold down a decent job, and then when she really hit the skids, she'd down anything she could get her hands on.

Her behavior lead to the Onendoga Department of Social Services caseworkers swooping down on us fairly frequently. They'd scoop me up and deposit me in some foster home that held on to me until my mom completed the required rehab for the zillionth time. They usually tacked on a few weeks of parenting classes, too.

I'm fairly certain my mother slept through the parenting classes or was in the ladies' room smoking up a storm with some of the other deadbeat moms because she never came back from those classes any more skilled in the parenting department than when she'd started.

When I was dropped off at the Orzinski household at age twelve, everyone was pretty sure I wouldn't be going back to my mom anytime in the near future. Mainly because my mom had moved on to heroin, and the chances of her kicking the habit for good wasn't what the caseworkers called *promising*.

I'd been told pretty clearly in family court that if I didn't make it at the Orzinskis, the next stop was an RTF—residential treatment facility for out-of-control adolescents. But Charlie and Claire worked their magic on me, more magic than any RTF would have done. Their love, patience and belief in me turned things around. And yeah, I did start getting A's in high school. And I did have two brain cells that knew how to spark against each other, just like Charlie had told me.

It had simply been too hard for me to believe what he said, even when it happened. Somewhere in the deepest, darkest place in my heart, I believed that it was Claire and Charlie who held the key to what I was able to accomplish. I was never able to believe—to accept—that I had anything to do with the miraculous turnaround in my behavior, no matter how hard Claire and Charlie tried to convince me otherwise.

And now Claire was dead, and Charlie was dying. It felt as though everything in my world was falling apart, crumbling in on me like a house of ill-stacked cards, destined to bury me and leave me with nothing to hang on to. The fear deep in my gut was almost too much for me to bear or to even think about.

"What are you thinking?" Jack asked as I pulled around the circle leading to the house's front door. "I can tell from that brooding look that you're talking negative to yourself."

He knew me too well. I unsnapped my seatbelt. "I'm fine. And I'm not thinking anything."

"Yeah, right. And the Pope sleeps naked."

I ignored him and his warped sense of humor. There was no sense in telling him. Jack had always known where he was going and what he planned on doing with his life. There had never been any question in his head that he was going to follow in Charlie's footsteps and become a cop. And then he had betrayed Charlie, sold him out for whatever gain he thought he needed at the time.

I didn't understand his behavior then, and I sure as hell didn't understand it now. And because of that, there could be no forgiveness in my heart.

I pushed open the car door, retasting the bitterness of my anger, but if I didn't cling to the anger, what ammunition could I use to shield me from more heartbreak? I strolled up to the front door and pressed the doorbell a little harder and longer than I probably needed to.

A few minutes later, a woman in a dark maid's uniform and a crisply starched apron opened the door. "Yes, may I help you?"

"We'd like to speak to Mrs. Renault, please," I said.

"Is she expecting you, Miss?"

I pulled out my badge and held it up for the woman to see. "I'm sure if you explain to her that Deputy Sheriff

Cray would like a word with her, she'd be more than happy to speak with me."

"Of course. Won't you come in." The maid stepped back and allowed us to enter the front hall.

It took every ounce of strength not to let my jaw drop to the floor and to turn around in a full circle like some kind of impoverished, impressionable kid. The place was unbelievable. A damn palace in the middle of little old northern New York. Even Jack couldn't hide that he was suitably impressed.

"If you'll wait here, I'll let Mrs. Renault know that you'd like a word with her."

The maid headed down the marble hallway for the back of the house.

"Holy mackerel," I said softly. "This place looks like something out of *House Beautiful*."

"I'm impressed that you get *House Beautiful*," Jack said with a wicked grin. "I'll be even more impressed if you tell me that you actually read it."

"I read it at my dentist's office," I said flippantly over one shoulder as I walked over to run a finger along the edge of an elegantly etched gold-framed mirror hanging over an antique hall table.

"Don't touch anything. If it breaks you'll have to pay for it and I have a feeling neither of us could afford to buy anything in this hall—including the umbrella in that stand over there."

I laughed. "You have no idea how right you are. That's a malacca cane umbrella and retails for around $285."

"For one little umbrella?" Jack shot me a look of surprise. "How the heck would you know how much one of those things costs, let alone the brand name?"

"I pulled over some idiot in a Porsche one evening and he tried to brain me with it when I didn't agree to let him off with a warning. I confiscated the dang thing and all the guy could do was moan the whole time I was booking him that he wanted his umbrella back. By the time we were done booking him, everyone in the squad room was ready to stick that umbrella in a place the guy would never forget."

I wandered a few feet down the hall, surveying the ancestral portraits hanging on the wall. "Something tells me that Dr. Renault or Mrs. Renault comes from a very moneyed background. You don't buy stuff like this on a doctor's salary. Not even if you're a cardiac surgeon."

"Mrs. Renault will see you now."

Startled, I whirled around to see the maid standing a few feet away.

She led us down the hallway, past several formal living rooms, a library that would make a small-town librarian weep with envy, through a study that had a woman's touch—French Impressionist furniture in snow-white paint with gilded trim, a flower-patterned couch and chairs—and through double glass doors leading to a beautiful and spacious greenhouse attached to the study.

The maid stopped and pointed toward the rear of the greenhouse. "Mrs. Renault is working on her orchids. Just follow the main corridor and you'll find her."

She scurried back inside, leaving us among the lush greenery and exotic flowers lining both sides of the corridor she had pointed out. The pungent smell of fresh earth, fragrant flowers and moisture filled my nostrils. It was a strange sensation after coming from the bone-chilling cold outside. I could only wonder how much it would cost to keep a place like this warm during the winter.

"I feel as though I'm in a freakin' jungle," Jack said, loosening the collar of his shirt. "And it's so damn hot I'm tempted to strip down to skivvies."

"Better not. Something tells me that Mrs. Renault might not be too appreciative." I reached out and gently cupped the petals of a delicate peach-colored tea rose. The bud was so fresh that tiny drops of dew clung to the tip of each perfect petal. "It's beautiful."

"Go ahead and pick it," Jack teased. He glanced around. "No one will even miss it there are so many."

"Oh, but I would know," a soft cultured voice interrupted. "In fact, I know every flower, every leaf, every petal, every tiny baby shoot that grows in this greenhouse."

Startled, I snatched my hand back and turned to see a woman emerge almost magically from the greenery overflowing a side corridor a few feet from us.

She looked to be somewhere between the age of fifty-five and sixty, immaculately groomed with perfectly coiffed blond hair with strands of bright gold strategically shot through the shoulder-length expensive cut.

Her hands were covered by a flower-patterned pair of gardening gloves, and one hand grasped tiny pruning shears.

She wore pants—expensive tan trousers with a perfect crease down the middle—that clung to her slim legs. A bright turquoise silk shirt, with the sleeves rolled up to showcase her tanned arms, was open at the neck. Not too many women her age could get away with wearing such a bright color. The lines on her face were barely existent. She smelled of money, class and expensive plastic surgery.

"Mrs. Renault," Jack greeted, his expression and stance saying that he wasn't in the least bothered by the fact that he'd been caught suggesting I pick one of the woman's flowers without her consent. He turned the charm on full wattage and held out a hand. "I'm Jack O'Brien. This is Essex County Deputy Sheriff Killian Cray. We were wondering if we could have a few moments of your time."

The woman barely gave my badge or me a glance. Her attention zeroed in on Jack and stayed there. Now, as I mentioned earlier, I'm never surprised when the female of my species passes me over in favor of feasting their eyes on Jackie Boy. But this woman took it to the extreme. It was as if I wasn't even there.

"Of course, Mr. O'Brien, won't you come this way," Mrs. Renault said, leading the way down the middle corridor toward the back of the greenhouse. "I was just going to sit down for a bit of tea. I've been working diligently all morning on one of my newest species of orchids." She glanced over her shoulder at Jack. "Do you know anything about growing orchids, Mr. O'Brien?"

"No, ma'am, I can't say that I do."

"A pity. They are quite delicate and respond well to a gentle touch. Something about your hands tells me that you'd have the patience and gentleness for such an undertaking."

I hid a smirk. Jack, patient? Gentle? Jeez, either the woman was coming on to him in a major way or she was cultivating him as her gardening soul mate. Either way, it was pretty amusing.

We stepped out into a bright airy area with a collection of elegant white wicker furniture clustered around a small table.

Brightly patterned cushions occupied the furniture, and the table held a silver serving tray, a teapot sitting beneath a tea cozy, a plate of scones, a crock of clotted cream and small jar of strawberry jam. There were exactly three tea cups clustered around the gilt-edged teapot.

Apparently, Mrs. Renault had been expecting us. No doubt Ms. Pratt had suspected Jack would meet up with me and made a quick phone call.

"Nice to know we were expected," Jack said, never one to mince words.

Mrs. Renault smiled, a stiff stretch of carefully glossed lips with no show of teeth. "Yes, as a matter of fact, my good friend Catherine Pratt called to tell me she thought you were on your way out."

"Then I assume you also know why we're here."

Mrs. Renault nodded and motioned for us both to take a seat. "Of course. As I mentioned, Catherine is a good friend, and she didn't want me taken by surprise if and when the two of you showed up."

She removed the tea cozy and steam rose from the spout of the pot. As she poured, she continued, "Catherine was also concerned that I might be upset that Deputy Sheriff Cray had discovered that I was paying Mr. Orzinski's legal fees."

At my raised eyebrow, she said, "Catherine isn't stupid, Ms. Cray. She realized when you left that you had probably used her computer to find out the information you were looking for. She apologized to me for being so lax in her security."

I shrugged, unwilling to admit whether or not I'd gained the information illegally. Mrs. Renault simply handed me a cup of tea.

"Were you upset that the information was leaked?" Jack asked.

"Not in the least, Jack...." She paused. "You don't mind if I call you Jack, do you?"

"Fine by me."

She gave him another cooly polished smile. There was no mention of calling me by my first name. Obviously I was going to remain Deputy Sheriff Cray, which didn't bother me a bit.

"May I ask why you were paying Charlie Orzinski's legal fees?" I asked. "Were you friends with him?"

Mrs. Renault laughed in a mildly indulgent manner. "I hate to be crass, but do I really look like I might move in the same social circles as Mr. Orzinski?"

Jack accepted a cup of tea from the woman and then shot me a sideways glance. I knew he was sizing me up to see if I was going to explode any time soon in regard to Mrs. Renault's obvious snobbery toward Charlie and his current lot in life.

"So if you weren't personal friends with Charlie, why were you paying his legal fees for such a high-class lawyer?" I asked, holding my rising temper back tightly. "From what I was able to tell, Gibson doesn't come cheap."

Mrs. Renault settled back in her own chair, crossed her long legs and carefully balanced her own cup of tea. She took a delicate sip before responding. "No, he isn't cheap at all. Quite expensive, actually. But good-quality lawyering always does cost, don't you think?" The question was directed at Jack. Again, it was if I didn't even exist.

Jack shrugged and took a healthy gulp of his tea. He refrained from making a face, but I guessed that he'd have preferred his with a splash of Jack Daniel's in it. That, or a plain shot of Jack Daniel's and skip the tea.

"I haven't been in the position to hire any high-class legal help recently," he said. "So I wouldn't even hazard a guess."

I was getting tired of the games. "You want to tell us why you were paying such an exorbitant fee for Charlie's lawyer if you didn't even move in his social circle?"

"Oh, I knew Charlie. We just didn't socialize. When I said we didn't move in the same social circle, I simply meant we weren't what you'd call close acquaintances."

I don't know about Jack, but her little cat-and-mouse game was really beginning to wear on me. "I don't think I can get any plainer than this—why the hell were you paying for his legal fees, Mrs. Renault?"

The woman stiffened slightly, as if someone had stuck a rod straight up the middle of her bony backside. The sharp glare she shot me over the rim of her gilded tea cup told me she didn't appreciate my sudden intrusion in her polite repartee.

I simply smiled sweetly and helped myself to a scone and a generous dollop of clotted cream and a spoonful of strawberry jam. As I took a healthy bite, I shot her my look of bland expectation.

"I met Charlie Orzinski during one of my charitable outings," Mrs. Renault said, as she set her cup down and waved breezily, refocusing her attention on Jack. "I often take my two older boys down to the soup kitchen at the Salvation Army to work during the holidays. I feel it helps to build character. Teaches the boys a bit about life and humility."

I had to bite my bottom lip to keep from laughing out loud. Somehow the thought of her two pampered children living in a house like this and then going down to the local Salvation Army to ladle out a few pounds of buttered noodles and couple of slices of SPAM loaf was ludicrous. Did the woman really believe that was going to teach them about the great unwashed?

"How exactly did this adventure of yours result in you paying for Charlie's legal fees?" I asked, ignoring the sharp glance Jack shot in my direction. Apparently he thought I was moving a little too fast. Or maybe he didn't like my tone.

But I didn't really care what he thought. I was the cop and I was the one conducting this interrogation. He was simply along for the ride. Besides, I was getting tired of sitting around, playing at attending a genteel tea party in Jeannette Renault's personal jungle.

"Charlie is an excellent cook, and I found him to be quite an articulate man. In fact, I found it a bit disconcerting to find such an educated man working as cook. During one of our conversations, he mentioned that he needed someone to take care of some legal matters for him and he asked for a recommendation. I mentioned Craig Gibson." She shrugged one bony shoulder beneath her silk blouse. "Craig has done some work for my husband over the years."

Before I could ask another question, her gaze wandered to a growth of daisies off to one side. She frowned slightly, got up and used her pruning shears to trim several of the flowers back.

She returned to her seat, placing the delicate but decidedly common flowers in her lap. "Of course, I should have realized that a man working in a soup kitchen couldn't afford Craig's exorbitant fees. But I guess I wasn't thinking too clearly.

"When Charlie's check bounced, Craig called me. I felt responsible and I paid for the bounced check and the bank fees." She raised on artfully arched eyebrow in my direction and smiled indulgently. "End of mystery, Officer Cray."

"But why would Gibson hold you accountable for Charlie Orzinski's bounced check?" Jack asked.

Mrs. Renault shrugged again. "Perhaps because Mr. Orzinski mentioned my name when he called for an appointment. I never really inquired. I simply made good on the check." She smiled again, as if she couldn't understand why we were making such a big deal out of such a minor incident. "Actually, I simply considered my action a charitable contribution. I liked Mr. Orzinski. He treated my boys well when they worked in the kitchen, and I felt that he was doing the community a great service for very low pay. I felt that paying off the debt was the least I could do for the man."

"Did Mr. Orzinski ever contact you and offer to repay the money?" Jack asked.

"Of course not. I told Mr. Gibson to tell the man that it was from an anonymous donor." She wrinkled her patriarchal nose slightly. "I didn't want things to get messy. I didn't want Mr. Orzinski coming out of there thinking he had to thank me or pay me back.

The last comment didn't surprise me a bit. This woman didn't want any messiness to appear unexpectedly on her doorstep, and that included Jack and myself. She saw such things as putting a major crimp in her view of her perfect little family.

As if on cue, Mrs. Renault stood up, signaling that our chat was over. "I'm so glad you stopped by." As she held out her hand and casually shook Jack's hand, her dark blue eyes seemed to search his face. It was if she was memorizing it.

I couldn't help but feel an oddness or strangeness to her attraction toward Jack, as if she couldn't get enough of him. But in spite of the attraction she held for him, she seemed to know that she had to let him go. Had to get him and me out of her house.

When she turned to me, the vulnerability that had been

on her face a moment ago vanished, and it its place was a frozen mask of cool remoteness.

Instead of shaking my hand, she took one of the daisies that had been sitting in her lap and slipped it swiftly behind my ear. "Much more your style, my dear. The rose was a little too classic for such a wild display of red hair. Always stick with what fits your overall nature."

I smiled, feeling tightness at the corner of my lips. No one needed to tell me I'd just been insulted. But I'd been insulted by better than Mrs. Renault.

I think I surprised her when I thanked her for the flower. Maybe she was looking for a fight, I'm not sure. But when she turned toward Jack again, a flash of sadness seemed to flicker in her eyes. Something about her expression told me that Mrs. Renault wasn't as far from the streets as she wanted me to believe.

Perhaps she'd hidden her hardness behind a veneer of polish and sophistication, but she didn't fool me. She and I were cut from a similar cloth, and I intended to find out just where her bolt of cloth had started out—just as soon as I ditched Jackie boy and could come back here on my own.

THERE WAS NO MAID to show us out this time. We simply retraced our steps to the front door. As Jack's hand touched the knob, the door swung open from the outside and two boisterous young men tumbled into the front hall. Both were dressed in the latest ski gear, their cheeks red from the cold, laughter tumbling unchecked from their young mouths.

"Oh, excuse us," the youngest apologized, pulling off his cap and revealing a mop of strikingly gold hair, shot through with streaks of Scandinavian-white. His green eyes, exuberant and mischievous, danced with some unrevealed merriment, and he glanced behind him at the other young man.

The second boy was older, less extravagant in his mannerisms, but when he smiled at us, he seemed to ooze an easy charm. He whipped off his ski cap too, revealing the same strikingly blond hair as his younger brother. But instead of green eyes, his were a deep China Sea blue. There was more of a sense of composure to the older brother, a confidence lacking in the younger one.

"I hope we didn't interrupt anything, Mother?" he said softly, his voice already deep, a man's voice.

Surprised, I glanced over my shoulder to see that Jeannette Renault had followed us out to the front door.

"Of course not, dear. This gentleman and his companion were just leaving." She held the door open for us, not bothering to even make a show of introducing us. "How was the skiing?"

"Awesome," the younger of the two said. "You should have come with us. You would have been the most stunningly beautiful snow bunny on the mountain."

For the first time since I'd laid eyes on Jeannette Renault, I saw something soft—something almost warm—enter her classically featured face. She reached up and touched her youngest son's wind-kissed cheek and patted it indulgently. "Next time, sweetheart."

Jack moved past the older son, who was standing to the right of the front door, and for a brief moment, it as if the two occupied the same space. I stared in disbelief. The resemblance was overwhelming. Astonishing.

One was golden blond and the other as dark as a raven's wing. But when they smiled at each other, there was the same slight indentation in their right cheeks, the dimple I used to kiss and tease Jack about mercilessly when we were lovers.

But it was their eyes—the amazing blue beneath thick, lush lashes—that defied one to deny the remarkable, uncanny resemblance. The resemblance was so frighteningly close it could only be called eerie.

Startled, I glanced at Mrs. Renault; for the briefest of moments, our eyes met. I could see the shiver of fear circle in the depth of her eyes, a fear so intense, so desperate, that I knew she was willing me mentally not to question what I was thinking.

She rushed forward. "Go put your gear away, boys. Your father said he hoped to be home in time for dinner tonight, and you know how he hates for us to be late when he's tired and worn out from a day in surgery." She fairly urged them down the hall, her hands fluttering at their backs like a mother hen protecting her chicks against the possibility of violent intruders.

The boys seemed confused for a moment, as if their always prim and proper mother was acting out of character, but they simply shrugged and complied. Both politely said their goodbyes and then disappeared down the hall, poking and jockeying for position as they entered one of the back rooms.

"Nice boys," Jack commented.

"Yes, they're a blessing. A blessing I hang on to each and every day. They seem to grow up much too fast."

For a moment, her gaze went to Jack's face again, and I felt she might say something else, but the moment seemed to pass and she didn't. Instead, she glanced at me. "Please give my regards to your foster father. He's a good man."

She opened the door and ushered us out, closing the door firmly after us. I had the distinct impression she never wanted to lay eyes on us again.... Or perhaps I should say that she never wanted to see *me* again. The wistfulness in her gaze when she looked at Jack was just a little too intriguing for me to believe that she wouldn't want to see him again. I intended to find out why.

Chapter Seven

A few minutes later, we were out on the driveway and the front door of the Renault mansion was locked securely behind us. I had a sudden urge to tweak Mrs. Renault one last time by ringing the doorbell again and pressing a few additional questions on her. But then I decided we'd bothered her enough for one day. I knew I'd be back.

Unfortunately, my unplanned mental pause cost me the driver's seat. When I turned around, I found Jack sitting behind the wheel of my trusty little Neon.

Naturally, that didn't sit real well with me. A bit presumptuous on his part. I rounded the car and stood next to the window. He didn't glance at me but simply sat there, letting the engine idle. The window stayed rolled up.

Ticked, I yanked open the door. "Shove over."

He didn't budge. "I got here first. Besides, you left the keys in the ignition, and I hate sitting in the passenger seat." He glanced up at me and smiled that damn easygoing smile of his. The smile that told me he wasn't about to give me what I wanted no matter what I said.

For a moment, I considered ripping the door off its hinges and chucking his fanny out of the front seat of *my* car.

But then I reconsidered. It was a fight I wouldn't win and one I wasn't ready to lose.

Besides, something told me not to make a scene. I had the oddest feeling that Mrs. Renault was watching us from one of the huge windows lining the front of the mansion.

Sighing, I rounded the car again and got in on the passenger side.

"For your information, I would never hop on your Harley without first getting your permission," I grumbled as I wedged one shoulder into the far corner of the seat, my mood dark and pensive.

"I'd have thought you would have picked up some manners from Claire in all the years you lived with her and Pop."

"She gave up on me. Realized I was a hopeless case. Lucky for me she turned her attentions on you."

By the time we were headed out of town, the silence between us had gotten more than heavy; it was oppressive. A few times, Jack shot a few glances in my direction, as if he might actually be concerned about my reaction.

Maybe he was getting antsy that I wasn't continuing to snap at him the whole trip back to the city. That seemed to be our pattern. Or perhaps he simply sensed my moodiness and had decided not to push things any further.

I have to admit I appreciated the silence. I needed to get my head on straight. I needed to try to understand—to get a handle on—the strange undercurrent that had filled the room while we visited with Jeannette Renault. My cop radar had gone off like an alarm the entire time we'd been inside the house. Something was up.

Much of what the woman had said to us didn't make sense. I knew unquestionably that she was hiding something. Something important. But for some reason, Jack hadn't seemed the least bit concerned. It was as if he was willing to take everything the woman said at face value. Maybe working as a paramedic had dampened his legendary sharp cop instincts. Sad thought.

I glanced over at him, but his gaze was shifting back and forth between the highway and the rearview mirror. There was a deeply etched frown between his dark brows, giving him a fierce look of concern.

"Problem?" I asked. "You've got that look of someone who just lost his best friend."

"No, but it seems as if we might have gained one." His gaze didn't move off the rearview mirror, but as I started to turn around, his hand clamped down on my left thigh, keeping me from moving. I tried to ignore the flush of warmth that shot through me at the touch of fingers wrapping around the inside edge of my leg. Damn my body. It was more traitorous than I'd ever imagined.

"Don't turn around. Keep your eyes front and center. I don't want whoever is back there to realize we're on to him. A black SUV—big. Looks like an Escalade. It's been hanging back there since we left Skaneateles."

"Who do you think it is?"

Jack shrugged. "It could be some rich lake dweller heading into Syracuse for a bit of shopping. Or it could be someone who is a little too interested in why we were out visiting the rich and infinitely gracious Mrs. Renault."

I snorted at his *infinitely gracious* comment. If the woman could have thrown us out of her house any faster, I think she would have suffered a hernia to do it."

"She was afraid."

"Of what?"

"Of the fact that one of us would bring up the fact that she used to be Handler Ortega's main squeeze."

"Get out!" I scoffed.

"I'm not kidding. She dated him for years, until he tired of her and moved on."

"Could Mrs. Renault have sicced them on us?" I asked. "She seemed pretty antsy about all the questions we were asking."

"True. But I don't think this tail has anything to do with her. She's hiding something for sure, but I don't think it has to do with her dating Ortega. But it will be easy enough to find out what she's hiding."

"Well, thank you, Lord." I glanced heavenward. "I was beginning to think that you bought her story hook, line and sinker."

Jack laughed. "Hardly. I simply figured I'd get a better handle on her by getting Standish to run her through the computer."

I didn't bother hiding my anticipation of that activity. "Excellent. I'm curious to know what she's hiding, too."

He shot me a look that said, *Dream on, kiddo.* "You're not going anywhere near Standish or the police station. I'm dropping you off at the hospital and then calling Standish once I get back to work. I'll swing back around and pick you up around six or so. I should be off by then."

"What do you mean, *forget it?*"

I set my jaw, clenched my back teeth and kept my eyes faced forward. I needed to be strong for this next part, and for some reason I was pretty sure that if I looked at him while trying to say it, I wouldn't be able to say what I wanted to say.

"I'm not staying at your place again. The agreement was for one night and one night only."

Jack shook his head, his jawline tightening in anticipation of the argument that was sure to follow. "That was before a cop was shot outside my apartment and you received a threatening phone call. Not to mention the fact that there is a car following us right now. You're staying at my apartment until this whole thing is cleared up."

"No."

"I'm not arguing with you about this, Chili. Get used to not getting your own way every time you disagree with something I say. It's the reality of life right now." He concentrated on the road, as if ignoring me after issuing his ultimatum would shut me up. Guess he didn't know me as well as he thought he did.

"I decide where I stay and who I stay with. That's reality in my world."

"Well, you're back in my world now and this is a non-negotiable item. You're at the apartment until I figure out what's going on." He turned and glanced at me, his blue eyes hard, unflinching. "Of course, I could always have Standish put you in protective custody and lock your pretty little ass up in some hotel."

"You wouldn't do that."

"Try me."

I was indignant but still trying to ignore the flush of pleasure that shot through me at the thought that he had actually described my ass as pretty and little. I can't remember the last time any guy had described it in those particular terms.

"Dammit!"

Jack's gaze was again glued to the rearview mirror.

"What's wrong?" I was smart enough to know that he didn't want me turning around to gawk out the back window.

"The guy behind us is coming up on us pretty fast. He was staying back there, but he's gaining on us now."

We had reached the loneliest, most desolate stretch of Route 20. Not another car was in sight.

My little Neon started up the hill leading to Route 81. The engine kicked into high as the car strained to get us up. The wind was whipping across the road, practically blinding us with blowing snow. My car hugged the road, determined not to be blown off the pavement.

Even though I wasn't driving, I could tell the tires' grip on the pavement was tenuous at best. The hill was covered with a fine sheen of black ice.

"Hang on, Chili, he's coming in fast," Jack said.

I glanced over my shoulder. The SUV was closing in, going at least sixty. I barely had a chance to brace my hand against the dashboard before we were hit from the rear. Hard.

The weight of the massive vehicle shook my entire car, metal shuddering and shaking under the impact. I felt my belt tighten and dig into my shoulder as I pitched forward under the force of the hit. A second later, I slammed back against the seat, bumping my head hard on the headrest.

Beside me, Jack's hands moved with lightning speed as he tried to compensate for the hit from the rear. He was able to keep the Neon on the road, but we skidded into the opposite lane. Luckily, no one was coming down the hill in the opposite direction. There would have been no way to avoid a head-on collision.

We hit a patch of black ice and the car skidded back into the right lane. Behind us, the SUV hit us again, this time on the back left end. It sent my car into a full 360.

The winter scenery whipped past the windshield in a blur of white and I slid sideways in the seat, my cheek slamming up against the side window.

I yelped in pain, but then everything seemed to go into slow motion. It felt as though each passing second lasted an hour.

From what seemed like a great distance, I watched Jack continue to fight the wheel, doing everything in his power to keep us on the road and upright. I opened my mouth to say something, but nothing came out. It was if my words were caught in my throat, as frozen in time as the accident unfolding in front of my eyes.

But then, I was pushed out of my stupor as the heavier vehicle rammed us again. Jack frantically fought the wheel, but this time, my car popped off the side of the road like a slippery melon seed. We slid down a steep embankment and rolled over twice. Papers and CDs flew around the cab.

By the time we came to a stop, we were hanging upside down. Shattered glass covered the ceiling of the car below me. Tiny shards covered me from head to toe. The windshield had gotten punched in.

I'm not sure if I lost consciousness or not. I don't think so. But I couldn't speak for a minute or so. I just hung there upside down, trying to figure out what happened.

By the time my brain had wrapped itself around what had gone on and why I was hanging upside down, Jack was already out of his seat belt, kneeling gingerly on the glass shards below, reaching up to get my belt undone. His hands seemed to be everywhere, checking me over, making sure nothing was broken.

"You okay?" he asked. "Can you talk? Do you hurt

anywhere?" He lifted me down onto the ceiling of the Neon, which was now the floor. I collapsed against him, my body feeling as though it were the consistency of warm rubber. He wrapped an arm around me, pulling me close, his touch reassuring, warming.

I rubbed the back of my head. "I think I'm okay. My head hurts a little. But I don't hurt anywhere else."

"You will tomorrow," Jack said dryly. He reached up and touched my cheek, his hand coming away with a smear of blood. "You must have hit your cheek on something."

"The window, I think," I said.

He reached up and yanked open the glove compartment and grabbed a couple of tissues. "Here, just press this against it. It's not deep but the pressure will stop the bleeding."

I nodded and did as he said.

He jammed his shoulder against the passenger side door, pulled on the handle and shoved open the door. A blast of icy cold air flooded the interior of the car. He crawled out and I followed.

"The damn idiot nearly killed the both of us," he said, standing up and lending a hand to help me get up, too.

"I get the feeling that was his objective, don't you?"

"No, I think it was simply a warning. If he had wanted to kill us, he would have come down and finished the job."

The black SUV was parked on the side of the hill where we'd gone off. The break in the guard rail was wide and gaping.

The vehicle's darkly tinted windows kept us from seeing anyone inside. It gave me the same eerie feeling I'd had the night the other car had sat across from Jack's apartment. Whoever was inside was staring down at us, taking it all in.

Suddenly, the driver took off, a cloud of white smoke shooting out the back end of the huge vehicle. He was headed straight back toward Syracuse.

"I guess it's too much to hope that he called us a tow," I quipped.

Jack pulled his cell phone out of his pocket. "No need. I can take care of that."

Less than fifteen minutes later, a tow truck from Skaneateles was there to pull the wrecked Neon out of the ditch and the talkative driver drove us back to the quaint little village.

Jack deposited me in a small cafe with hot chocolate and a bowl of warm soup while he went in search of a rental car to get us back to Syracuse. I used his cell phone to put in a call to Shawna.

"Where the hell have you been?" Shawna's voice was taut, her irritation evident.

"I'll be there shortly." I didn't want to get into the details of the accident over the phone. "What's going on? You sound upset."

"Just get here. Now!" She clicked off the phone.

A few minutes later, we squeezed into a rented Honda Civic and headed back to Syracuse, a little sorer and a lot less knowledgeable about who the heck was so damn determined to put the fear of God into us that he'd run us off the road and leave us to fend for ourselves.

A FEW HOURS LATER, we stood outside Charlie's hospital room. Jack had insisted I get checked out in the E.R. this time. So after a couple of X-rays of my head, a butterfly bandage on my right cheek and a quick once-over by the E.R. doc, I was released.

I wasn't mad at Jack for making me get checked out; I was just angry at how much time it took. Now I was dealing with a bellyful of guilt about not being at Charlie's bedside as quickly as I had promised. And I knew without a doubt that as soon as we walked into Pop's room, the occupants might not be too pleased with me, but they were going to be even more hostile when they saw Jack at my side.

My regret about Jack getting grief from the family actually surprised me. I mean, it seemed a bit out of character. Two days ago, I would have been at the head of the pack, kicking his butt out of Charlie's room and telling him he had no rights, no say in anything that had to do with Charlie. And now here I was actually feeling sorry for him having to face his fellow foster siblings.

I was beginning to feel as though I was living on an emotional roller coaster when it came to Jack O'Brien. But then I remembered that was pretty much how I felt when the two of us had dated all those years ago. I needed to keep that in mind whenever I felt myself weakening toward him.

"I'm sorry, but I'm guessing that you're going to have to put up with a bit more hostility," I said.

He reached up and lifted my chin with the edge of his hand, his dark blue eyes searching out mine. There was no regret, no sorrow in them. They were as cool and placid as a pond at dawn.

"Don't sweat it, Chili. They don't mean any harm. Like you, they're just hurt. They're worried Pop isn't going to make it through this, and they have to have someone to blame. I'm an easy target and believe me when I say I'm a big boy. I can handle it."

"But it still isn't exactly fair. No matter what happened

in the past, Pop loves you as much as the rest of us, and he'd want you to be a part of any decision about his care."

"You know what my decision is—I want the docs to do whatever they think they can do to bring him back. But I also respect Pop's wish that the heroics don't go too far. You know as well as I do how he feels about living his life as a vegetable. He wouldn't want that."

I nodded, a small tear slipping out the corner of my eye and sliding down my cheek.

Jack reached up and caught it on the tip of his finger, gently touching it to his own lips, as if he needed to taste me, to take me inside him.

Without thinking, I reached out and laid the flat of my hand on his hard chest. I could feel the steady beat of his heart against the palm of my hand. At that moment, I wanted to soak in his strength, his endless supply of serenity. I wanted to slip into his skin and become him for the battle I knew lay ahead. For some reason, I didn't think I could do it alone.

As if he could read my mind again, Jack said, "You're worrying too much. You know how to advocate for Pop. He knew what he was doing when he appointed you his executor."

"But I'm a real chicken when it comes right down to it. You know I've never been able to stand up to Richard."

I leaned my head against his upper chest, listening to the steady beat of his heart. *Please save me from this,* I whispered deep inside me, wishing that we were again so tied to each other that he'd hear my plea and rescue me for the job ahead.

But in the end, he didn't save me from anything. He pushed me back a step and stared down at me, his eyes holding their familiar calm, placid gaze. But it imparted a message to me. It told me he believed in me. Had faith that I could do what needed to be done.

"You'll do fine."

"He'll bulldoze right over me. You know how he is."

Jack laughed. "Richard has nothing on you, sweetie. He's a blowhard who is more afraid of his own shadow." He reached into his pocket. "Besides, I picked up a power charm for you today."

I frowned. "A what?" Fear immediately entered my belly. A gift? I couldn't accept any gifts from him. I was already too close to him. A gift meant I owed him something, and I couldn't take that step. I held up a hand. "I can't take any gift."

He ignored me and opened a small black box and pulled out a chain. "I found this in a shop in Skaneateles—while I was out renting the car for us. I was just walking by the shop and there it was, hanging in the window. I think it actually called out to me—yelled at me to be exact."

He held up a necklace with a small perfectly formed chili pepper hanging off the end. The red of the pepper was so brilliant, so glossy, that it seemed to sparkle in the dimly lit hall of the hospital.

In spite of my fears, I reached out and lightly touched the charm with the tip of my fingers. The pepper swung gently on the gold chain, the color flashing a radiant warmth of redness in the light as if it truly held something powerful and potent in its structure.

"It's beautiful." But I pulled my hand away and shook my head. "I can't accept something like that, Jack."

"Of course you can."

He ignored my refusal, put his hands on my shoulders

and twirled me around with ease. Before I could speak again, he slipped the necklace around my neck and worked the clasp. His fingers brushed the nape of my neck and sent a familiar chill down the center of my vulnerable spine.

The charm sat comfortably in the hollow of my throat, cool and warm all at the same time. My first instinct was to immediately rip it off and return it to him. We weren't dating anymore. Gifts were for lovers. They meant giving and receiving. And I wasn't sure I had anything to give him back.

It signaled a connection, a mystical connection that had existed between us for so long, so deep, that it had never vanished as I thought it had. Somewhere inside my head, a soft voice whispered that I had stepped into dangerous waters. I'd allowed the infamous thread to reconnect, to re-route itself and draw us closer.

But for the life of me, I couldn't reach up and remove the charm. I liked the feel of it sitting there against my warm skin, knowing he had seen it in a window of a shop and thought of me when he bought it. It was pure unadulterated seduction at its worst. But somehow, I didn't seem to care. I was truly losing it.

"Thank you. It's beautiful."

He grinned, leaned down and gently brushed a kiss across my lips. "I'd have liked to make that kiss a little something more significant, but I have a feeling one of your siblings might charge out of the room at any moment and rip out my throat for molesting you."

He lifted his head and I already missed the taste, the feel of his lips on mine. I wanted to deny the feeling, push it away, but it was impossible.

I wanted him more than I think I'd ever wanted anything

in my life. But I shielded my eyes, refusing to let him see how he was getting to me.

Instead, my fingers went to the tiny pepper hanging against my throat. I smoothed my fingers over it, imagining the feel of his own hands on it. The feel of his hands on every part of my body.

I suppressed a shudder and pushed the feelings away. Squaring my shoulders, I glanced at Pop's room. "Okay, I'm ready. Let's get this over with."

I marched into the room, with Jack on my heels.

As I entered the room, I carried more than a little guilt. This was my first visit since this morning. And the fact that I was in the company of Jack O'Brien wasn't going to escape any of my siblings' scrutiny, either.

My guilt came from realizing that the others had picked up the slack, and in the interim, I hadn't heard any complaints that I'd been traipsing all over the city with Jack, the most hated person—outside of Sweetie Pie—in the entire Orzinski foster clan.

Not that any of them knew I'd been getting it on with the guy…. Wait, change that to *almost* getting it on with the guy. It was important to recognize that in spite of all the heat and sweat the two of us had been generating between us, we'd both shown more than a little self-restraint. Not a hell of a lot, but some. At least we hadn't fallen into bed yet.

Pop's hospital room was filled to capacity, every nook and cranny taken up by one of his former kids. It was as if a giant powwow had been called and someone had forgotten to let me in on the plan. I was somewhat relieved, however, not to see Richard anywhere among the crowd.

Shawna sat at Pop's beside, stroking his hand and talking to him softly. The soft hiss of the respirator accompanied her words.

Nicole stood on the other side of the bed, her blond hair long and unbraided, looked slightly unwashed. It wasn't an unusual look for her. Her hair hung in her face, hiding her long, narrow features behind a shield of shining gold. She lived in a studio apartment above a smoke shop on North Salina Street, eking out a living as a painter.

When I used to visit her, we'd walk down to the Columbus Bakery and buy a loaf of Italian bread made by the Greek owners. They made the best bread in the city. We'd just tear off huge hunks of it and gnaw on them as we walked back to her apartment, chatting up a storm about the family and what was going on with everyone.

The memory was sweet, and the thought that I'd missed out on a lot these past nine years hit me hard.

Nicole nodded briefly in my direction and then went back to smoothing a wet washcloth over Pop's forehead.

Courtney, the youngest of the clan and the last to leave home, shortly before Charlie was arrested, had taken up a position on the windowsill, her small, booted feet propped up on the radiator, her elbows jammed on top of her knees, covered by faded, distinctly frayed jeans. A fierce scowl occupied her pale, pinched face. Earlier, Shawna had told me she was attending Columbia on a full scholarship and was doing well.

David and Brian, the two self-proclaimed Syracuse Romeos, had claimed two high-backed chairs they must have found somewhere in the halls of the I.C.U. and confiscated for Pop's room. Both had propped their long legs up on the end of Pop's bed.

"It's about time you showed up," Shawna said, lifting

her head and giving me a hard, searching gaze. I tried not to squirm under her close inspection, but I was pretty sure I failed miserably.

A quick, knowing look entered her dark eyes, and I knew without her even saying anything that she'd spied the necklace and knew exactly where it had come from. I was never able to put anything over on her. She knew exactly where I'd been and what I'd been up to, especially in regard to one Jack O'Brien. The look on her face clearly stated she wasn't happy with me.

I could only hope she'd wait until we were alone before she started peppering me with questions that I knew I couldn't answer, or, if I did, that they would embarrass the hell out of me.

A voice from behind the open door broke the connection between us. "It's about time you got here. We've been waiting for over three hours."

I leaned forward and peeked around the door. My stomach clenched and a wave of nausea washed over me. My luck had just run out.

Richard stood behind the door, his arms folded over his narrow chest, dislike infusing every bone of his skinny body. I shouldn't have been so quick to think he wouldn't show up.

This kind of drama was right up Richard's alley. He wasn't on my list of favorite foster siblings, but then I'm pretty sure I wasn't on his, either. Nor was Jack, for that matter. It wasn't hard to see the slight tightening of displeasure at the corners of Jack's mouth.

The two were close in age, coming into the Orzinski family around the same time. Way before I had ever arrived. Both boys were out of the house and on their own by the time I showed up on Claire's and Charlie's doorstep. But, like Jack, Richard had visited often, and his visits were always volatile and frequently filled the house with discontent.

Selfish and opinionated, Richard often managed to set Charlie and Claire off with his pompous spouting of his conservative views and narrow-mindedness.

Unfortunately, he had a keen intellect and had gone to law school. Of course, that only inflated his sense of importance and upped his need for control.

As a kid, I used to watch his interaction with Pop and Jack and I'd drawn a pretty quick conclusion that he'd been insanely jealous of the closeness of Jack's and Pop's relationship. He hadn't appreciated the intimacy, the easy camaraderie the two shared. At every opportunity, Richard had tried to downgrade or belittle Jack.

But his behavior always seemed to backfire on him because Jack never bought into his little tantrums. Of course, that only served to increase Richard's anger and resentment.

"I'm sorry," I said. "We had a little accident on the way here."

"Accident?" Shawna straightened up, concern immediately crossing her dark face. "What kind of accident? Are you both all right?"

"We're fine," Jack said, speaking for the first time. "Just some idiot going too fast when he was passing us, and he forced us off the road."

"You're sure you're okay?" Nicole asked me, her gentle face racked with even more worry. She used one delicate hand to shakily brush back several silken strands of hair.

"We're fine," I reassured her. Jack had made the right

decision. None of them needed to know it had been no accident. They had enough to deal with.

I glanced at Shawna. "Now, what's this about us having to make a decision?"

Richard glared pointedly at Jack. "It's a decision of a personal nature—regarding Dad."

Richard never could bring himself to call Charlie Pop. He thought it was too undignified. Too pedestrian for his tastes.

His flat gaze dug into Jack but, to Jack's credit, he didn't flinch or seem in the least perturbed.

I could see the rage start to simmer in the back of Richard's eyes. An argument was about to break out between these two, and I was pretty sure that wasn't something Pop needed to hear, even if he was in a coma.

"We're all Pop's kids, Richard. Just spit it out. What do we have to decide?" I asked.

Richard didn't even glance at me. "We don't need any outsiders hanging around, O'Brien. Time for you to vacate the premises."

I felt a brush of anger heat the back of my neck and flush my cheeks. All of us harbored some deep resentment toward Jack, but that didn't change the fact that he was still an Orzinski foster kid, part of the family.

"Jack has as much right as the rest of us to be here to hear what's on the table. He's one of Pop's kids, too."

"Not in my book, he isn't," Courtney snapped from her perch on the windowsill.

She popped an oversize pink bubble of gum and sucked it in before continuing, "Not after he testified in court crucifying Pop. In my book, he relinquished all rights to his relationship with Pop on the day he walked into court and ratted him out."

There was a distinct murmur of agreement from the others. Richard's smile couldn't have been more smug. I had misjudged how busy he'd been these past few hours, working the room to get everyone to see things his way. It was a mistake I shouldn't have made.

Jack shrugged his broad shoulders, his exquisitely handsome face devoid of emotion, totally blank. "No problem, gang. I have some work to finish up downtown." He glanced at me, a slight smile of reassurance peeking out. "I'll be back to pick you up around six or so."

He nodded to the others pleasantly and backed out of the room.

I watched him leave, terribly torn. I still couldn't forgive his destruction of Pop's career and everything Pop had believed in. But there was a strange tugging sensation in the pit of my stomach, a tug that told me that I might have misjudged him.

But I let him go. I wasn't about to argue with or go against my entire family simply because my hormones were most likely raising their overactive heads and getting in the way of my thinking clearly.

"What's the decision we have to make?" I asked briskly, turning back to the family.

Courtney jumped down off the windowsill and brushed off the seat of her jeans with both hands. "Pop's doc wants to meet with us in the family room. He wants to give us an update on Pop's condition and then he wants us to make a decision about where we want him to go from here."

"He wants us to decide?" I asked. "Am I missing something here but isn't he the doctor who is supposed to be tell us what should be done?"

Behind me, Richard sighed. There was a distinct flavor of exasperation in the sigh, letting me know that he resented having to explain everything to me. "Unfortunately, Dad wasn't thinking too clearly when he appointed you the executor of his health proxy. That means the doctors have to go through you when they want to do anything medical."

I glanced at Richard and shot him a quick grin. I just loved yanking his chain. "And that just eats at you, doesn't it, Richard? Ticks you off royally that Pop didn't appoint you the executor, right?"

"If he'd been thinking clearly, he *would have* appointed me. But Dad was having some memory problems these last few months—age, probably. He's been pretty distracted, but then you wouldn't know that because you haven't been around."

No big surprise that he'd resorted to a little backstabbing. "Pop and I talk every week. He was planning to come up for a visit later in January. So don't try to snow me with talk about me being out of touch."

"Well, he should have known that I'm the most knowledgeable when it comes to these types of decisions. If he had talked to me, things would be done differently."

I raised an eyebrow. "Oh, really? And when was it exactly that you went to medical school and gained all this vast medical expertise?"

Richard's frown darkened. "I'm speaking in regard to the fact that I'm the most qualified of all of us to deal with this situation legally. You've been running around upstate, ignoring Dad's pleas to return home to the family, playing cops and robbers in the mountains and who knows what else for the past eight years. What would you know about what Dad needs?"

My hands squeezed into fists at my side. "You pompous son of a—"

"Stop it, both of you," Shawna interrupted. "Pop doesn't need to hear us squabbling like this. He might be in a coma but he can hear us and we don't need to be upsetting him with these petty arguments."

She jerked her chin in the direction of the door. "Now that Killian is here, we need to meet with Dr. Mannus—Pop's physician—and make a decision."

Richard opened and then closed his mouth. Even he knew when not to argue with Shawna. He nodded and stalked out the door, his shoulders rigid. I knew he wasn't finished with me yet. He'd save his best ammo for later.

I allowed the others to file out before moving over to the bed and standing next to Charlie. His eyes were still closed, his massive chest rising and falling to the rhythm of the respirator.

I reached out and touched his cheek. It was smooth and baby-soft. Someone had recently shaved him and put on a splash of aftershave. It must have been something Shawna had brought in because it had the familiar scent of Old Spice, a favorite of Pop's. When we were kids, every Father's Day, he'd get gallons of the stuff. I think he had a lifetime supply of it somewhere in some closet.

The thought of a *lifetime,* brought tears to my eyes, and I leaned down and kissed his cheek. The smell brought back sweet memories of him hugging me.

Hugging the stuffing out of me, he used to call it. A hard, unrelenting hug that conveyed deep caring, uncompromising compassion and pure unadulterated love for a rebellious, ornery teenager who used to stiffen in his arms and try to pull away. A teenager who pretended she didn't want the affection or the love. But Pop knew better and he never let go, not once.

He had never given up on me. Every chance he got, he hugged me, letting me know in his own way that he cared about me with every fiber of his being. It had taken a while, but I had learned the lesson of trust and love in his huge, forgiving arms.

As I laid my cheek against his, I willed him to open his eyes and hold me again. Just one more time, Pop, I thought. Just one more time. Let me have your reassurance that I'm capable of making the right decision one more time. But he didn't respond. Instead, he slumbered on, oblivious of my needs for the first time in my entire relationship with him.

Pressing my lips to his forehead, I left, wandering down the hall and finding the consultation room. I slipped into a chair between Shawna and Nicole. Beneath the table, Nicole grabbed my hand and squeezed it hard. I smiled at her, letting her know I appreciated her tiny demonstration of support.

For the next twenty minutes or so, we peppered the doctor with questions. He was patient in explaining every aspect of Pop's care, and in the end, we all voted for a delicate operation, which should relieve some of the pressure on his brain. It was extremely risky and offered no guarantees, but it was the best chance he had to improve his chances of recovery.

All of us with the exception of Richard. He was for leaving things they way they were. He wasn't pleasant about the fact that he'd been outvoted, but the fact that he stormed out of the room didn't seem to bother anyone too much. I don't think any of the rest of us could have considered the possibility of not trying to have the man we loved so dearly back.

Chapter Eight

Dr. Mannus had already reserved the operating room in anticipation of us making the decision we had. He let us know that Pop would probably be in the O.R. for anywhere from nine to thirteen hours. We were in for a long wait.

I knew without question that my body would never sit still that long. It was a simple biological fact. So, shortly after we said our goodbyes and Pop disappeared through the double doors leading to the O.R., I headed for the bank of elevators at the end of the hall.

Shawna followed, her expression inquisitive. "Where are you going?"

"I have a few people I need to see." I held out my hand. "I need your keys. My car isn't driveable."

"Not until you tell me where you're going and who you're going to see."

I sighed. "I'm going to look up an old friend—Patsy Lowell. Have you seen her lately?"

"Candy Cane? You're going to try and look up Patsy 'Candy Cane' Lowell?"

Patsy, nicknamed Candy Cane in high school, for reasons even more embarrassing than the reason for my nickname, had been one of my closest friends from my old neighborhood. Shortly after I was placed with Claire and Pop, she visited once in a while. But it didn't take the Orzinskis long to regret that particular decision.

Candy's defiance, blatant sexuality and foul mouth had undoubtedly worried them. I'm not saying I was any prize package, but I had calmed some under their gentle but firm guidance. I'm pretty sure Candy's visits had them worried that I'd start reverting to my old ways of behaving.

But Pop and Claire hadn't tried to cut me off from everyone in my old life. They simply made sure Candy's visits were closely supervised.

After a few months, Candy got the message and her visits started to drop off. I think she realized I wasn't going to take off with her on some wild adventure. That there wasn't much chance that I'd run off and engage in the initiation rites of some local gang looking to recruit some fresh girls to join their ranks.

I punched the Down button on the elevator. "I thought it would be good to see some of the old gang."

"Old gang?" Shawna stepped into my space, her hands jammed firmly on her hips and her expression reflecting an obvious opinion that I'd gone off the deep end into major lunacy. "What would you want with the likes of Patsy 'Candy Cane' Lowell? That woman is pure unadulterated trouble."

"I just want to ask her a few questions. Candy always knew how to keep her ear to the ground."

"That girl knows how to be on her knees all right, but it isn't so she can keep an ear to the ground."

"No need to get insulting, Shawna," I said, even though I knew of Candy's, shall we say, wild reputation, despite not having seen her in a while. "Candy knows people. She keeps up with what's going on. Maybe she's heard something. Something that could give me some leads as to what's going on with Pop and these threats."

Shawna snorted in disgust. "The only thing that girl knows is trouble. She was born with *trouble* tattooed across her forehead."

I suppressed a grin. Little did Shawna know that that was exactly what Candy had tattooed on her body, but it wasn't located on her forehead.

"Someone mentioned they'd heard she bought a bar," I said, leaning forward and extracting Shawna's keys from her pocket. She didn't stop me. Mainly because she knew it was a useless cause.

"I heard Candy was doing okay for herself," I said as I slipped the keys into my own pocket.

"Oh yeah, she's doing okay. Candy is the type of girl who knows how to land on her feet. She bought some dive bar and did some renovations. She calls it *Candy Cane's Cave.*" The wrinkle in the center of Shawna's nose told me exactly what she thought of the place.

"Where is it?"

"It's down on North Salina. If the name doesn't tell you what kind of place it is, all you have to do is take a look around. Lots of those stores with trashy sex clothes hanging in the windows and pigeon poop all over the sidewalks. It's smack dab in the middle of a dump."

I grinned and poked Shawna's arm playfully. "So what you're saying is that it's a little on the seedy side. I bet you tell all your probationers that they have to stay out of there, right?"

Shawna slapped my hand away, trying to keep her own mouth from turning up at the ends. I mean, who wouldn't laugh. Candy had always had been a wildcat—nothing was too fast or too crazy for that girl. From the age of ten, she had demonstrated a startling attraction to anything and everything flashy, and she didn't care who knew it.

Sometimes, she'd scared even me with her crazy ideas of what constituted fun. But in those days I'd been too into rebellion to resist, and Candy had spelled rebellion with a capital *R*. I adored her, and we had driven our mothers and the school officials nuts with our antics.

"*Risky* is a pretty tame description for that bar of hers," Shawna said, getting her older-sister frown firmly back in place. "I don't let my probationers go down there, and I certainly don't want my little sister anywhere near the place. Are we clear on that?"

I ignored her last comment. I wasn't about to make any promises to her at this point. Even Shawna seemed to forget I was a grown woman with extensive police training. I went into dives all the time. Even the backwoods of the Adirondacks had its share of seedy bars. But I knew it wasn't worth arguing about. I just needed to do what I needed to do.

"Look, I'm going out for some air. I need to clear my head. I promise to be back later. Call me on my cell if there's any news on Pop."

"And what am I supposed to tell Jack when he shows up here to pick you up? He said he was coming back at six."

"Tell him I got antsy and went for a walk." I impatiently jabbed the Down button several times.

"You know he isn't going to take that well."

I shrugged. "Too bad. He doesn't own me. I go where I please. Jack knows only too well that he doesn't have any hold over me anymore." I folded my arms, determined not to get into this conversation with her. "I come and go as I please."

Shawna reached out and touched the chili pepper hanging at my throat. "No hold over you, you say?"

"Oh that was some crazy scheme of his to boost my confidence in dealing with Richard. It doesn't mean anything."

A sour taste of betrayal invaded the back of my throat, but I swallowed it down. Why did I feel the need to lie like that? Why couldn't I admit that he *did* mean something to me and I was just too chicken to admit it? What was so wrong about admitting that deep down inside I still needed him? Wanted him and that seeing him again had brought the feelings back full force.

"He's crazy about you, Killian, and you're crazy about him. You're just both too stubborn and pigheaded to admit it."

"Oh, so even though you agreed with the others that Jack should be barred from having any say in what happens to Pop, you're now telling me that I'm crazy and stubborn because I refuse to allow my hormones to rule my life?" I shook my head in amazement. "Are you actually telling me that it's okay to jump into the sack with the one person who single-handedly ruined Pop's life?"

Shawna simply stared back at me, her dark eyes flat with disappointment. Her expression told me that I was overreacting, not hearing what she was saying, but I didn't care. She was pushing my button and I intended to push back.

Finally, she said, "I didn't say anything about jumping into the sack with him. In fact, I'd highly recommend you *not* do that until you've both dealt with your unfinished business—namely, your feelings for each other. If you don't get a handle on where you both stand, you're both going to keep spinning your wheels. It's like the two of you are mired in emotional muck. Muck that you both created. Finish up that business and then decide on the jumping-into-the-sack business."

The elevator dinged and the doors slid opened. I quickly stepped inside. There was no meeting Shawna's gaze. I didn't want to hear what she was suggesting, probably because it made too much sense.

But Shawna had no intention of backing down. She stepped forward and wedged her boot between the doors, keeping them from closing. She obviously wasn't through pontificating.

"If that unfinished business means that the two of you need to get together and boink your brains out like two rabbits on steroids and then go your separate ways, so be it. But I think it means talking out your issues."

With that, she pulled her foot back, turned and walked down the hall toward the waiting room.

The doors closed, leaving me standing in the middle of the elevator, contemplatively chewing on my bottom lip. I decided that I really resented it when Shawna was right.

NOT TWENTY MINUTES LATER, when I was halfway across town, my cell phone vibrated in my side pocket.

Irritated, I pulled it out and flipped it open. *"What?"*

"It's me," Jack said.

"No big surprise there."

He laughed. "Damn, but I hate being predictable."

"Deal with it. You are."

"Why aren't you at the hospital? And where the hell do you think you're going?"

I ignored both questions. "Who ratted me out? Shawna?"

"No one. I just know you too well. There wasn't any

way you'd sit there for nine hours waiting to hear the out-
come of the operation."

"So you know we voted for the surgery?"

"Yeah, I was pretty sure that was the direction you'd all
take—except for Richard, of course."

I smiled. He really was psychic. He knew how each of
us would vote. I was silent for a minute, listening to the
tires of Shawna's car hiss on the slick pavement.

"We made the right decision, didn't we, Jack?"

"You made the right decision, babe. Pop wouldn't have
wanted it any other way. He wouldn't have wanted to live the
rest of his life hooked up to a respirator, living out his final
days unaware of his family. This gives him a fighting chance."

His reassurance meant more to me than I could ever ex-
press in words. We had done the right thing. But now we
had to wait to find out the results, and I couldn't sit by idly.

"Where are you headed?" he asked me again.

"To see an old friend."

"And the name of this old friend is…?"

"None of your business."

"Don't get difficult with me, Chili." His voice deepened
even more and I could hear the tension tighten around the
edges of it. He didn't like my evasiveness one bit.

"In case you've forgotten, someone is after you," he said.
"You're not supposed to be going anywhere unescorted."

"I won't be alone for long." I turned onto North Salina
and pulled into a parking space five doors down from a red-
and-white striped neon sign advertising Candy Cane's Cave.

The sign was of a nude woman sucking suggestively on
an oversize candy cane. I couldn't help but wonder what
the neighbors in the adjacent upstairs apartments thought
of having to look at that gem every day. But then from the

looks of the neighborhood, I decided that none of them were probably too concerned. More than likely, they were all regular patrons of the place.

Beneath the woman, the neon letters announced that exotic dancers and happy hour lasted from 4:00 p.m. until closing. It was a Monday night, but there was already quite a crowd pushing and shoving to get in the front doors. Obviously, Candy had hit on a gold mine of an idea.

A giant of a man, with arms the size of giant pythons folded across his massive, totally hairless chest, guarded the front door. A red silk turban, harem pants and a short sleeveless vest completed his outfit.

I couldn't help but wonder how the poor guy wasn't freezing to death in the getup. But he seemed oblivious to the cold as he carefully checked out the clientele as they presented themselves at the door. Most of the customers were guys, but there were some women, too.

"I'm not fooling around anymore. Tell me where you are," Jack said, his voice reminding me that I still had my cell phone pressed to my ear.

"Gotta go, Jack. Things to do. People to see." I flicked the cell phone off and shoved it back into the pocket of my pants.

I climbed out and wandered over to the bouncer. "Nice night, huh?"

He looked me up and down and if he could have gotten away with wrinkling his nose at my sloppy attire, he probably would have. "Shove off, sister. Even you are a little too trashy for this joint."

"Any chance that Candy Cane is in?" I decided to ignore the command to vacate the premises and the unelicited comment on my attire.

"Who's asking?"

"An old friend of hers." I took out a folded twenty and slipped into one of his hamlike fists. "Tell her Chili Pepper wants to see her."

He didn't appear real impressed with the twenty, and my nickname didn't seem to do anything for him, but he moved over to the intercom and punched the button. He spoke in low tones for a few seconds and all of a sudden his expression changed from bored insolence to all smiles.

He pulled open the club door and waved me inside. "Ms. Lowell says to go right on in. Her office is at the back, overlooking the dance floor. She'll be waiting for you."

"Thanks!" I started to walk inside and then paused. "If a good-looking, dark-haired guy with a rotten, overbearing attitude shows up here looking for me, tell him I left about an hour ago, 'kay?"

"Sure thing, little sister. Attitude isn't welcome here at Candy Cane's. We like to keep things peaceful."

He went back to his stonelike pose, and I moved through a darkened corridor with only a tiny strip of plastic white lights lining the edges of the rug to illuminate my way.

The entire hallway seemed to throb and vibrate with the beat of some pretty funky music. At a different time, I'd probably be hanging out at a joint like this just to take in the ambience. Even I appreciated good music.

When I entered the main club area, I was impressed. Candy had definitely outdone herself. The room, once a large warehouse, had been turned into a thriving, totally driving night club.

A curved mahogany bar occupied one entire side of the club. The guests were piled three deep around the bar, drinks being passed over customers' heads as five frantic bartenders tried to keep pace with the frenzy of orders.

Waitresses in skimpy shorts, barely covering their shapely bottoms, and tiny halter tops with fringes, moved in and out among the tables, efficiently dodging the swats some of the more obnoxious patrons.

To the far right, a gyrating DJ inside an enclosed booth played the music and encouraged the crowd on the dance floor to a higher level of craziness. More than a few women were being passed around over the heads of the other dancers, their laughter indicating a high level of intoxication. Apparently anything and everything was a go at Candy Cane's.

On either side of the DJ's booth, floating dance cages held exotic dancers. At the moment, two women had live snakes coiling and slithering up and down their almost-nude bodies. It made me more than a little nervous.

Personally, no one could pay me enough to dance naked, let alone with a huge snake crawling all over me. I shivered and moved my gaze elsewhere.

Behind the dance floor at the back of the club, elevated slightly above everything in the place was a long glass-paneled booth. I could see Candy standing on the other side of the glass, watching me advance into her establishment. Even from a distance, she looked as if she hadn't aged a bit. But one thing sure was different. She'd cleaned up nicely. Gone was the sulky teen with the green-streaked hair and spiked metal dog collar.

In her place stood a stunningly beautiful woman. Her red dress, exceedingly short and perfectly fitted to her petite figure, was exquisite. It wasn't something a person would find in any shop in Syracuse. But then, from the looks of the crowd and the cash flowing across the bar, I figured Candy Cane had reached a point in her career where she could shop in just about any store in any city she wanted. The club was a gold mine.

Her blond hair hung almost to her waist, pin-straight and with a sheen that seemed to glow white. I knew without question it was a dye job because when I'd originally known her, Candy's hair had been dirty blond turning drab brown.

As I climbed the stairs leading to her perch, she opened the door to her office and squealed my name. She jumped up and down on six-inch heels, and for a moment I was afraid she was going to take a header down the stairs and fall right on top of me. But she managed to stay upright.

When I reached the top, she embraced me and dragged me into her office, a lavish, over-the-top stylin' place with plush red velvet couches, lava lamps and rugs so thick and soft a person could drop down and fall asleep on them in seconds.

There were mirrors all over the place, including the entire ceiling. It didn't take much imagination to guess what went on in this place during the after-hours parties.

Candy had always aspired to be like the ladies who hung around the notorious street corner a short distance from our moms' apartments. The kind of women who were visited by all the lowlifes in town. She liked the kinky clothes the women wore, but perhaps even more, she envied the easy cash exchanged between the women and their "customers."

She stood back and gave me the once-over. "Girlfriend, you look positively drab! You need a total makeover and some serious fashion advice."

"Not much need for fashion in the wilds of the Adirondack Mountains," I countered.

Candy laughed and plopped down on one of the couches, propping her narrow feet up on the coffee table, the six-inch spikes hitting the glass top with a sharp snap.

"I never could understand you burying yourself alive up there in the wilderness. For what?" She flipped back her hair and gave a breezy laugh. "Because some player of a cop you were sweet on betrayed you? Hell, woman, haven't you learned yet that that's the way men operate? We women just need to learn to beat them at their own game."

I groaned inwardly and dropped down on the couch directly opposite her. From the looks of things, everyone in the entire city of Syracuse knew about my pathetic love life and Jack O'Brien's starring role in making it so damn miserable.

Candy leaned forward and pulled a bottle of expensive-looking champagne out of a silver ice bucket. She poured two tall flutes of the bubbly stuff.

She reached across, handing one to me. "All right, enough about the ignorance of men. Tell me what you've been up to lately. And you better tell me you're dating at least three studly lumberjacks with legs the size of giant spruces and their other even more critical appendages of similar size and length!"

I grinned and knew my face had turned several shades of red. Leave it to Candy to get right to the sex talk. "I'd rather hear about what's been going on with your life. Things seem to be really popping for you. This place is unbelievable."

A wide grin broke out across her face, lighting up her entire face. She was genuinely pleased with my compliment. She liked the fact that I was impressed with her accomplishments. I knew it hadn't been easy for her growing up. She hadn't had people like Charlie and Claire to look out for her, people who believed and encouraged her. Somehow, she'd gotten lost in the system when I'd been lucky enough to get rescued. Funny how life dealt us different endings to the traumas we experienced.

"Bet Principal Schmitz wouldn't believe how far little old Patricia Lowell got, now would he?"

I had to laugh. Schnozzle Schmitz, so named because of the incredibly huge honkin' nose that hung like a banana in the middle of his narrow face, used to torture the two of us in his office on a daily basis. He'd give us endless lectures on the proper demeanor of young ladies of quality, which, according to Schnozzle, neither of us had a chance in hell of ever being. Not that either Candy or I saw that description of young ladyhood as anything desirable.

"No, I'm pretty sure even Principal Schmitz would be pretty impressed with your current level of success."

Candy leaned forward, lifted her glass to mine and clinked. "To success."

"To success," I agreed.

I took a small sip and then swept a hand toward the bustling night club gyrating at full steam outside the glass window. "So, how'd you manage all this?"

The corner of Candy's lush lips turned up slightly, giving her a somewhat cunning expression. "Oh, I had a little help from a friend."

"Anyone I know?"

Candy shrugged, her expression becoming closed, sectioned off. She liked to talk, but she wasn't stupid. "Let's just say that I have a very wealthy silent partner. He helped with the financing." Her smile brightened. "But it still leaves me with plenty of dough left over for myself."

"Who's the silent partner?"

Candy tilted her head to one side and studied me. "Why the questions, Chili? You left this life behind aeons ago. You became the Orzinskis' poster child of model behavior—bought whatever it was that Charlie and that mealy-mouthed wife of his was selling."

The slam against Charlie and Claire irritated the heck out of me, but I held my tongue. I needed something from Candy and getting angry with her wasn't going to get me what I wanted. I stayed cool.

"I was just curious. Charlie's out of money, no life insurance and we're not sure how we're going to pay the bills that are piling up. I thought you might know someone who would float us a loan."

Candy moved to the edge of the couch, her gaze intense. "You really believe that Charlie is broke?"

"I don't believe it, I know it. I have power of attorney. I've seen his bank account. It's down to thirty-five bucks."

Candy laughed and shook her head. "Then he's stashed it somewhere, honey. He and Handler have been doing business for years. There's no way he's spent all the money he got over the years"

I tasted something bitter in the back of my throat, but I didn't let on. I sat back, resting my arms along the back of the couch. There was no way I was going to buy anything she was selling when it came to me believing that Charlie had ever been in cahoots with Ortega. Somewhere inside me, I had to believe that the money in the safe-deposit box had been planted there, that Charlie knew nothing about it.

After all, wasn't there plenty of evidence that Jeanette Renault had been Ortega's lover for years? Wouldn't be hard for her to open the box and hand the key over to Gibson. Jack had already said that Gibson's partner, Catherine Pratt, was Ortega's personal lawyer.

But I played along, needing Candy's information. She had her ear to the ground, and from all indications, she knew something. Something important.

"Handler Ortega gave Charlie money?"

Candy nodded and set her glass down on the table, a self-satisfied grin on her face. She liked holding the cards, knowing something I didn't have a clue about. Engaging in one-upmanship had always been a favorite pastime of hers. Some things never change.

"How do you know?" I asked.

"I keep current. You have to in this business." She studied her magnificently manicured nails for a moment, as if appreciating the red lacquer but more than likely carefully considering what she was or wasn't going to reveal. Candy wasn't a fool, but she was dying to tell me something. Something juicy.

Finally, she lifted her head. "I've been dating Handler for about four years now. Once he dumped his last girlfriend, who was getting a little too possessive, he was ready for something new. Something more stylin'. I happened to be in the right place at the right time."

"He's old enough to be your father, Candy!"

She giggled. "Yeah, ain't that the truth. But he's a real sugar daddy, and a girl never knocks a guy who can get her what she wants and needs." Her voice took on baby-like tones. "Whatever Handler's widdle Candy Cane wants, his widdle Candy Cane gets."

The baby talk made me nauseous, but again I feigned interest. I needed her information, and if that meant putting up with baby talk, then baby talk it was. "Well, I always said that you knew how to pick the right guy. The one who would get you what you wanted."

To anyone else, that might have been an insult, but to Candy, I had just paid her the ultimate compliment. "Ain't that the truth."

She liked being seen as the one in charge, the person who knew everyone and had all the right connections. She'd been like that since I'd met her at age eight when she'd been working the lunchroom, relieving the kindergartners and first graders of their lunch money. She loved wheeling and dealing. Someone like Handler Ortega would be right up her alley.

She leaned forward to pick up her glass again and took a sip, watching me over the rim for a few seconds as if trying to make a decision. I waited, figuring that whatever she had to offer would be worth the wait.

"Handler wants something that Charlie's got. Wants it bad. Apparently Charlie walked off with something of Handler's that he has a real *burn* for. If you know where it is, I'd advise you to get it to him. He'd pay you a good chunk of change—enough to take care of Charlie's hospital bills and a little more."

"Why would Charlie have anything that Handler Ortega wants?"

Candy raised a perfectly plucked eyebrow. "Still playing Miss Goody Two-Shoes, huh, Killian?"

"What's that supposed to mean?"

"That you're still buying that ridiculous story that your foster dad didn't sell information to Ortega back in the early nineties."

I sat up, the anger in my stomach tightening to such a

degree that I thought I might double over in pain. But I forced myself to calmly stare back at Candy.

"He didn't sell any information. I know Pop too well to ever believe that story. It was a setup, pure and simple. Someone used him as a scapegoat."

I worked to keep my voice from getting out of control. I knew I needed to keep the negotiations between Candy and me civil and open-ended. I needed her cooperation, and I knew she held the key to getting me in to see Ortega.

Candy shook her head, her expression suddenly sad, if you called a slight drooping of her pouty lips true sadness. "You really don't know, do you, sweetie? Your Pop was just like the rest of them. Always coming around with his hand out, information flowing out of his mouth faster than Handler knew what to do with it."

Devastation hit me like a Mount Everest landslide of pain. The small sips of champagne I'd taken earlier started to roll and pitch like crazy in the pit of my stomach, threatening to come back up. I swallowed hard and kept it down.

But I needed the information I came for. So, instead of arguing, I smiled benignly. "Then set up a meet. Let me talk to Ortega. Maybe I can help him out. Help him locate what he's looking for." I stretched my legs out in front of me, trying to relieve some of the cramping in my stomach, but also feigning an expression of benign interest.

"Charlie's put me in charge of his affairs," I said. "I'm more than willing to negotiate. I simply want Ortega's goons to leave Pop alone and see that he gets some cash to help him through this rough spot."

Candy tapped the tip of one of her nails against her brilliant white front teeth. Bleached, no doubt. They were so white they probably glowed in the dark. Her smile turned cunning. "You're less of a Pollyanna than I originally thought, Chili." Her grin widened. "Remember when that gang of sixth grade boys told us we couldn't be in their gang unless one of us ate an entire jar of red-hot chili peppers?"

I cringed inwardly. *Did I remember?* How could I ever forget. It was probably the reason I now battled a chronic case of acid reflux. "It's not something one forgets."

"You ate that entire jar without a whimper. Not even a single tear. I always knew you had it in you to play hardball. You just got soft going and living with the Orzinskis." She stood up and walked over to her stylish glass topped desk trimmed with gold and picked up the phone. "I'll give Handler a call, see if he's open to a meet." She paused a moment and then added, "You'd have to go alone. No thoughts of bring that hunky O'Brien with you."

"Jack and I aren't attached at the hip. I'm perfectly capable of going places all on my own." Which was true as long as I found a way of ditching O'Brien and keeping him from following me. I was pretty sure I could manage that.

She hitched one shapely hip up on the edge of desk and punched in a series of numbers. "Yeah, give me Handler. Tell him Candy needs to talk to him."

A few minutes later, a big smile broke across her face, and she seemed to preen herself like a prized bird, smoothing back her hair and wetting her lips. "Hey, sugar. Good to hear your voice." Her smile froze and a small pout turned down her lower lip. "Well, *excuse* me for interrupting. I called because I thought I had some good news for you."

She listened for a minute and then said, "I've got Killian Cray sitting right here in front of me. She says she might have what you're looking for, and she's willing to negotiate."

Her pout deepened. "I'm not stupid, Handler. Her boyfriend O'Brien isn't sitting on the couch next to her. It's just Killian."

Ortega talked a little longer and Candy did all the listening. Her head bobbed up and down so hard it was like watching one of those damn spring-headed dogs in the back of a person's car. It was interesting to see such an assertive, almost aggressive woman reduced to such submissiveness in a matter of seconds.

"Okay, I'll tell her." She hung up the phone. "He's engaged in some rather delicate negotiations at the moment. But if you can come to his restaurant tomorrow afternoon around four o'clock, he'll meet with you."

"He couldn't manage anything sooner?" I had Jack out of my hair at the moment and the thought of getting things wrapped up before he made a reappearance was critical.

"Not a chance. But he'll give you his undivided attention tomorrow."

"Guess I'll have to settle for that. Tell him when you see him that I'll be there."

Candy stood up. "He was pretty clear that you're to come alone, Chili. No O'Brien. If you show up with anyone, all bets are off."

"I got that."

Even though a small voice in the back of my head told me that I was totally off my rocker for even thinking of doing this, I knew there was no other way to do it.

I needed to talk to Ortega alone. Needed to find out what he thought Pop had that was his. If it was the money, he was more than welcome to it. But something told me it was something else entirely.

I stood up, setting my champagne glass on the coffee table. "Thanks for the drink and for setting up the meet. I appreciate it."

"You're leaving so soon? Why not stay around for a bit? Things are just heating up here at the club." She grinned and swayed her hips a bit. "Plenty of cute guys hang out at my place. You might find a bit of fluff to amuse you."

"Thanks, but it's been a long day and I want to stop by the hospital and check on Charlie."

I headed for the door, but stopped when Candy said, "Wait."

I paused and watched as she walked over to a closet, opened it and rummaged through an amazing array of dresses.

Finally, she turned and threw me a scrap of something. "Here, wear this tomorrow night. You'll make more of an impression on Handler if you arrive looking like a woman rather than a cop or whatever image you're attempting to project."

I held up a tiny slip of slinky green. It was a dress, or at least what passed as a dress in Candy's world.

It was a designer dress from the look and feel of it. A scooped neckline and a short, asymmetrical hemline that would probably fall about midthigh or higher on me.

Candy bent down and grabbed something else. Straightening up, she tossed me a pair of six-inch heels in a matching emerald green. "Packaging is real important when you're talking to Handler." Her eyes narrowed. "Just don't get any ideas about stealing him away. We might be friends, but I draw the line at anyone trying to steal my man."

"Relax, Candy, I'm not in the least interested in finding myself a sugar daddy. I can handle life on my own terms."

"That's what we all say, sweetie. Until reality sets in and you realize what you're missing. But you stay in la-la land. Meanwhile, I'll be grabbing whatever I can get."

I set the clothes and heels on the table next to the door. "As much as I appreciate the offer, I can dress myself."

She shrugged. "Suit yourself."

I turned to walk down the steel steps leading from Candy's office. I paused midway. There was no missing the sight of Jack leaning one broad shoulder against a pillar on the edge of the dance floor. Apparently, Mr. Harem Pants Bouncer hadn't pegged Jack as *the guy with the attitude*. He gotten into the club without a scratch on him.

The brilliant blue of his eyes met mine from across the room and there was no missing the fiery sparks of dark anger flickering around like fireflies in their depths. Obviously, Jackie Boy wasn't happy.

"Well, well, isn't this delicious. I was wondering when Jack O'Brien would take me up on my invitation to visit the club," Candy said from behind me.

"Oh yeah, Jack likes to visit at the most inopportune times."

Candy had always harbored a thing for Jack, but he had never given her a tumble. Not even when she practically threw herself at him at my eighteenth birthday barbecue in Charlie's and Claire's backyard. At least I never heard any rumors that they'd gotten it on. Nine years later though, I couldn't be sure they hadn't found each other. Syracuse was only so big, and Jack had a well-known appetite for pretty women.

"No time is an inopportune time at Candy Cane's Cave," Candy said, brushing past me on the stairs.

As she passed, she pushed back a few strands of her platinum blond hair with a swift flip of her head. Her eyes gleamed and she had the look of a woman grooming herself for the male of the species. Jack was in for a full-frontal attack. I could only hope he was prepared.

"I wonder if he'd like to make a little extra cash dancing on ladies' night. The ladies here would just about eat him up."

"Oh, do me a favor, Candy, and ask him," I said, barely able to contain my own glee at the thought of Jack's reaction to such an invitation. "I'm sure he'd jump at the chance to make a little extra cash."

Candy teetered over to Jack on her six-inch red heels, the sway of her hips a sight to behold. I figured I'd fracture a hip if I tried anything even close to a walk like that.

She reached up and lightly grasped his right bicep as she talked to him, her fingers gently caressing the curve of the muscle. She leaned in close, her lips brushing the edge of his ear as she made her request over the thundering volume of the music.

Even from a short distance away, I could see the sparks in Jack's eyes ignite even more than when he'd spied me. His look accused me of putting her up to the request. I simply grinned.

It was kind of nice to see the great Jack O'Brien not so serene and unruffled by a lady's request. Obviously, Candy's invitation had hit a sore spot with him, and I was only too glad to oblige.

He shook his head, letting her know he wasn't interested, then brushed past her and made his way over to me. "Gee, thanks for the recommendation." He eyed me suspiciously "I'm right in, assuming it was you who put her up to that request?"

I blinked my lashes innocently. "I have no idea what you're referring to, Jack."

He took my arm and headed for the door, his stride purposeful and no-nonsense. "This is not where you need to be right now. Let's go."

"Killian!" Candy called after me. We both paused and turned to glance at her. "Don't forget what I said."

I knew she was referring to the fact that Ortega wanted me coming to the restaurant alone. I simply nodded.

As we headed out the door, Jack asked, "What was she talking about?"

"Oh, she got me an appointment at her hairdresser's. She says I need an updated do and some new fashion sense. She swears this guy will change my life in the date department."

Jack grunted. "Forget it. You're fine just the way you are."

I think I might have fainted if he didn't still have my arm in his grip. Did he really think that?

"Grunge is your style. Leave it at that."

My heart took a steep nosedive. Jeez, how'd he manage to always do that? Compliment me one moment and take it away in the next breath.

"Where are we headed?" I asked.

"Back to my apartment. Shawna says that Pop still isn't out of surgery and she doesn't want to see you back there until you've eaten a decent meal, showered and slept for at least five hours. I'm simply following orders."

I didn't argue. I figured it would be easier to ditch him back at the apartment or even at the hospital later in the evening.

THE RIDE BACK to Jack's apartment was pretty quiet. His anger fairly simmered with heat between us. I figured if I reached out and touched the space between us, I might singe my fingers.

For some reason, his anger pleased me. I think I saw it as a means of keeping us apart. It kept us from dealing with the issues Shawna had already told me we needed to sort out.

If Jack stayed mad, then I didn't have to bring the subject up and we could remain blissfully ignorant of what we felt for each other on a deeper level. I told myself that it was safer that way.

As soon as the elevator door opened and we stepped out on his floor, we both knew something was wrong. His apartment door stood ajar, the wood around the lock splintered. Someone hadn't demonstrated much finesse breaking in. It looked as though someone had taken a crowbar, jammed it between the frame and door and pried it open like a reluctant clam shell.

"Stay here," Jack ordered.

I stopped him as I reached into my jacket and pulled out my revolver. "In case you've forgotten, big guy, I'm the one with the weapon." I nodded at the stethoscope dangling from his pocket. "Personally I don't think that thing is going to give you much protection."

He swore softly but let me brush past him. He followed so close behind that I could feel his breath on the back of my neck, and I knew from the harsh cadence of his breathing that he was tempted to grab the gun out of my hand and shoulder me aside. But I had to give him credit—as much as it must have tempted him, Jack followed protocol.

The place was pitch-black. The only light filtered out

into the main room from the single bulb lit over the bathroom sink. Behind me, Jack quickly turned the knob of the closet next to the door and opened it. He reached onto the top shelf and pulled down a revolver.

I eyed the weapon with suspicion.

"Don't worry," he said softly, "it's registered."

He slid in a clip as we surveyed the damage to his apartment. It had gotten the same, if not worse, treatment as Pop's.

Everything was trashed. The couch cushions and the mattress on the bed were slashed open and the contents spilled out on the floor. Each panel on the Japanese screen was ripped to shreds, and the wooden frame broken into a pile of splintered pieces.

Pictures from the wall were torn down and the backs cut open. Someone wasn't taking any chances. They'd checked every possible hiding place.

The refrigerator and freezer compartments were wide-open, the food pulled out, the containers opened, the contents dripping on the floor.

As we moved farther into the apartment, our footsteps echoed loudly on the hardwood floors. It seemed as though whoever had done the damage had already departed.

I was concerned because there was no sign of Sweetie Pie. My heart went out to the poor beast. He was probably beside himself with shock at the same thing happening a second time.

"I'll take the kitchen," I whispered. "You check out the opposite side of the loft."

Jack nodded.

No sooner had I gotten into the kitchen than I heard a loud curse and then the sound of someone running.

"Hold it!" Jack shouted.

Glass broke and a harsh expletive from Jack told me that whoever had been hiding in the living room when we entered wasn't giving much credence to Jack's demand.

I ran out into the living room just in time to see Jack using the butt end of his revolver to knock out the remaining shards of glass sticking out of one of the large windows on the opposite end of the loft. Apparently, the burglar had crashed through the window in an effort to escape. Jack climbed out onto the fire escape after the intruder.

Moving over to the window, I glanced down. Nothing.

I looked up. Sure enough, a figure in black was racing up the iron fire escape, Jack right behind him. I picked up the cell phone, dialed 911 and reported the break-in.

Then I followed Jack out the window and up the fire escape.

Chapter Nine

Climbing the metal fire escape wasn't easy. The temperature had turned cold again and a light, freezing rain had been falling since dusk. Ice had formed on everything. The steel steps and railing fairly dripped with the stuff.

I couldn't believe Jack and the guy he was chasing were actually running up the slick surface. If one of them slipped and fell backward, we were all in trouble; we'd tumble down the steps like three dominoes in free fall. I clicked the safety on my gun and shoved it into the waistband of my pants.

I crawled up the steps, my right hand tightening on the railing until my fingers ached from the cold. Halfway to the top, my foot slipped and I skidded sideways. My feet slipped outward, one leg swinging out into black nothingness.

I scrambled to regain my footing, terror hammering a quick beat against my breastbone. I grabbed the railing and kept myself from pitching over the side. In the process, I bumped the railing and my gun clattered onto the steel steps.

"Damn."

I tried grabbing for it, but it skittered across the icy surface and fell onto the landing below. I paused for a brief second. Did I go after it or keep going?

I glanced up. The intruder had reached the top and was on the roof. Jack followed. No time to stop. Jack had his gun. It would have to be enough.

I clattered up the steps after them.

The roof was pitch-dark. In spite of the recent renovations to the condo, some idiot hadn't thought to install any lighting on the roof.

I could hear Jack and the other guy running, the sound telling me that they were headed for the opposite end of the roof. Their feet hit the frozen tar paper with hard thuds. They were running all-out. I followed.

Midway across the roof, the light from the roof next door gave off enough illumination for me to make out their silhouettes. I arrived in time to witness Jack take a flying leap, tackling the guy from behind.

They went down hard, Jack on top of the other guy. They both grunted as they fell, but it was immediately obvious that the hit wasn't hard enough to convince the other guy to give up. He struggled beneath Jack's weight, reaching out a hand and groping for something—anything to use as a weapon. Jack struggled to keep him down, but they seemed pretty evenly matched in the strength department.

I saw Jack fumble with one hand in the pocket of his jacket. I knew he was trying to control the guy and get to his gun.

But he was too late. The guy ripped the top off one of the air vents. He twisted around and slammed the metal piece up against the side of Jack's head. I could hear the crack of the steel on Jack's skull from a few feet away. He fell sideways onto his attacker, his body boneless.

Dread slid into the back of my throat, clawing and choking me. Please, God, let him be all right.

The guy shoved Jack aside, giving him a wicked kick as he scrambled to his feet.

A vicious urge to wrap my hands around the man's throat and squeeze shot through me. How dare he treat Jack like that?

Jack moaned and sat up, his hands going up to touch a spot over his left ear. He glanced around, his expression dazed. Disorientated.

But he'd moved. That meant he was alive and functional. Sweet relief washed over me.

The perp took off, running for the edge of the roof. I headed for Jack, bending down to see if he was okay.

"Where's your gun?" I asked.

He stared up at me, his eyes unfocused and blood streaming down the side of his face, soaking the collar of his shirt. The metal vent had left a six-inch gash down the right side of his face. I knew he was confused, not processing what I said.

I patted him down, found his revolver in his side pocket. But as I pulled it out, I glanced up to see the perp climb the roof wall. He scanned the distance between Jack's building and the adjacent one.

"I wouldn't try it if I were you," I warned, moving closer.

I kept the gun trained on him, figuring he wasn't stupid enough to think he could jump the chasm. He was trapped and any moment he'd give up.

I miscalculated. He leaped out into space, stretching for the opposite roof.

I held my breath, willing him to make it. Even if he was

a dirtbag, I wasn't in the mood to see anyone splatter himself on the pavement below.

The guy hit the opposite wall, grunted and curled his fingers over the top edge of the adjacent roof. He had the audacity to turn and glance over his shoulder, shooting me a triumphant grin before starting to pull himself up.

But he had made a mistake. The ice coating the opposite ledge was thicker than he'd anticipated, and his taking the time to shoot me a grin had loosened his hold. His grin turned to panic. I watched in horror as his fingers started to slip.

Jack climbed to his feet. He stumbled toward the wall, and I knew without him saying anything that he was already contemplating making the same jump. I ran after him, grabbing his shirttail. He shook me off.

"Don't do it, Jack. It's too far," I pleaded.

He ignored me and climbed the wall. My heart pounded in the back of my throat. I could feel a well of dark fear build inside me.

He took the leap. But somehow, in spite of his head wound, he had more power, more stamina, than the perp. He reached the opposite roof, hit and rolled. When he came to a stop, he jumped up and ran back to the wall. Reaching down, he grabbed for the guy dangling by one hand.

Frantic, the guy scrambled to hang on. But it was obvious he had weakened. His fingers slipped a fraction of an inch down the length of Jack's arm. Jack leaned out farther, his powerful shoulders bunching and straining to keep from slipping over the side along with the thug. His feet scrambled for better footing.

Terror gripped me. I knew without question that he was

in danger of being pulled over the side. The burglar was big; his grasp was becoming more frantic, more desperate. I could hear him pleading with Jack to hold on to him, not to let him fall.

I stepped back, got a running start and ran for the wall.

I heard Jack yell, "No!", but I was already in the air, jumping out into space.

For a moment, I seemed suspended in midair, the hard pavement fifty feet below, the opposite roof miles away. Across the divide, my gaze met Jack's. The fear in his eyes surprised me.

But before I could contemplate the meaning of that, I cleared the opposite wall and hit the rooftop of the building. I rolled, my injured shoulder screaming with renewed protest.

I lay on my back, stunned for a brief second, and then scrambled to my feet. I ran for the ledge.

Jack's body was inching across the top of the wall as the man below pulled on him, dragging him closer and closer to diving over the side headfirst.

I dove for Jack's legs, wrapping my arms around his thighs and hooking my feet around the nearby air shaft. I hung on, my heart feeling as though it might beat right through the center of my chest.

I skidded on the ice, my knuckles hitting the frozen cement of the opposite wall. They were being cut and sliced as I slid with the movement of Jack's body. My mind begged and pleaded for my body to give Jack the ability to haul the man to safety before all three of us were dragged over the side.

But a few seconds later, the man seemed to lose all power and strength in his fingers and he simply let go. He screamed once and then plunged to the pavement below.

I turned away and slid down, my back to the wall. I sat stunned, unable to think straight. No one should have to die that way. Not even some creep who had broken into Jack's apartment and ransacked it. I felt the champagne I'd drank earlier rise up into the back of my throat and I leaned over, gagging violently.

A few seconds later, I felt Jack's hand on my shoulder as he jerked me upright. "What the hell were you thinking? Are you nuts? You could have killed yourself making that jump."

At least his roughness kept me from making a fool of myself by puking on the rooftop like a rookie.

"Oh, so it was okay for you to make the leap, but not me?" I wiped my mouth with the back of my hand and swallowed down the sourness of my own fear. "And by the way, you're entirely welcome."

He frowned. "Welcome? For what?"

"I saved your butt. In case you're having trouble grasping the fact that I kept you from becoming pavement art right alongside the guy you were trying to hold on to."

"I had everything under control. There was no need for you to take the risk."

"Yeah, right. And the fact that I anchored your sorry butt to this roof has nothing to do with why you're still here able to reprimand me like I'm a child."

He had the decency to look chagrined. "Sorry. I didn't mean to lecture. Thanks for the help."

"Better." I climbed to my feet and stuck a raw knuckle in my mouth to keep myself from really blasting him.

"I simply wish you hadn't made the jump. You could have been seriously hurt, if not killed."

"You think I was ecstatic watching you make it with a head wound?"

He shrugged, one hand going up to wipe blood out of the corner of his left eye. "I'm okay. We're both okay." He paused a minute and then added, "I guess what I'm really trying to say is that it scared the hell out of me to see you do that."

I think my jaw dropped and I stared at him. Holy Toledo. Jack O'Brien had actually admitted to a real emotion.

I also realized I was feeling the same thing in regard to him, but I wasn't as brave when it came to emotional confessions. Much too risky. I couldn't open myself up to possible rejection.

There was no way I could put into words how I'd felt watching him slide toward certain death. I glanced away.

"I was worried, too," was all I could manage. The words were so soft that they were barely audible even to my own ears.

Jack laughed and reached out one hand to tilt my head back. "What? Is this the same Killian Cray who keeps telling me to get lost and that she could care less what happens to me?"

Unable to deal with his directness, I pushed his hand away. But Jack was never one to be put off. He pulled me to him, pressing me up against his long, lean body, and I sank into him, burying my head against his shoulder and inhaling the sweet smell of his cologne mixed with the pungent odor of male sweat. I didn't speak. I couldn't find the right words.

Speaking meant admitting that I truly felt something for Jack, and that was impossible. There was too much risk of finding out that the feelings weren't reciprocated, weren't experienced in the same way that I experienced them. It was simply too dangerous.

Part of me whispered that too much time had passed and the window of opportunity had closed nine years ago when I had walked out on him. Too many hurt feelings had flowed under the fragile relationship bridge we had once shared. It was too late to try to rebuild what we had.

Jack seemed to realize I couldn't respond. But he didn't seem to need an answer. He bent his head and pressed his lips to mine, caressing my mouth with the sweetest, most sensuous touch.

His hand moved up to stroke my neck and pull me closer, his body pressing against mine, deepening the kiss with a caress of his tongue along the length of mine, encouraging, asking and receiving me with a gentleness I hadn't expected.

I wrapped my arms around his neck, touching the warmth and smoothness at the back of his neck, my fingers tunneling into the soft strands of hair, curling and twining themselves into the twist of familiar curls.

He slid his hands up beneath my jacket and shirt, touching the length of my naked spine, his fingers stroking each indentation and smooth upward curve. I shivered in anticipation of the swell of emotion that flooded my veins and marveled at how easily he made my blood sing.

As he deepened the kiss, I savored each stroke, each touch of his hands against my bare skin. A liquidlike heat filled my belly and seeped lower. I held on to him as if my life depended on it, and in a way, it did. I needed him so badly that the heat flooding my entire body seemed uncontainable, bubbling to the surface and stirring my blood to a boil so hot and mercurial that I thought I might burst into flames. Nothing like the awareness of one's mortality to bring those kinds of feelings to the surface.

Off in the distance, I heard the sound of a police siren drawing closer. Jack lifted his head. "You called the police?"

I nodded. "Right before I headed up the fire escape after you two."

"Good girl. How's the shoulder?"

"Fine." As much as it hurt, I wasn't about to admit it to Jack. I couldn't imagine an examination of the same caliber as the previous one. Such an undertaking would only lead to the kind of trouble we both needed to avoid with a passion. Our kiss a moment ago proved that.

"Hopefully, one of Syracuse's finest will come up on the roof and we can get them to unlock the door to this building." He glanced at the space yawning open between the two buildings. "I don't know about you, but I'm not real keen on the idea of having to make that jump again."

"Not on my list of things to do, either."

"I wonder what the guy was looking for?"

"Whatever it was, he appears to have been under the impression that I brought it here to your apartment." I leaned against the low wall and tentatively looked over the side, contemplating the jump I'd made a few moments ago. I must have been nuts. "I'm getting the distinct impression that I'm being followed."

Jack nodded in agreement. "Whatever it is this person thinks you have has got to be somehow connected to Pop. And the only thing you've gotten out of this deal is that damn cat and Pop's health proxy. Shawna has already told me that there isn't any money left."

I almost opened my mouth to tell him about the safe-deposit box, but then I shut it again. I needed to sort that out before telling Jack. "Speaking of that *damn cat,* I didn't see Sweetie Pie anywhere downstairs. Any chance he might have snuck up onto the roof during the ruckus?"

"I doubt it. He's too smart to come out on a night like this." Jack glanced around. "I guess it's possible, but more than likely he's downstairs hiding like he did last time. He'll show up." He gave a short laugh. "Not much chance of anyone stealing that beast. No one can even get near him except Pop and you."

I paused, realizing that what Jack had said was dead-on. Sweetie Pie was the one constant in Pop's life. The one thing that had remained steady and unchanging over the past nine years.

When he'd been sent to prison, Sweetie Pie had lived with me. But as soon as Pop had been released, the mangy cat had gone back to living with him, his relief evident in the satisfied smile I swear he got whenever he was near Pop.

Sweetie Pie was Pop's lifeline, his connection to the love of his life—Claire. The thought made me pause. We had all failed in our attempt to get through to him in the hospital—to reach him deep in his coma. Maybe Sweetie Pie was the key, the single element that would coax Pop out of his seemingly endless sleep. I knew at that moment that somehow I had to find a way to get Sweetie Pie to Pop.

Chapter Ten

By the time the coroner and the police were done with us, it was late—around 10:00 p.m. The paramedics who had arrived on the scene were all well acquainted with Jack and none were above razzing him a bit for his impromptu heroics on the rooftop. But both saved me the trouble of acting like a mother hen by insisting that he get the nasty gash on his head checked out at the hospital.

True to form, Jack wasn't real thrilled with the idea of going, but he didn't dare argue. Not after glancing in my direction and catching my glare. He knew better than to resist after insisting I go to the E.R. the other day.

He did, however, draw the line at going by ambulance. Instead, he told his buddies I'd drive him over. Lucky me. I knew I'd be on the receiving end of all his griping, but I'd try to get out of it. I had a mission to accomplish and it meant going back to the hospital, anyway. I needed to see Pop.

Before we left, Sweetie Pie made his appearance, drifting out of the kitchen where he'd been hiding behind the refrigerator. As he passed Jack, he took a swipe at him as if to say that the night's free-for-all was his fault. But when he reached me, he weaved himself in and out of my legs, purring like a well-oiled motor on high octane.

"Told you he'd show up," Jack mumbled, shrugging into his jacket. "Too bad he didn't take off when the door was left open."

I sniffed in disagreement and went over to the bed to grab my duffel bag. The intruder had already dumped all my clothes out, leaving them in a scattered pile on the floor. I brought the empty bag over to the couch.

"What do you think you're doing?" he asked. "If you think you're moving out after what just happened, you'd better reconsider and fast."

"Relax, big guy. I have no intentions of moving out. I'm as spooked as Pie at this moment. I intend to stay in someone's company at all times." With the exception of when I had to go meet Ortega, but I wasn't about to discuss that. That was one thing Jack wasn't going to hear about any time soon.

I bent down and scooped up Sweetie Pie, stuffing him inside my bag, leaving one end unzipped for air. He wasn't happy about this new arrangement and gave off an indignant howl, but he didn't try to claw his way out.

"What are you doing?" Jack's expression took on a concerned cast. "I really didn't mean that you had to get rid of the damn cat."

"Good, because that'll never happen. Pie is family. I'm simply taking him with us."

"To the hospital?"

I nodded. "He needs to see Pop."

"Are you insane? You can't take that mangy cat into the hospital. You can't take *any* cat into a hospital."

"Who says?"

"Health laws. Besides, you'll never get him past the nurses."

"Wanna bet?"

Jack sighed. "Look, Chili, I know you're worried about Pop, but bringing a cat into the I.C.U. isn't going to go over real well with the staff."

I ignored him, heading for the door. "Pop needs Sweetie Pie. He's Pop's closest connection to Claire. She gave him to Pop as a gift, remember?"

Jack nodded. His eyes said he understood on an emotional level, but the clear lines of skepticism bracketing his mouth told me he wasn't supportive of this arrangement in the least.

I tried softening him up. "Remember how Pop would stretch out on the couch to take a nap and Pie would leap up onto his chest, curl up and go to sleep with him? Remember how we'd all argue about who snored louder, Pop or Pie?"

Jack's sigh was louder this time. "You and I both know how important that damn furball is to Pop. But the hospital staff isn't going to see things the same way. They're going to look at him as a flea-ridden bag of disease."

I clutched Pie and the bag closer to my chest. "They don't have to know he's there. I'll bring him in hidden in the bag and just let him lie on Pop's chest for a little while." I let my eyes plead with Jack. "Remember how he'd tuck his big head right up under Pop's chin?"

I caught my lower lip with the edge of my teeth, holding it steady for a minute, willing it with all my might not to tremble. I didn't want to lose it in front of Jack.

But I also knew that I didn't have much left in the way of persuasion. I resorted to pleading. "It could help. You know it could. I feel as though if Pop could feel Pie snuggling up against him he might find his way back to us."

"Honey—"

A single tear slipped down my cheek and Jack stopped his protests. He shook his head and I could tell he wouldn't argue anymore. He understood my plea and I loved him for that.

I could feel the ice around my heart, the ice that had been there for so long that I'd been sure it was harder and more frozen than the ice caps at the South Pole, begin to melt a fraction. I could feel the coldness slip away, warming me inside.

"Well, don't blame me if the head nurse kicks our collective butts out of there and doesn't let us back in." He opened the door and motioned me toward the elevator.

A short time later, Jack was in the E.R. waiting to be stitched up and I took the elevator to Pop's room. I had told Jack I wasn't up to seeing a grown man cry while having his cheek stitched up.

Naturally, Jack wasn't happy about my sudden desertion. He'd been pretty clear that he didn't want me out of his sight. But there wasn't much he could do to stop me, not with a needle stuck in his cheek and the doctor injecting some kind of anesthetic. Even Jack realized it wasn't the time to try to anchor me to one spot.

So, in a matter of few minutes, I waltzed out of the E.R. with Sweetie Pie in the bag, knowing Jack would be otherwise occupied for a while.

In the I.C.U., I nodded to the private security guard outside Pop's door and walked in. I stopped short. None of my foster siblings were anywhere to be seen.

Instead, sitting at Pop's bedside was Jeanette Renault. Her chair was pulled up close to the head of the bed and she was holding Pop's hand. Her other hand gently stroked his forearm.

There was an oversize bouquet of fresh flowers sitting on his bedside table—an overabundance of orchids. I almost gagged. No need to guess who had brought them.

I couldn't wait until she was gone so I could throw them in the trash. Orchids were for funerals, not for the bedside of a man who was going to wake up and rejoin his family. But first I needed to get her out of there.

"May I ask what you're doing here?" I demanded.

She glanced up, her expression calm, unruffled, not in the least startled to see me. "I came for a visit."

"Where's my family?"

"I sent them down to get some dinner. They were pretty exhausted after waiting all day for Charlie to get out of surgery."

"Who let you in? You're not a family member. Only family members are supposed to be visiting." I knew my voice wasn't the least bit welcoming, but I didn't care. Her presence felt like an invasion, one I had no desire to tolerate. I simply wanted her out of Pop's room.

What had the rest of the family been thinking when they allowed the former mistress of Handler Ortega, the man who had ruined Pop's life, to be in his room alone with him?

Jeannette seemed to read my thoughts. "Believe it or not Charlie and I used to be quite good friends."

"You're right, I don't believe it." I kicked the door shut and deposited my duffel bag on the bed. Sweetie Pie let out an indignant howl, letting me know that I had better handle him with a bit more finesse.

"What in God's name do you have in there?" Jeannette asked.

"One of Pop's *true friends*." I unzipped the bag and

Sweetie Pie jumped out. The mangy beast hunched his back and snarled in Jeannette's direction. I grinned. Pie's unfailing good instincts about who to trust came through loud and clear.

He slunk up to the top of the bed and jammed his scarred nose up against Pop's face, sniffing. I swear that crazy cat smiled.

He nudged his big head against Pop's chin and the purring commenced, a loud, buzzing sound that rumbled in the back of his throat. He curled up against Pop's neck, his head resting comfortably on Pop's chin as if waiting for the expected petting to begin.

"Ah, this must be Sweetie Pie," Jeannette said.

I glanced at her in surprise. "You know Sweetie Pie?"

"I know *of* him. But we've never actually met. Charlie told me that Claire had given him Sweetie Pie for their thirtieth anniversary. I believe it was originally a joke. But it turned out to be one of his all-time favorite gifts. Especially after Claire died. I think Charlie saw Sweetie Pie as his reminder of Claire."

Her knowledge of my family shocked me, her comments telling me that she truly did know Charlie, better than most people. Perhaps even better than some of my foster siblings.

I pulled up a chair on the opposite side of the bed. "How do you know all this?"

Her blue eyes, sharp and unrelenting, met mine. "I'm guessing that since you're asking me this you haven't been inside the bank box yet."

I wasn't giving her anything, least of all access to that information. "That's none of your business. Just answer the question."

"A long time ago, almost thirty-six years ago, I met Charlie when he was a patrolman. He used to patrol down in the area I hung out. I worked as a singer in one of the local dives."

"You were a lounge singer?" Somehow the thought of rich, sophisticated Jeannette Renault crooning in a microphone in some dive of a bar didn't quite fit the image she projected now. But then I remembered how I'd originally thought she seemed closer to my side of town than she'd want anyone to realize.

She smiled, something soft, vulnerable and infinitely sad. It seemed strangely out of place next to the string of perfectly matched cultured pearls, the Donna Karan suit and the faint whiff of Chanel No. 5.

She leaned against the cushioned seat and her eyes went a little hazy, as if she was reaching for a memory. "Once in a while, after they were done with their shift, Charlie and his partner would come into the Chain Reaction. That was the bar I sang in. It was a place where they could unwind, throw back a few shots of Jack Daniel's and de-stress after a tough night on the street."

She sighed. "On more than a few occasions, Charlie's partner hit on me. Tried to buy me a drink, get me to sit at their table or talk to them after my set."

The cardiac monitor overhead beeped out of sync a few times, and both our gazes jumped upward, our faces reflecting our shared moment of panic.

But the beat settled back to its usual pattern, and Jeannette continued, "I wasn't interested in his friend. He was a typical lowlife, a cop looking for a quick tumble. But Charlie—Charlie was different."

She smiled across the bed at me, her eyes so pensive,

so defenseless that I almost smiled back. I say almost, but in the end I didn't.

I forced the tenderness in my heart to disappear in the blink of an eye. She was the enemy, and she deserved no mercy. I refused to lower my wall of distrust.

"Charlie, he was something else entirely. He was always the gentleman. Always polite. Sweet, even. A true innocent in a world of corruption and filth."

"He was married to Claire," I said from between stiff lips.

Jeannette nodded. "Yes, he was. And he loved her very much, but at the time he started coming into the bar, they were having marital problems."

I frowned. This was *not* what I wanted to hear. Sure it was way before I was even in their lives, but the thought of this woman alluding to trouble in the Orzinski paradise made me highly suspicious. Something told me I didn't want to hear what she was offering in the way of an explanation.

But she ignored my obvious resentment and continued. "At the time, they had learned that they couldn't have children. Something to do with Claire, I think. It devastated the both of them."

She paused as if considering whether she wanted to go on. She picked at a piece of imaginary lint on her skirt for a moment.

"They might not have been able to have children, but that wouldn't have destroyed their love."

"Marital problems creep up on a person. Do strange things to them. They both wanted a family, and the news put Claire into a deep depression. She pushed Charlie away and that hurt him. He didn't know how to handle it."

"Pop would have handled it by getting Claire help. By supporting and loving her no matter what."

I was angry that this woman would even hint that Charlie and Claire couldn't have worked things out. I knew them. They were the experts at working everything out. They were the ultimate communicators.

Jeannette shrugged one elegant shoulder and leaned forward to gently brush several strands of hair off of Charlie's forehead. I gritted my teeth, angry she would dare touch him.

"Claire was hurting. She coped the only way she knew how. She withdrew inward and pushed Charlie away."

"Charlie wouldn't have allowed that to happen."

"Oh, he pleaded with her. He even went with her to see a therapist. But in the end, Claire simply withdrew."

"But she came out of it."

"Oh, indeed, she did. But not for a while. And Charlie was a young man. Strong. Virile. Passionate. He was terribly hurt by Claire's rejection. And I liked Charlie, and I wanted him."

She smiled with one corner of her perfectly glossed lips, a smile that spoke of her personal knowledge of her own weaknesses. Gone was the pensive, vulnerable expression of a few moments ago.

"So, I took advantage of his vulnerability and got what I wanted."

An ill taste of bitterness hit my belly, and my fingers tightened on the arm of the chair. "What's that supposed to mean?"

I knew what it meant, but my knees shook and my denial raged. It was all I could do to keep from leaping across the bed, clamping my hands around her throat and tightening down, refusing to allow her to speak anymore. I didn't want to hear what she was about to tell me.

But for some reason, I couldn't stop her. Couldn't demand she shut her mouth and keep the secret forever. It was like a train out of control, barreling down the track right at me, and I couldn't get out of its way fast enough.

Those blue eyes, so similar to Jack's, but so cold in comparison, stared across the bed at me. She knew what I was feeling, but she continued, anyway. "What it means, my dear sweet Killian, is that I seduced Charlie and he let me."

I jumped up. Anger surged through every nerve in my body. I turned away and then turned back. "I don't believe you! Charlie would have never cheated on Claire."

On the bed, Sweetie Pie lifted his head and hissed at me. He didn't like the fact that I was disturbing his nap. I didn't either, but I couldn't seem to get control of my anger or the terrible pain that ripped a path through the center of my heart.

Jeannette shrugged. "Believe what you will. But we had an affair—a short one—but an affair, nonetheless."

She crossed her legs, her nylons whispering slyly in the quiet, dimly lit room. "He called it off fairly quickly—two months, maybe less. He was racked with guilt, unable to handle the intensity of his feelings. He confessed everything to Claire, and that's when they started communicating again. They worked things out."

"Claire knew? She forgave him?"

"Of course she forgave him. Besides, do you really think Charlie could have kept a secret like that from the woman he adored more than life itself?"

I dropped back into the chair and Sweetie Pie nestled his head back against Charlie's chin, content that my rampage was under control. "I—I guess not. It wouldn't have been in his nature."

"Charlie and I didn't see each other again until I contacted him about a year later." She swallowed hard and then continued, "I'd had a child and realized fairly quickly that I couldn't raise him in the environment I was living in. He was in the way. I told Charlie it was his child, and that I wanted him to adopt the boy."

I stared at her across the bed, my heart pounding so hard I thought it might come through my chest. "The child was Jack, wasn't it?"

"I knew the day you came to my house that you had noticed the resemblance Jack has to my youngest son. Quite an astonishing resemblance, isn't it?" She smiled knowingly. "Yes, Jack is my biological son."

"But he isn't Charlie's biological son, is he?"

Jeannette's eyes widened. "You're actually more astute than I imagined." She reached out and threaded her fingers through Charlie's; the sadness in her eyes deepened. "No, in spite of my wishing he was, I found out shortly after Jack was born that he wasn't Charlie's."

"But it didn't stop you from trying to scam him into believing he was."

"Charlie knew as soon as he looked at Jack that he wasn't his." Air whispered between her slightly parted lips. "He knew I was lying, but he still wanted Jack."

"Why?"

"I'm not really sure. We never talked about it. Personally, I think he fell in love with Jack the moment he set eyes on him. And Jack, a baby hungry for attention and love, bonded to him instantly. And since Charlie and Claire wanted a family so badly, they agreed to take Jack."

"Why didn't they adopt him?"

"Jack's biological father wouldn't sign the release papers. He had no interest in Jack, saw him as a nuisance, actually. But I think it pleased him to keep me dangling. And I knew better than to push the issue by going to court."

"Why?"

"Because he would have fought for custody of Jack just to spite me. I didn't dare take that risk. So I asked Charlie and Claire to raise him as their own without the adoption papers. And they agreed." She tightened her fingers around Charlie's. "They insisted that Jack keep my real last name—O'Brien. They told me that was for Jack's sake. That if he ever wanted to seek me out, he'd be able to find me with their help. They told me that no matter what, he was still my child." She was silent for a moment. "But that time never came. He never asked to meet me or find me."

I was surprised to see a single tear squeeze out from between her carefully made-up lashes. The drop splashed onto the back of Charlie's hand.

She made no effort to wipe it away. The tear lay there, a tiny drop of pain and sorrow, the deepness of that sorrow so enormous that I almost wanted to get up and go around the end of the bed to comfort her.

I say almost because I was pretty sure she wouldn't accept the gesture, and to be truthful, I wasn't quite sure I could bring myself to do it. Something told me there was more to her story, more pain, and that pain and grief was something that would make Jack suffer.

"So who is Jack's real father?" I asked.

Jeannette's narrow chest expanded and contracted as if she was preparing to make a giant leap into some unimaginable void.

"Handler Ortega."

I gasped, my fingers tightening on the arms of my chair. I had expected something tragic, but finding out that Jack was the biological son of Handler Ortega was definitely *not* what I'd expected to hear.

I dropped against the back and stared across at Jeannette in stunned silence. "Did Charlie and Claire know this when they agreed to raise Jack?"

"They knew." She leaned down and gently kissed the back of Charlie's hand, her lips brushing and erasing the small tear from his skin. "They kept their silence all these years. Raised Jack as their own, made him strong. Straight. Honest. Filled him with integrity. I couldn't have asked for better parents for my child."

Silence hung heavy in the room.

Then she said, "They never wanted Jack to be touched by the filth that his biological father wallowed in."

"So, you're telling me that you had an affair with Ortega at the same time you were sleeping with my foster father?"

Her lips twisted into a tragic smile. "I never claimed to be perfect. In fact, I can pretty much admit to being imperfect for much of my youth. But over time, Charlie and Claire helped me see the error of my ways. I stayed with Ortega for a few more years, but when he finally threw me over for a younger, newer model, Charlie and Claire helped me get a loan on a small flower shop."

She reached up and gently stroked the tip of the petal of one of the orchids in the nearby vase. "I discovered I had a talent for growing and nurturing things."

"Not your son, obviously." It was a cutting comment, meant to hurt, but Jeannette seemed oblivious to my need to wound her.

."He was better off where he was. Claire and Charlie couldn't have raised a better man than Jack O'Brien."

"Does he know any of this?"

"He does now," a new voice said.

Stunned, I whirled around. Jack stood in the doorway, the line of stitches on the side of his face standing out in stark contrast to the paleness beneath his bronze skin. The shock and pain on his face told me that he'd heard most of our conversation.

"I'm sorry, Jack," Jeannette whispered. "I never meant for you to hear the truth this way. I had hoped Charlie would explain things to you. But he always seemed to feel that as your mother it was my duty to tell you. I just never had the courage."

"My *mother* was Claire Orzinski." The words fell from Jack's lips like icicles falling from a great height, cutting and sharp.

Somehow, I'm not exactly sure how, Jeannette kept from flinching. "I realize that. And it's one of the reasons I never interfered. Never asked to be a part of your life. Claire and Charlie kept me up to date on your progress, sending me pictures and clippings of your accomplishments."

Jack's expression remained unmoved. Unforgiving. "Let's get honest here. Your secrecy had more to do with selfish reasons than for any need to protect me." He stepped up to the end of the bed. "You were involved with Ortega. You lived with him for years. If he didn't want a child, you were willing to do anything to keep that status quo, right?"

"I won't deny that."

"What did Ortega want with Charlie?" Jack asked. "How did he get him to cooperate with him."

"He's a clever man."

"Why did he come after him now? Charlie had nothing to offer him after getting kicked off the force and left penniless."

"He wanted what I took from him when I left him."

"And what exactly was that?" There was no softness or gentleness in Jack's voice. He was using his interrogator's voice, the one meant to get what he wanted.

"I knew after all the years of living with Handler that I couldn't leave him without a security plan in place. It was my means of making sure that he could never touch me or hurt me again."

"What kind of security are we talking about?" Jack asked.

"A microchip of his books. An accounting of all of his deeds up until the time I left."

Jack nodded. "No wonder he's been so relentless in his pursuit of the information. Where is it?"

Jeannette shrugged. "As soon as I got out, I gave the chip to Charlie. I told him to use it in any way he wanted. He tucked it away, told me it was security for you."

"For me?"

"Handler might not have wanted you when you were an infant, Jack, but as you grew, so did his interest in you."

"How so?"

"When you were about thirteen, do you remember giving Claire and Charlie a run for their money—getting a bit mouthy and running with a wild crowd?"

Jack nodded. "I was doing the usual teenage rebellion bit—smoking, dabbling in some drinking, going on a few joyrides with a bad crowd. Minor stuff."

"Handler found out about it and saw your actions as

your being a chip off the old block. He claimed to be getting nostalgic for a family, and he told Charlie that he wanted you back. Claimed that he'd seek custody of you through the courts as your biological father."

"He couldn't do that after so much time had passed," I protested.

Jeannette's smile was bitter. "Handler could do anything he wanted. He knew he could claim that I never informed you of his parental obligation. He had the kind of money to hire any kind of shyster lawyer he wanted to get what he wanted. He had more than a few judges in his back pocket."

A sinking feeling rumbled deep in the pit of my stomach. I could only imagine the fear and terror such a possibility would have struck in Claire and Charlie.

They would have dreaded the loss of their impressionable, beloved son disappearing into Handler Ortega's fold, coming under his influence during a time when most teenagers had little ability to morally walk away from everything being handed to them on a silver platter. A silver platter Ortega would have made all too irresistible.

"So Charlie made a deal with him instead?" Jack said quietly.

I stared in disbelief at what Jack was suggesting. But even as I tried to push the thought away, to deny what he was saying, I knew it explained perfectly the neatly stacked and wrapped bills sitting in Charlie's safe-deposit box. It explained the evidence against Charlie at his trial. He *had* sold the information. I just hadn't been able to see any of this, couldn't believe anything bad of the man I loved so deeply as a father.

A great sadness ripped through me, followed with regret. Jack hadn't lied or sold out Charlie. He'd told the truth. Charlie had sold his soul to save Jack, the son he loved more than life itself.

Jeannette smoothed her hand over Charlie's, her gaze roving gently over his empty expression—the once intelligent and loving eyes closed and shuttered against knowing or acknowledging anything we were discussing.

She sighed and glanced up at Jack. "Charlie sold himself to Handler to save you. Personally, I think it was Handler's plan all along. He wanted an informant inside the police department and Charlie was pretty high up in the information chain. But Handler was no fool. He knew your father's reputation. He knew how upstanding, how incorruptible he was. But Handler has always known how to find a person's Achilles' heel, and you were Charlie's."

"So, Ortega used Jack as the bait," I finished for her.

Jeannette nodded. "Handler *said* he wanted to play daddy, but he was more interested in grooming Charlie to be his own personal pipeline into the police department." She shook her head, reaching out to smooth the sheet resting against Charlie's chest. She ignored Pie's hiss of warning. "I think Charlie knew Handler wasn't really interested in suddenly becoming a father, but he couldn't take the risk. He did as Handler asked."

Jeannette stood up. "I'm guessing that I've overstayed my welcome." Her gaze sought out Jack. "When I left you with Claire and Charlie, I knew you would have a good life. I never wanted any of the stain from my relationship with Handler to touch you."

Jack's gaze settled on Charlie, the pain in his eyes only too evident. "But it appears that it has."

"Yes, it would appear so." She leaned down and picked

up her coat and purse. "Don't ever trust Ortega. Don't ever believe anything he says or offers. He lives only for himself. Don't ever make the mistake of getting sucked in."

She nodded in my direction and exited the room, her perfume the only lingering evidence that she'd even been there.

Jack walked over to stand next to Charlie, his hand reaching out to gently touch his forearm. "You old fool. You should have trusted that I would have come back to you even if I flirted with Ortega's offer of family."

"He couldn't take that chance," I said.

"He still shouldn't have compromised himself. Ortega asked for too much and it swallowed Charlie up in the end."

I nodded. There was no disagreeing with that.

Before we could continue, Shawna and Drake entered the room, looking refreshed from their short excursion down to the hospital cafeteria.

"Any word from the doctors?" I asked.

Shawna's dark eyes misted slightly and Drake reached out to gently capture her against him, comforting her. "It's not looking good," he said. "Dr. Mannus removed a large clot. Said that the damage was pretty extensive. They're talking about doing a trach because he won't be able to breathe without the respirator."

"They're going to do another EEG tomorrow. I guess that tells them how Pop's brain is functioning. The one they did earlier didn't show any activity." Her voice caught for a moment, sounding choked and hoarse. "Dr. Mannus isn't being too optimistic."

"What does it mean?" I asked.

"That he probably won't come out of the coma. He'll

live in a vegetative state until his organs give out. That he's brain-dead." Drake swallowed hard, his despair evident. "We'll know more tomorrow.".

"We'll have some decisions to make tomorrow," Shawna said, moving up to take the seat vacated by Jeannette. "Until then, we wait."

I nodded, unable to voice the deep sense of fear that had opened inside of me. It wasn't hard to guess what kind of decision she was referring to.

Pop's health proxy was pretty clear. He'd voiced his desire not to be forced to live out his life propped up by machines, unaware of his surroundings. I knew I wasn't strong enough, courageous enough, to make the decision alone. I could only hope that Jack and the others were.

Chapter Eleven

Exhausted and barely able to keep my eyes open, I left the hospital with Jack. Shawna had insisted that I return to Jack's apartment to get some sleep. She didn't want me back until the next day.

I didn't argue. There was no strength left in me to do so. But I didn't leave the room until I'd grabbed the orchids and heaved them into the trash bin out by the nurse's station. I couldn't bare seeing them sitting next to Pop's bed.

Although Sweetie Pie wasn't happy about being removed from his spot on Pop's chest, I also knew that he'd be kicked out once one of the nurses came in and found him. I tucked him back in my bag and exited the hospital.

Our ride back to Jack's apartment was quiet. Strained. There wasn't much either of us had to say, each of us locked in our own worlds of pain and confusion. He had to work out his feelings about his father's destruction of the man he adored, and I had to come to grips with my rejection of Jack on the basis of a betrayal that truly didn't exist, except in my own mind.

I don't think either of us slept much that night. Several times, I heard Jack get up and wander around the apartment, a familiar insomnia plaguing him as much as it did me. Perhaps that was when I should have reached out to him, helped him deal with the pain and anguish he was feeling. But I couldn't. I kept my own feelings locked inside too tightly, and talking to him would have meant allowing the floodgates to open.

I still had one more job to do before I could allow that to happen. I had to meet with Ortega and convince him to leave the two men I cared most about in this world alone. If I opened up to Jack, I knew without question that I'd tell him what I planned. I also knew him well enough to know that he'd never agree to Ortega's demands that I meet him alone.

When I awoke the next morning, later than usual, I found Jack already gone. He'd left a note, telling me that he'd gone in to work to finish up some paperwork and arrange for some time off. He told me that he'd meet me later at the hospital.

His absence brought a strange sense of relief. I was free to go to the hospital alone and then on to Ortega's to straighten things out. I knew it was risky, but Ortega would never go through with the meet if I showed up with Jack in tow. And if I didn't meet Ortega alone, then everything Charlie had sacrificed—his career, his honor, his integrity—was for nothing.

LESS THAN AN HOUR LATER, I was downstairs, freezing my tootsies off in a pair of chunky heels while trying to pry open the frozen lock on Shawna's Jeep. Why I'd even listened to Candy's advice and put on a dress was beyond my comprehension. But I'd gone and done it, anyway.

Following a quick shower and a useless ten minutes trying to tame my hair and apply a bit of makeup, I had pulled out a black dress I'd stuffed in my duffel bag at the last minute. It wasn't anywhere near the calibre of fashion that Candy had offered last night, but I figured if Ortega responded better to a woman in a dress, then I was willing to try anything.

I knew on some level that I looked slightly ridiculous in the short dress, heels and my oversize parka. But more than likely, by the time I got to Ortega, I could slip off the jacket and look semi-sophisticated.

But first I needed to visit the hospital and check up on Pop before heading over to Ortega's restaurant for my four-o'clock meeting. Hopefully, Jack would be tied up most of the day.

News on the hospital front was not in the least encouraging. The second EEG had shown no improvement. Pop's brain was continuing to limp along, unable to function on its own. It was looking more and more like the family was going to have to sit down and make a decision. The doctors and nurses were already beginning to talk about organ transplants. I begged the doctors for one more day. Dr. Mannus readily agreed, recognizing on some level that facing the inevitable wasn't something to be rushed.

When Shawna, Drake and David showed up around three o'clock for their shift, I was waiting at the door, eager to get out of the place before Jack made an appearance. If Shawna was suspicious of my antsy behavior and my clothing, she didn't let on. She simply took up her seat next to Pop and started telling him about her day.

Her actions told me that she hadn't given up hope, either. But Drake and David were looking pretty haggard and resigned. I had a feeling that Shawna and I would be the final holdouts on any decisions.

Ortega's restaurant, The Onion Eater, was located on Salina Street in the old Syracuse Bank and Trust. It wasn't far from the hospital, so I took my time driving the few miles to the location. A light snow started to fall and the radio DJ announced in rather gleeful tones that the temperature had dropped to a chilly thirty degrees.

I turned up the heat, blasting it on my legs in a futile attempt to stay warm. I wasn't used to wearing a dress, but on another level I knew full well that the coldness I felt had more to do with fear and trepidation than it did with the weather. The thought of meeting the man who had put Pop in the hospital and who had undoubtedly been terrorizing me for the past few days was more than a bit disconcerting.

The restaurant was upscale. Very upscale. The marble entrance and the elaborate sign outside spoke volumes on the expense Ortega had gone to make the place classy. Everything he wasn't.

It was exactly what I would expect. I glanced around. As usual, there wasn't a single vacant parking spot on Salina Street. I drove up to the front of the restaurant and a man stepped out, rounding the car to the driver's side to gallantly open the door. Cold air blasted the interior of the car.

"You Cray?" he asked.

I nodded.

He held out his hand. "Give me your keys."

"Why?"

"I'll park your heap around back."

"I can park it." I didn't like the thought of giving up the keys. In my mind, they were my only source of freedom.

He glared down at me with muddy brown eyes. "Just

shut up and give me the keys. Mr. Ortega doesn't like being kept waiting."

I handed him the keys.

"You got any weapons on you? Or do I need to frisk you?"

The thought of the jerk's beefy hands touching me any-where brought on an unexpected shudder. I shook my head. "No weapons…unless you have an issue with nail clip-pers."

He snorted in disgust and jerked his head, indicating I needed to vacate the car. "Go on in. Mr. Ortega is expect-ing you."

"Be careful with the car. It isn't mine."

He shot a smart-ass grin over one beefy shoulder. "Yeah, I know. Yours is sitting in a repair shop, isn't it."

He didn't wait for an answer, but he'd gotten his mes-sage across. I didn't have to wonder any more about whether or not Ortega and his group of goons were respon-sible for my little Neon looking like a squashed bug.

The inside of Ortega's restaurant was as impressive as the outside, all brass, dark rich woods and pristine white table linens set with fine crystal and sparkling silverware. The former tellers' cages had been turned into the bar, all polished wood and brass fixings.

There were a few customers scattered across the large dining area, all over the age of sixty and probably there for the early-bird specials prominently displayed on an ele-gantly scripted blackboard sitting next to the reservation desk. None looked up when I entered. Obviously, Ortega catered to a crowd that knew curiosity wasn't encouraged.

A maître d' in a black tux approached me. "Ms. Cray?"

I nodded.

"I'll take your coat. Mr. Ortega will see you in his private office." He snapped his fingers and a young man in a white shirt, black pants and white waiter's apron jumped to attention. "Please show Ms. Cray to Mr. Ortega's office."

I shrugged out of my jacket and handed it to the maître d'. He held it away from his body as though he thought bugs might crawl out of the seams and attach themselves to him. He handed it to the waiter. I followed the silent young man to the back of the restaurant.

He knocked once on a huge, oak door, turned the brass handle and then stood aside to let me enter. When I stepped inside, the door closed after me with a finality that made my heart thud.

The room was dimly lit, the only light coming from a small desk lamp sitting on a huge desk on the other side of the room. Someone sat behind the desk, but I couldn't quite make out his features due to the low level of light illuminating the room. The drapes hanging behind the man were thick and heavy, keeping out any remaining daylight.

"You're punctual. I like punctuality," the man said. His voice was immediately recognizable, the smooth silky tones infused with a grating undertone that stirred a bad memory. He was the voice on the other end of the phone. The one who had called me several times in the last few days.

"Charlie was always a stickler for teaching his kids to learn to be on time for important events, even the unpleasant ones." I was surprised my voice and sarcasm were unflinching in the face of the fact that I was now face-to-face with the man who had ruined Charlie's life and probably had similar designs on ruining Jack's.

"Our meeting doesn't have to take on unfriendly undertones." He motioned toward one of the chairs in front of his desk. "Sit."

I did as instructed, curious to get a look at him. As I settled into the chair, his face came into view, shadowed some, but still visible.

During Pop's trial, Handler Ortega's face had been plastered all over the papers. But his shyster lawyer had skillfully gotten him off on all charges of bribery, mainly because Charlie wouldn't or couldn't implicate him as the one who had hired him.

He hadn't changed much. He was a powerful-looking man with broad shoulders and handsome chiseled features. But the handsomeness was marred by cruelty and a touch of something sadistic. The hair, which had once been jet-black, was now more white. But it was him. This was a man who liked getting his own way and didn't mind how he went about getting it.

"Did you bring what I asked for?"

"I'm here to negotiate," I said. "You say Pop has something of yours, and I say you get it when you pay for it."

A slow, predatory smile spread across his face, but none of the amusement he might have felt reached his cold, flat eyes. They regarded me as unfeelingly as a wolf might study a terrorized rabbit that was about to become his dinner.

"I don't negotiate for what belongs to me, Ms. Cray. Give me the computer chip and we'll call things a draw. Charlie gets to live out his days sucking on the end of a respirator tube, and you get to go home…alive."

"It's Officer Cray, and I don't think you're in a position *not* to negotiate."

The smile disappeared as quickly as it had appeared. "I

don't care if you're the head of the FBI, Officer Cray. I want the chip and I want it now."

We were at a stalemate. I had no idea where the computer chip was, and he didn't seem inclined to give me any more information that would allow me to stall him until I found it.

"I don't have it on me."

"Now, that is truly a shame."

Something told me he wasn't whistling Dixie here. There weren't going to be any second chances with this guy.

"I need to get it out of the safe-deposit box," I lied.

His grin turned colder. "You and I both know it isn't in there."

Apparently his shyster lawyer, Catherine Pratt, had been a busy little beaver, getting access to Pop's safe-deposit box before I'd even opened it.

Before I could respond, there was a knock at the door. "Come," Ortega ordered.

The thug who had taken my keys stepped into the room from a side door, followed by another man.

"O'Brien just pulled into the parking lot," the valet said. "He's on his way in."

Ortega's hooded gaze tracked across the room and settled back on me. "How nice of you to invite my son to these delicate negotiations. I'm assuming that Charlie somehow failed to teach you to follow the rules of engagement. A pity."

I opened my mouth to deny that I'd invited anyone, especially Jack, but Ortega wasn't interested in excuses. He glanced at his two minions. "Take her out to the location. Ralph has his instructions. I want some time alone with O'Brien."

His gaze shifted back to me. "If you cooperate, they'll dump you back off at O'Brien's apartment. Play games and you won't be going anywhere ever again. Learn from your old man's mistakes. Don't cross me."

I stood up and edged toward the door. If I got there first, I might be able to call out and warn Jack what he was walking into. But the thugs were on me in two seconds flat, slipping a gag in my mouth and a hood over my head.

They hoisted me up and hustled me out the side door, carrying me down a long hall. We must have passed through the kitchen because I could hear pots and pans clanging and the smell of food cooking. Whoever was doing the cooking didn't seem the least bothered by the fact that someone was being carried out of the restaurant with a hood over his head. I guessed it happened fairly frequently in Ortega's establishment. That fact didn't bode well for me.

Cold air hit me as the restaurant door opened and then slammed shut behind us. I knew that they'd taken me out into the back alley. The faint sound of cars passing on wet pavement out front filtered down the alleyway.

I heard the click of a car lock and then the thug carrying me threw me into something. My head bumped up against hard plastic, a tire well. I figured I was in the trunk of a car. A second later, the lid of the trunk slammed and deep, relentless silence engulfed me.

I was scared, the gag in my mouth drying up my saliva and making it difficult to breathe. Hot air whistled in the back of my throat. I didn't know where they were taking me, but I knew without a doubt that Jack had no idea I'd been carried out of the same restaurant he'd just entered.

I had made a fatal error coming alone to meet with Ortega. I had ignored Jack, Charlie and the police academy's golden rule. *Never go anywhere without backup.* Now I was paying the price for my arrogance, and rescue didn't seem like a viable option.

Chapter Twelve

Someone lifted the trunk and a hand pulled off the hood. The trunk light blinded me for a brief second, and I blinked and turned my head. But the blinding sensation only got worse. Someone was shining a flashlight directly into my face. I raised an arm, trying to shield my eyes.

"Get her out of there, Tony," my valet snapped.

The larger of the two men leaned over the lip of the trunk and lifted me out. He smelled of beer, cheap cigars and dried sweat layered on dried sweat. If the guy had bathed in the past year, it would have been newsworthy.

I gagged slightly, my mouth dry from the cloth pulling at the corners of my mouth. I panicked for a minute, thinking I was going to choke on my own vomit. But Tony seemed to grasp what was happening, and he reached up and loosened the gag.

I gulped in a mouthful of fresh air. "Thanks. One small suggestion, Tony, you might consider slapping on a little Right Guard once in a while."

Tony laughed, his huge belly jiggling against my body. At least the thug had a sense of humor and didn't seem terribly offended that I'd just insulted him.

"Where are we?" I asked now that I figured Tony and I were bonding on a buddy level.

"None of your damn business," the other thug snapped. He was smaller than Tony and definitely more fastidious about his personal hygiene. Every piece of clothing he wore looked as though it had been starched and pressed at a high-class laundry. The smell of some type of cloying aftershave rose up off his baby-soft cheeks.

Tony set me down on my feet, but kept his hands clamped tightly on both my forearms.

"Don't bother screaming," he rumbled, his voice deep and nonchalant, as if he couldn't care whether I listened to him. With his hands on me, he probably figured I wasn't going anywhere. "There ain't no one within twenty miles of here."

I swallowed and nodded, taking a minute to look around now that my eyes had adjusted.

It was dark outside, pitch-black. But the moon was already up, casting a pale white light on us. There were no street lights, and that told me we were pretty far outside the city. But then, I had expected that. After all, we'd been driving for a while and my legs had started to cramp up from my position in the trunk.

Off to the right was a small lake. The ice, smooth and blue in the moonlight, was frozen solid. Except for the moon, the only other light came from some twinkling white Christmas lights strung along the pilings of a small dock sitting at one end of the lake, not too far from us. The sight of them gave my heart a small lift. Maybe someone was nearby.

But the cabin, situated on a snowy knoll overlooking the dock, was completely dark. No one home. Not that I was surprised. As stupid as these guys seemed, they wouldn't have brought me out here if there was anyone around to witness what they were up to.

On the opposite end of the lake, pretty far off from us, I could see lighted cabins, which obviously belonged to people who stayed through the winter months. But on this end of the lake, all the little camps were dark and closed up pretty tight.

"Where ya want her, Ralphie?" Tony asked.

"Hold your horses, Tone." Ralph glanced around. "Pete should be here somewhere. I told him to meet us here."

My heart sank a little lower. Three of them. The situation had gone from bad to worse. I might have been able to give two bozos the slip but with three on me, my odds had gone from bad to worse.

"He's probably already down by the lake," Tony offered.

Ralphie nodded, looking none too pleased. A quick glance down at his feet told me that he was wearing thin leather street shoes, not boots. Poor Ralphie was going to get his feet wet walking through the snow leading down to the lake.

But then I realized I wasn't in much better shape. Heels were definitely not snow-hiking apparel. Ralphie and I were both in for a bad case of frostbite if we stayed out here too long.

"So are we going to just stand here in the snow?" I asked.

"Shut up," Ralphie snapped. He cupped his hands over his mouth and yelled, "Hey, Pete!"

"Down here!" a voice called. It came from down near the lake.

"Damn, now we've got to walk through the snow. You'd

think the idiot would have shoveled a path for me," Ralphie grumbled. "Bring her along."

He gingerly stepped into the tracks leading down to the lake. Tony and I followed close behind. Tony was careful to keep a tight grip on my upper arm. I wasn't going anywhere if he had his way.

A few minutes later, we reached the edge of the lake. We were in a small cove off the main lake. Pete stood out on the ice in the middle of the cove. He waved to us.

Ralphie pushed me closer to the shoreline. The ice was soft near the edges, and we had to jump onto a more solid section. The ice cracked and moved beneath our weight. Ralphie looked nervous for a minute.

"You stay on shore," he said to Tony. "I don't trust the ice with your fat ass on it."

He pulled a gun out of the pocket of his jacket and motioned to me. "Don't try anything stupid, sister, or I'll shoot you right there."

I nodded and watched with some regret as Tony clumsily jumped back onto shore. For some reason, I had this misguided feeling that the big guy would be a little gentler with me than ole Ralphie.

The Ralphster's eyes had that creepy vacant look to them, as if he wasn't firing on all cylinders upstairs. Like the empathy thing was missing in his repertoire of affect. Not a good sign.

I had no doubt Tony would take me out if Ralphie ordered him to, but I also had the feeling that Tony would do it with a bit more compassion than his buddy.

Ralph and I walked across the ice to the spot where Pete stood waiting for us. As we got closer, I noticed the huge auger leaning up against Pete's side. An ice spud lay at his feet. The guy was breathing kind of heavily, as if he'd been working hard for a while. Anxiety hit my stomach with a major splash of acid.

I knew what an auger was used for. A transplanted Adirondacker, I couldn't help but know that ice fishermen use them to cut holes in the ice to drop their lines into. An ice spud was a tool used to widen the hole. Pete had made his ice hole pretty big. Something told me he wasn't out here fishing for lake perch.

I stared down at the hole. The underlying lake current moved tiny chunks of ice in the middle of the hole back and forth like miniature corks. They bumped against each other, jockeying for position.

The hole looked like the top of a giant slushy drink. Unfortunately, I knew only too well that I wouldn't survive too long in the water, and I had no doubt that was Ralphie's plan for me.

"Okay, sister, you're gonna tell us what we want to know or you're going in the lake. A few seconds in that frigid water and you'll be begging to tell me what I want to know."

"Look, I'm not trying to be uncooperative here, but I don't have what Ortega wants. There really isn't any need to throw me in because I can't give you what you want."

I spoke in what I thought was a reasonable tone, trying to ignore the slight tremor in my voice. I really did want to cooperate. "My foster dad, Charlie, was already in a coma when I arrived in Syracuse. He wasn't able to tell me anything. As far as I can tell, he wasn't able to tell *anyone* anything. He's been in a freakin' coma for five days. How could I possibly know anything?"

Ralphie didn't look too convinced. In fact, I was getting the distinct impression that this guy was dying for any excuse to throw me in, as if it were going to give him some kind of sick thrill.

"Jeez, why won't anyone believe me?" I glanced at Pete, deciding he might be my better bet. "You believe me, don't you, Pete?"

Pete shrugged, his brown eyes flat and unemotional. There wasn't a lot of intellect behind those eyes, either. He was a gofer, Ralphie's drone. "I just cut the holes, sweetheart. Talk to Ralphie. He's in charge of this operation."

Great, two psychos for the price of one. I turned my attention back to Ralphie. "Look, I already told your boss Ortega that I didn't know anything."

Ralphie laughed. "Mr. Ortega didn't quite believe you, sweet thing. He thinks you need a bit of persuasion. And what Mr. Ortega wants, Mr. Ortega gets."

"Well, why didn't he say so when I talked with him? No need for us to get all in a twist here. Take me back and we can talk in the nice, warm, cozy environment of his restaurant."

"Nah, Mr. Ortega doesn't like dealing with this kind of stuff." Ralphie elbowed Pete. "He considers the two of us much better equipped than him to handle the important stuff like this."

"Throwing some defenseless woman into a freezing cold lake is important stuff?" I asked incredulously. "I thought having your own turf and a few guys to order around made you one of the important ones in Ortega's operation."

I guess I shouldn't have taunted the guy. His narrow face darkened. "Take off your jacket."

I backed up a step, glancing around in a frantic effort

to figure a way out. No way did I want to be lowered into that icy hole. Besides, I didn't have anything to tell them. I'd freeze to death before they got anything out of me. And as creative as I could be with my stories, I didn't think I'd be able to come up with one that would satisfy Ralphie.

Pete grabbed a handful of my jacket and yanked me over to him. I hit at his hands, but he simply pinned them behind me and Ralphie yanked down the zipper of my coat. Pete pulled it off and dropped it on the ice at his feet.

The bitter night wind hit me like the slam of a sheet of ice traveling at ninety miles an hour. I knew I shouldn't have worn a dress. Damn Candy and her stupid ideas. I started to shiver, my teeth chattering in the darkness.

"Cold enough for ya, sweet stuff? Feeling a little more cooperative, maybe?" Ralphie asked.

I crossed my hands over my chest and jumped up and down, trying to generate some energy. Some heat. These guys were morons if they thought I'd put up with this just to keep a secret from them. I would be only too glad to spill my guts if I knew what it was they wanted me to spill.

"Put her in the hole," Ralphie ordered.

"Wait! Can't we discuss this in a more civilized fashion?"

"You gonna tell us where the microchip is?"

"Well, I don't know *exactly* where it is, but I'm sure I could locate it."

Ralphie scowled. "I don't have time for games. Put her in the hole."

Pete picked me up and I squirmed, trying to kick him where it would do the most good. But he manhandled me over to the hole and dropped me in feet first.

I sunk like a rock, the icy slush closing over me greedily, sucking me down. A second later, I popped to the surface. The shock of the water tore my breath away, forcing it out of my mouth in a single whoosh of release.

Suddenly, it was as if I couldn't breathe. I knew my mouth was open and I knew my lungs were screaming for oxygen, but inside of me, my muscles couldn't move. Couldn't function.

Nothing moved. I was shock still in the water. I felt as if my heart had stopped in midbeat. It was like dying with your eyes open and being able to watch everything around you go totally still.

And then I heard this strange, high-pitched sound. Like someone going, "Oh… Oh… Oh… Oh…" over and over again. And then I realized the sound was coming from me.

A moment later, just as I thought I might simply slip beneath the undulating icy water, Pete reached down and plucked me out. The icy wind hit me and I felt even less capable of breathing. But he quickly wrapped me in a big blanket and its warmth seeped into me. Suddenly I was able to breathe again.

Ralphie leaned in, a grin on his thin lips. He was enjoying this way too much. "Change your mind about cooperating?"

Through chattering teeth, I managed to say, "B-believe me, Ralphie, if I-I had any idea w-where this microchip is that y-you're looking for, I'd be the f-first to tell."

Ralphie's face twisted in the moonlight. He didn't like my flippant attitude, and I knew I wasn't scoring any brownie points with him.

"Shove her in again," he ordered.

Pete ripped off the blanket, but I held on to the end of

it, fighting for survival. But Pete simply yanked it off and threw it onto the ice.

Frantic, I glanced around, getting a bead on the dilapidated dock with the twinkly Christmas lights a few yards away. I knew the ice around the pilings would be thin.

The dock was my only chance. Too many more times in the hole and there wouldn't be anything left of me. I'd be a single block of ice.

Pete picked me up. I emptied my lungs and then took in several deep, gut-filling gulps. He dropped me in the hole again.

I let myself sink, the cold water surrounding me. I kicked my feet, my heels dropping off and sinking. I ignored the numbness that seemed to envelop my entire body. I could do this. I could get away from them. I could reach the dock.

I tried not to think about the fact that I was swimming away from the hole cut in the ice. That I was leaving behind the only escape hatch available to me.

I was now under solid ice. Ice so strong and solid that no amount of crawling or hammering with my fists would break through if I ran out of air. I would be trapped beneath the surface. I pushed the thought out of my head.

I swam with every ounce of strength left in my frozen limbs. A strange dizziness seemed to seep into my brain. I felt as though I was moving in slow motion. That I was getting nowhere. That I was standing still in the freezing water.

But somewhere in my brain, a voice urged me on, telling me that I was swimming with the current and that was a good thing.

Overhead, I thought I heard a muted shout. But I didn't

bother looking up. I was sure that if I saw the solid sheet of ice overhead, I'd panic. Better just to swim.

My blood slowed, seeming to move through my veins and arteries with the consistency of cold molasses. My lungs felt as though the air in them had frozen into blocks of immovable ice. I could feel myself sinking, my body and mind giving up.

But then, I hit my forehead on something hard.

I reached out and wrapped my arms around wood. It was the dock.

I put my feet down, touching mud. I leveraged myself upward, pushing myself to the surface and, with the force of my body, shattering the thin ice that had formed around the dock piling.

Shaking so hard I could barely move, I crawled up on the dock, collapsing in a heap. I lay there for a minute, trying desperately to breathe. All around me, the Christmas lights twinkled a cheery welcome. Only trouble is, they were also highlighting the fact that I was now on the dock.

"There! There she is!" Ralphie shouted from somewhere out on the ice.

I didn't bother looking. I pulled myself to my feet and ran barefoot across the wooden planks, headed for shore. They'd be on me any minute, but first they needed to get off the ice. They weren't cold and dying a slow death from exposure like I was, but I knew if I reached shore and blended into the woods, they'd have a harder time finding me.

The farther I got from the dock, the less light I had. I stumbled over some boulders covered with snow and ice, but I managed to stay on my feet. Ice cut at my feet, shredding my nylons and destroying what little protection I had.

I entered the woods behind the cabin, the thick pines closing in around me. I don't know how long I ran. It could have been minutes, it could have been hours. I had lost all sense of time. I wasn't even really running anymore. It was more like a pathetic stumble. A frozen shuffle. I knew my body was about ready to shut down.

But then I saw something. A yellow glow filtering through the pines. A campfire flickering in the darkness. Someone was camping in the woods. I could hear high-pitched voices laughing and talking. Warmth. People. Safety.

I could reach them. I just had to keep putting one foot in front of the other. I stumbled over a log hidden in the snow and fell.

Somewhere behind me, I could hear the three men calling to each other. They sounded close.

Cold snow stung my hands and ice shards cut my cheek. My feet had gone totally numb. I pulled myself up, reeling slightly, totally disoriented.

But then I heard someone laugh again, and I headed in that direction. I stumbled into a clearing. I could see a ring of faces sitting around a campfire. They stared up at me in total surprise, as if I had just materialized within their midst from another planet.

My heart sank. Kids. They were just kids out for a night of partying. None of them looked older than twenty. Ralphie and his men would make mincemeat of them.

I teetered slightly and then fell face-first into the snow. As hard as I tried to get up again, my body wouldn't move.

Someone rolled me over. A kid with a fuzzy goatee and electric-blue eyes. Blue eyes like Jack's. Handsome like my Jack. My brain turned on its side and I lost focus of the boy, his face replaced with Jack's.

"I'm sorry, Jack. I'm sorry I messed things up so bad," I slurred.

"I'm David Warren, ma'am. Are—are you okay." He didn't wait for an answer but snapped to one of the others, "Get one of the sleeping bags over here, quick. This lady is in shock."

"W-we need t-t-t-to get out of h-h-h-here," I chattered. "They're c-c-c-coming for m-m-me."

"You're safe, ma'am. No one is going to hurt you. You've had a bad accident."

"Her car must have gone into the lake," one of the young women said from some distance off.

I grabbed the young man's arm. "Y-you don't under-stand. They're c-coming for me. They'll hurt all of you. We n-need to get out of here."

Something in my face or in my words seem to get through to David. "Put out the fire, Ian. Heather, you and Mindy get on the snowmobiles—but don't start them up yet."

He glanced down at me. "If someone is out there, we don't want to alert them to where you are until we have you out of those wet clothes and into one of the down sleeping bags. We'll get you to safety."

"Here's the bag," one of the boys said.

"Help me get her undressed and into the bag," David ordered. They stripped me naked, rubbing my numb limbs as they stuffed me into the bag. It didn't seem much warmer in there. My entire body shook so hard that I thought I might break a limb.

David scooped me up and carried me to one of the snowmobiles.

"We'll take her to my house. My dad's home." He sat me in front of him and pushed his own body up against

mine in an attempt to pass some of his warmth on to me.
"My dad's a physician's assistant. He's got tonight off.
He'll help you out, and we'll call an ambulance."

I nodded, no longer able to speak. All I could do at this
point was concentrate on breathing in and out without bit-
ing my tongue due to my chattering teeth.

"Hey! You kids! Hold up there!"

Ralphie, Tony and Pete broke into the clearing.

"Oh jeez, t-those are the guys," I whispered.

David didn't even bother answering, he simply revved
up his snowmobile and took off down the trail. The other
two vehicles followed close on his heels.

"Stay off the roads," I said. "They'll go back and get
their car."

"We'll stay to the woods for a while, but we have to get
on the main road at some point to reach my house," David
said, leaning down to whisper in my ear over the roar of
the powerful snowmobile engine.

It wasn't a smooth or quiet ride. The snowmobile en-
gines roared and the noise rebounded off the trees lining
the wide path. But it was a fast ride. The wind whipped
my face, and I slid down deeper into the sleeping bag trying to hide my face from the bitterness.

Up ahead, I could see the lights of cars on a highway.
Frantic, I tugged on the front of David's jacket, and he
leaned down, placing his ear close to my mouth.

"Don't go near the main road. We don't know if they
sent the other guy by car to find us."

David shook his head. "We have to cross the road. No
other way to get to my house."

My heart sank. I didn't want these kids involved in this.
Tony, Ralphie and Pete didn't care who they took out.

David drove his snowmobile up on the snowpack and waited for an approaching car to pass. But, just as I expected, as the car got closer, it slowed. But a few feet from us, the bubble-top lights of a police car snapped on and a police cruiser pulled up in front of us. The sense of relief inside me was so full, so gratifying that I almost passed out. Two men stepped out of the car.

"We're only crossing the main road, officers, to get home," David protested. "We've got an injured woman here. Some creeps are following us."

I didn't even see the policemen's faces until they approached the side of the sled and pulled back the hood of the sleeping bag. I stared into the brilliant blue of Jack's eyes. Eyes that were never so welcome in my entire life. Right behind him stood Standish.

"You have a hard time listening to no, don't you," Jack said with more gentleness than his face portrayed.

"They jumped me at Ortega's place and dragged me out of there just as you arrived."

"I figured as much."

"I didn't have much hope that you'd be able to find me."

He reached down and gently ran a finger underneath the Chili Pepper charm he'd given me yesterday. "I had a feeling you'd try something like this. I had one of the men in the lab put a tracking device in the charm."

I sat up. "You what?"

He grinned. "I put a tracking device in the charm. Someone has to look out for you. You've certainly shown you don't give a damn what happens to you. And you definitely have a stubborn streak a mile wide."

Considering my current predicament, I didn't have the strength or inclination to argue. I simply kept my mouth shut for the moment. Or as shut as I was able to with my teeth rattling against each other as crazily as those ridiculous, Halloween windup skeleton teeth.

He leaned down and scooped me off of David's lap. "I'll take it from here, son. You and your friends hightail it home and don't stop for anyone."

"My dad's a P.A.," David said. "I thought he could help. She's suffering pretty bad from exposure."

"Not a bad idea. Where do you live?"

David pointed to a large rambling farm house about a mile down the road.

"Okay, we'll take her there first. I'll bring her in the car, we've got the heater going." I knew he could feel the tremors still wracking my body.

David nodded and drove his sled down off the snowbank and headed across the road." He shouted over his shoulder and the two other sleds followed close on his heels.

Jack slid me onto the front seat of the police cruiser and then climbed in after me. He pulled my body up against his, wrapping an arm around me and snuggling up close. Reaching around me, he turned the heater to full blast and the hot air shot out of the vents like a gift from the gods. Standish got behind the wheel and took off, siren blasting and lights flashing.

But in spite of the heat, my body refused to warm up. I shook inside the sleeping bag, my limbs seeming to have a life of their own.

I opened my mouth to speak, but nothing came out. I reached up and tugged on Jack's sleeve. He leaned closer.

"H-how did you give Ortega the s-slip?"

"He was pretty uncooperative when I arrived. Denied

you'd been there. But then Elliot and a few fellow officers stopped by. We found Shawna's car parked out back." He grinned at Standish. "A few of the guys escorted Ortega downtown for a friendly chat. Elliot and I used the locator to zero in on you."

I nodded and wearily rested my head on his shoulder, soaking in his warmth. It felt almost too sweet to contemplate.

A short time later, we were inside the farmhouse that housed my rescuer, David. His dad, a kindly looking man who didn't seem much older than his son, with light eyes and lean youthful face, motioned for Jack to bring me into the downstairs bedroom.

The quilt on the bed had already been drawn back and the man's physician's bag sat on the bedside table. He told everyone to leave the room as he quickly checked me over. He tried his best to keep me covered because my body continued to be racked with terrible waves of chills. Nothing seemed to warm me.

Finally, he pulled the blankets back over me, opened the door and motioned Jack to come back in.

"In a hospital, we'd put her under a special warming blanket. Maybe even start warming her blood. I've called the ambulance and it's on its way. But the ice storm outside is pretty bad. It might take a while for them to get here." He glanced at Jack and Standish. "The best way to get her core temperature up is body-to-body heat. I'm guessing that Killian would prefer that one of you performed that service rather than me."

The words were barely out of the man's mouth before Jack was stripping off his jacket and unbuttoning his shirt.

"Hey, don't I get a say in this?" I asked, barely able to speak through my chattering teeth.

Jack shook his head, a thick strand of black hair falling across his forehead. "Not one word. Not even one little protest."

Standish grinned. "I left the patrol car in the driveway with the lights flashing. I don't think Ortega's goons would be foolish enough to try stopping by, but I'll keep a lookout." He left the room.

Jack's eyes never left my face as he stripped off his jeans and underwear and slid beneath the quilt and into the sleeping bag. He pressed up against me. His body felt like a furnace stoked to the max.

"Jeez, you're like a stick of ice," he said, wrapping his arms around me and pulling me close.

As David's father backed out of the room, he said, "I'll be sure to give you plenty of warning before the ambulance arrives."

"Why'd he say that?" I asked, snuggling closer and resting my chin on Jack's shoulder, soaking in his glorious warmth.

"I'm assuming he doesn't want us to be embarrassed by anyone walking in on us."

I glanced up at Jack, watching his eyes crinkle with something very close to mischievous delight.

"You can't possibly mean that he thinks we're going to do the wild thing in his bed and in my weakened condition?"

"Oh, I believe that even in your weakened condition you could do just about anything you wanted," Jack whispered in my ear, his lips moving down to softly, sexily taste the side of my neck, nibbling gently on the pulse pounding beneath my skin.

His hands, warm and strong slid down the length of my

back, his fingers stroking and smoothing my cold skin. They settled on my round behind, pulling me tight against his naked flesh, a sly finger tracing the crease and erotically teasing me.

A wonderful and totally unexpected stream of warmth and something even more startling, flooded my entire body. My heart beat faster, and my limbs, a moment ago cold and unresponsive, started to tremble. But this time it wasn't from the cold.

He nuzzled my neck, his teeth nibbling a tiny bit like some kind of wild animal marking his mate. I lifted my chin, giving him greater access, loving the feel of his lips and teeth as they moved across my tender, heated flesh.

His mouth covered mine, first soft and gentle and then more demanding, harder. More insistent and unremitting. A low hum trembled in the back of my throat and I opened my mouth, allowing him inside. The taste of him was sweet and oh so familiar.

I slid my hands around his neck, tunneling my fingers in the thickness of his hair, pulling him closer still. I felt his hardness press against me, hovering near the core of my heat. I pushed my hips against him, urging him on, wanting him now more than I'd ever thought possible. All the memories of the past, of our time together, seemed to collapse into one moment, one golden opportunity of unlimited, uncompromising passion.

"Slow down," he whispered. "We have some time. First, we need to warm you up."

"I'm about to burst into flames," I protested, my leg sliding over his and pulling him on top of me. I nudged him again, letting him know that there would be no more waiting.

He slid into me, filling me with himself and a small cry escaped from my lips. I moved beneath him, clinging to him with desperation and need.

As he moved to meet me, I shuddered, feeling waves of something wild and infinitely wonderful wash over me. This was what I had missed, what I had forsaken. He captured my cry deep inside his own mouth and I let go, tumbling and catapulting over the edge. I could feel my heart hammer against my chest, answering the violent beat of his own heart pressed against mine. My body shook, awash in the beauty of the moment.

And as I climaxed, a soft whisper of satisfaction hissed in my ear as he followed me over the edge. It was like coming home.

Chapter Thirteen

With a sigh of satisfaction, Jack slid off of and settled next to me, his long legs still entangled with mine. Sweat poured off both our bodies, mingling and heating my body core to an even higher temperature. I was pretty sure even the hospital's treatment of hypothermia couldn't come close to Jack O'Brien's unique method of body warming. Maybe Jack could write this up for the medical community.

"What did they want from you?" he asked. I knew he was referring to Ortega and his men.

I slid the flat of my hand across his bare chest, delighting in the smoothness contrasted with hard muscle. "They kept asking me to hand over the microchip. They couldn't seem to get it through their thick heads that I had no idea where Pop hid it."

He bent his head and pressed his lips against the center of my throat. I moaned softly as his tongue slipped from between his lips and gently lapped the tender spot between my breasts. "Keep doing that and I won't be able to talk."

"Interesting possibility," he said, his mouth moving over to gently suck on one taut nipple. "What's on the computer chip?" he asked, lifting his head for a brief second before returning to his delightful attention to my body.

Air hissed between my teeth. "Everything the D.A. would need to put Ortega away for a long, long time. At least according to Jeannette Renault."

The gentle pull on my nipple had turned to a deep, sucking tug that sent shivers down my belly and liquefied my already burning insides.

"Why did you go there alone? You know better." His mouth switched to my other nipple and I figured he'd discovered a whole knew interrogation technique. It was proving quite effective, but I sincerely didn't want him using it on any of his other female suspects—I wanted him all to myself. The revelation was startling.

"Because I knew Ortega wanted to pull you in. To corrupt you just as he corrupted Charlie. I thou—"

I couldn't finish the sentence because his hand had traveled down to intimately stroke the warmest, most sensitive part of me. I gasped and my head arched off the pillow. I called out his name, begging him to stop, but in reality I didn't want him ever to stop.

"Ortega knows better than to mess with me. Why couldn't you have trusted that I could handle him as easily as I'm handling you right now?"

"Because I love you too much and I couldn't take the chance that he'd win," I said. Even as I said the words, my heart seemed to stop, to pause in anticipation of the rejection I knew was right around the corner.

"Finally," Jack said, his words caressing my ear. "Finally you are able to say it."

"I never wanted not to. I was just too afraid. Too frightened you wouldn't feel the same way, especially after my rejection. After I turned my back on you and refused to speak to you again after the indictment of Pop came through and I realized your involvement."

"I understood, Chili. I knew how hurt you were. How wounded you were by what you thought was the ultimate betrayal of Pop."

I tightened my hold on him, clutching him to me, secretly frightened he might change his mind and pull away. "I'm sorry I couldn't see the truth. Couldn't believe Pop when he told me that you'd done the right thing."

"I'm glad you're back," he said softly, his clever tongue sending waves of ecstasy rolling over me. My body shook, and I clung to him, every ounce of coolness leaving my blood at once, leaving behind only heat, passion and an unabiding love for him.

"I've missed you more than you can imagine," he said.

I've missed you, too, I thought. More than even I imagined.

"You'd better stop," I panted. "The ambulance guys will be here any minute."

"Who cares? You don't need them now. You're as warm and sweet as hothouse honey."

No argument there. I felt like a blast furnace, ready to ignite into uncontrollable flames.

I gasped for breath. "For some reason, they seemed to think that Charlie left the microchip with me."

Jack's lips nibbled along my collarbone, their smoothness sending new waves of something excruciatingly sinful through me. Would his seduction never end?

"Where would Charlie have hidden something like that?"

His tongue ran along the edge of the necklace he'd given me, sending an army of goose bumps to pop up all over my body. When he reached the charm, he gently sucked in the chili pepper, holding it between his teeth. Holding me captive with his mouth and clever hands. "Careful, you might swallow the tracking device," I teased.

"No chance. Too well hidden."

Too well hidden? It was then, out of nowhere, I realized where the computer chip was hidden. I sat bolt upright in bed. The chili pepper popped out of Jack's mouth and the sleeping bag and quilt pooled down around my waist.

"Sweetie Pie!" I shouted.

Jack propped himself up on one elbow and frowned. "What the hell does Sweetie Pie have to do with any of this?"

"He has the computer chip. Sweetie Pie has had the computer chip all this time."

I scrambled out of the sleeping bag, practically falling face-first on the floor in my haste. I ran around trying to find my clothes, but then realized the boys who had rescued me had probably left them back in the woods when they stripped me naked.

"Clothes!" I said. "I need clothes."

"Jeez, will you calm down?" Jack said, sitting up and swinging his own legs out of the bed. "Tell me what you're thinking so I can catch up here."

As he stood up, my brain went slightly off kilter at the sight of his long, powerful body totally naked. It had been a while since I'd gotten a good look at it in full light.

Oh sure, I'd been feeling its lean hard muscles pretty well a few minutes ago, but seeing him wasn't too bad, either. It brought back a rush of pleasant, totally erotic memories of being in the sleeping bag with him for our more than a few body-heat-enhancing minutes.

Jack waved a hand in my face as he picked his own

clothes up off the floor. "Earth to Killian. Talk to me, girl. How does Sweetie Pie fit into all of this?"

Yanking myself back to reality, I opened the closet in the corner of the room and pulled out a flannel shirt and a pair of the P.A.'s scrub pants—the kind with the tie waist. I figured our kindly host wouldn't mind if I borrowed them until I could locate some of my own things.

"Pop left Sweetie Pie in my care. He knew without question that I was the only one he'd allow to touch him."

"An understatement if I've ever heard one," Jack grumbled.

"Well, Sweetie Pie has a brand-new collar, hand tooled by Pop. What do you want to bet that we pop that charm open and find the microchip that everyone has been looking for?"

Jack paused in the middle of snapping his jeans, his expression pensive for a moment and then a lazy grin slid across his face, dimpling his left cheek. "That crazy old coot. It would be just like him to hide the evidence in plain sight."

"Problem is, Ortega knows about the existence of Sweetie Pie. I told him that the cat and the safe-deposit box were the only things Pop left me in charge of. Since Catherine Pratt had the key to the box, I'm sure he knows that there's nothing in it he's looking for. He essentially told me that. That leaves Pie as the only other option."

"We'll discuss the fact that you failed to mention the safe-deposit box at another time. Right now, I agree that we need to get to Sweetie Pie before Ortega and his men figure out he's the key."

I nodded, tying the scrub pants around my waist and pulling on a heavy knit sweater over the flannel shirt. I made a mental note to get the stuff back to our host once this whole mess was cleared up.

THE AMBULANCE CREW wasn't happy when they arrived to find their patient dressed and on the way out the door. No amount of convincing on anyone's part, the P.A.'s or the paramedics', got me to change my mind. I wasn't going to the hospital. I was going after Sweetie Pie. Jack was smart enough to know this was one argument even he wasn't going to win.

The ride back to Syracuse was a wild one. Standish handled the icy roads with finesse, but we still had a few close calls. He radioed ahead at Jack's insistence, asking that several patrol cars converge on Jack's apartment.

The officers were instructed not to go into the apartment. They were simply told to make sure no one but Standish or Jack was allowed inside. None of us wanted to take a chance that someone would get to Sweetie Pie before we did.

Thirty minutes later, we were in the elevator and headed for the top floor. I pressed the button again, staring up at the numbers flashing overhead.

"That won't make it go any faster," Jack said calmly.

"I realize that, but I have to do something," I snapped.

Standish grinned. "You two argue like an old married couple."

Jack and I exchanged glances. We sure didn't make love like an old married couple, but we kept that between ourselves. As we exited the elevator, two policemen moved toward us, half holding, half dragging a familiar figure—Ralphie.

He looked as though he'd been through a wheat thresher. His narrow face was cut to shreds, his hands a bloody mess. Strips of his expensive silk shirt were hanging around his waist, and more scratches marred his skinny chest.

"What the hell kind of beast do you keep in there, O'Brien? A freakin' tiger?" one of the officers asked. "This bozo came flying out the door when we got off the elevator. He was screaming like a banshee."

. I grinned at Ralphie. "Got more than you bargained for, didn't you?"

He wiped a bloody hand across his cheek and winced. "That is one crazy-ass cat. He's a menace to society. Someone should put him down."

"Not likely," I said as I brushed past the hood to get into the apartment.

I spied Sweetie Pie immediately, sitting on top of Jack's prized leather couch, more than a few strips of leather hanging off the sides, indicating the level of fight he'd put up. He was casually licking his paws, appearing completely nonchalant about his recent attack on the Ralphster.

Considering what he'd been through the past couple of days, I was pretty sure he had enjoyed the opportunity to take some of his aggression out on the unsuspecting Ralph.

I walked over and picked him up, holding him close. He purred, welcoming me home. His big head bumped up against my chin and he smiled his familiar cat grin. Yep, he was definitely proud of himself. It was almost as if he knew he'd protected the chip entrusted to him by his beloved master.

Sitting down on the edge of the couch, I carefully removed the collar and used my nail to pry up one edge of the charm hanging from it. A microchip fell into the palm of my hand. I held it up for Jack and Standish to see.

"Here's your evidence," I said, reaching out to place the chip in Standish's open hand. "I have a strong feeling that this should put Mr. Handler Ortega away for a long, long time."

Standish carefully placed the chip in an evidence bag. "You ever want to think about joining the Syracuse police force, Killian, you just let me know. We could use an officer of your caliber."

He glanced over at Jack. "And when you decide to stop playing pseudodoctor, you need to think about coming back, too. I think you've sulked long enough."

Without another word, he turned and left, dragging along Ralphie and the other officers.

Epilogue

Orchids are for funerals. Claire had always said that, refusing to have them in her house. But today I found myself sitting at Pop's grave site, staring at a glossy black coffin with gold fixtures, covered in a cloying blanket of a seemingly endless array of orchids.

A terrible sadness flooded every chamber of my heart, seeping out into my blood and filling me with a deep sense of emptiness. The flowers had been Jeannette Renault's final tribute to a man she had both loved and hurt over a lifetime. No amount of orchids would ever make up for what she and Ortega had done to such a good and loving man.

The delicate petals of the orchids appeared frozen in the frigid temperatures, and I wondered how the workers had been able to dig into the hard, frozen earth in preparation for Pop's final resting spot.

I knew Jack had had a part in getting things done. I'd overheard him on the phone telling the funeral director that he'd better get out the blasting caps if need be because Pop wasn't going to sit in some freezer waiting for the spring thaw to come. Jack knew we all needed closure, and he was determined to see that happen.

He had also taken care of the money in the safe-deposit box, making sure that I didn't have to go back to the bank to deal with the one thing that had the power to mar my memory of Pop. I didn't ask him what he'd done with the cash, but I was pretty sure the D.A. had gotten a visit from Jack sometime in the past few days.

So, instead of worrying about loose ends, I sat at Pop's graveside and listened to the preacher drone on.

At one point, I gave serious consideration to jumping up and grabbing the fragrant flowers off the top of Pop's coffin and ripping them to shreds, scattering them to the wind. But I didn't. Pop and Claire had always taught us patience, humility and honor. And as much as I hated her, I knew that even Jeannette deserved her chance to honor Charlie.

So instead, I sat in stunned silence, Jack's arm wrapped around my shoulder, a bouquet of simple daisies clutched in my damp, cold hands.

On either side of us sat our family. No longer foster siblings. I could never think of them in that way again. They were real flesh-and-blood family. We'd all been through too much to ever think of ourselves as anything less. Claire and Pop had bonded us, made us whole. We weren't half of anything. We were a full-fledged family, with all the gifts and faults that went into the makeup of a real family.

I leaned closer to Jack and whispered, "Pop deserved more. It should have never ended this way."

Jack's dark head brushed against mine, his lips inches from my ear. "I know that, babe. But Charlie wouldn't have wanted it any other way. The other option just wasn't for him." His strong, capable fingers tightened on my shoulder, as if he could press his incredible strength of will directly into my weeping heart.

"We all made the right decision. Pop wouldn't have wanted to spend the rest his life hooked up to a machine, unable to talk. To laugh. To lecture us about how to live our lives. This is how he would have wanted things done."

I knew he was right and somehow, in the deepest part of my psyche, I could almost hear Pop's voice talking to me, telling me that I had shown the strength of character to do the right thing, to make a critical decision without him there to guide me.

I hadn't realized until that moment that all these years I'd been carrying him inside of me—the essence of his teachings, his love, his compassion, his self-sacrifice. He'd been right there with me each and every day, inside my heart and mind, guiding and comforting me in my most difficult moments. It had been his gift to me.

And finally I had the courage to recognize that I did possess all his strength and knowledge of life. All the things he'd taught me, whether he was at my side or not. I just hadn't wanted him to leave so soon. There were still so many things I had wanted to say to him, to thank him for. But now he was gone, and I knew I needed to make his legacy of deep caring and compassion live on.

I leaned against Jack. "Do you think they let single women become foster parents?"

"Without a doubt. But who says you have to do it alone?"

Startled, I glanced up at him, and he smiled that sweet smile of his, the one that reminded me of Pop. "You're not the only one who feels the need to give back, Chili. The need to make a difference. I think we'd make a pretty good team, don't you?"

"Are you asking me to marry you?"

Jack shrugged. "Maybe this isn't the most romantic spot for a proposal, but somehow I think Pop would approve."

The sun broke through the clouds overhead and spilled down a shaft of surprisingly warm sunshine on the cold, hard ground. The daisies in my lap fluttered softly in the breeze, and I touched their petals with the tips of my fingers. "I think Claire would approve, too."

Jack nodded and leaned over to gently kiss away the single tear that slid down the curve of my cheek. "We'll make them proud, Chili. We'll make them proud of all the hard work they did to make us the people we've become."

I nodded, letting go of some of the sadness that seemed endless. He was right. Pop and Claire had done a good job, and now it was time to let go. To get on with our lives and love each other through it all.

"You do realize, of course, that Sweetie Pie is part of the bargain?"

Jack sighed. "If I can handle you, I can handle a lifetime of that damn cat."

I smiled and stood up. I walked over to Pop's coffin and placed the tiny bouquet of unassuming daisies at the head. A simple tribute to a man who had made mistakes in life, but who had always cared for the people he loved most. I only hoped I could make the sacrifices needed when it came to my own family.

Somehow, I was fairly certain that I could with Jack standing at my side.

"Take care, Pop, and give Claire a warm welcome when you see her," I whispered softly.

Jack wrapped me in his embrace and we walked away, down a path to a new life.

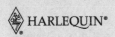

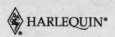

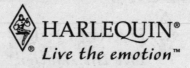

If you enjoyed what you just read,
then we've got an offer you can't resist!

Take 2 bestselling
love stories FREE!
Plus get a FREE surprise gift!

A SELECTED LIST OF
CORGI TITLES

WHILE EVERY EFFORT IS MADE TO KEEP PRICES LOW, IT IS SOME-
TIMES NECESSARY TO INCREASE PRICES AT SHORT NOTICE. CORGI
BOOKS RESERVE THE RIGHT TO SHOW AND CHARGE NEW RETAIL
PRICES ON COVERS WHICH MAY DIFFER FROM THOSE ADVERTISED IN
THE TEXT OR ELSEWHERE.

THE PRICES SHOWN BELOW WERE CORRECT AT THE TIME OF GOING
TO PRESS (APRIL '84).

☐	12092 8	No Time for Tears	Cynthia Freeman	£1.9
☐	11730 7	Portraits	Cynthia Freeman	£2.5
☐	11775 7	A World Full of Strangers	Cynthia Freeman	£2.5
☐	11776 5	Fairytales	Cynthia Freeman	£1.9
☐	11925 3	Come Pour the Wine	Cynthia Freeman	£1.7
☐	11660 2	Princess Daisy	Judith Krantz	£2.9
☐	11959 8	The Chatelaine	Claire Lorrimer	£1.9
☐	12182 7	The Wilderling	Claire Lorrimer	£1.
☐	12309 9	Flames of Glory	Patricia Matthews	£1.
☐	12080 4	Embers of Dawn	Patricia Matthews	£1.
☐	12118 5	The Debutantes	June Flaum Singer	£1.
☐	07807 7	Valley of the Dolls	Jacqueline Susann	£1.
☐	08523 5	The Love Machine	Jacqueline Susann	£1.
☐	11575 4	A Necessary Woman	Helen Van Slyke	£1.
☐	12240 8	Public Smiles, Private Tears	Helen Van Slyke	£1.
☐	11321 2	Sisters and Strangers	Helen Van Slyke	£1.
☐	11779 X	No Love Lost	Helen Van Slyke	£1.

All these books are available at your bookshop or newsagent, or can be ordered dir
from the publisher. Just tick the titles you want and fill in the form below.

CORGI BOOKS, Cash Sales Department, P.O. Box 11, Falmouth, Cornwall.

Please send cheque or postal order, no currency.

Please allow cost of book(s) plus the following for postage and packing:

U.K. CUSTOMERS. 45p for the first book, 20p for the second book and 14p for e
additional book ordered, to a maximum charge of £1.63.

B.F.P.O. & EIRE. Please allow 45p for the first book, 20p for the second book p
14p per copy for the next three books, thereafter 8p per book.

OVERSEAS CUSTOMERS. Please allow 75p for the first book plus 21p per copy
each additional book.

NAME (Block Letters) ....

ADDRESS ....

....

FAIRYTALES

BY CYNTHIA FREEMAN

The storybook romance of two strong-willed passionate people trapped in a fairytale of their own making ...

CATHERINE ANTOINETTE FRANCES POSATA ROSSI – fabulously beautiful, enormously rich and spoiled. But she would fight for what was hers, even if it meant destroying and losing – her man.

DOMINIC ROSSI – charming, ambitious and ruthless, he was marked by destiny. The brilliant son of proud Sicilian peasants, he had everything a virile man could want ... except the love he needed and demanded.

552 11776 5

A WORLD FULL OF STRANGERS

BY CYNTHIA FREEMAN

The story of a family you'll never forget! A rich, dramatic saga of
passion and love, of sin and retribution, spanning three generations
of family life – from the ghettos of New York to the glittering hills
of San Francisco ...

DAVID   who destroyed his past to live a life of power and
        glory.

KATIE   who lived with her past, whose roots and memories
        were too deep for her ever to be able to forget.

MARK   their son, who had the courage to struggle toward
        the sacred heritage his father had denied him.

MAGGIE the successful and glamorous woman David wanted
        because she was everything Katie was not.

0 552 11775 7   £1.95

PORTRAITS

BY CYNTHIA FREEMAN

The tempestuous rags-to-riches novel of an immigrant family in America – their dreams and heartaches – their struggle to survive in an alien country ...

JACOB   whose newfound wealth could never fill the aching void inside him.

SARA   who sacrificed everything in the name of love – even her daughter.

SHLOMO   who kept the family's disgrace a secret, and paid the price.

RACHEL   whose forbidden love for one man drove her into the arms of another.

DORIS   a Cinderella who achieved fame and happiness beyond her wildest dreams.

0 552 11730 7   £2.50